Elven Roots

Book 1
Finding the Past

Book 2
Preserving the Present

Book 3
Forging the Future

Preserving the Present

Elven Roots Book 2

Jennifer Abrahamsen

ISBN: 979-8-9899852-4-1

Cover Art by Darren C. Leonard

Printed in the United States of America

This book is dedicated to my friends at High Point K-9 Center.
Don't we all wish we knew what our dogs were thinking?

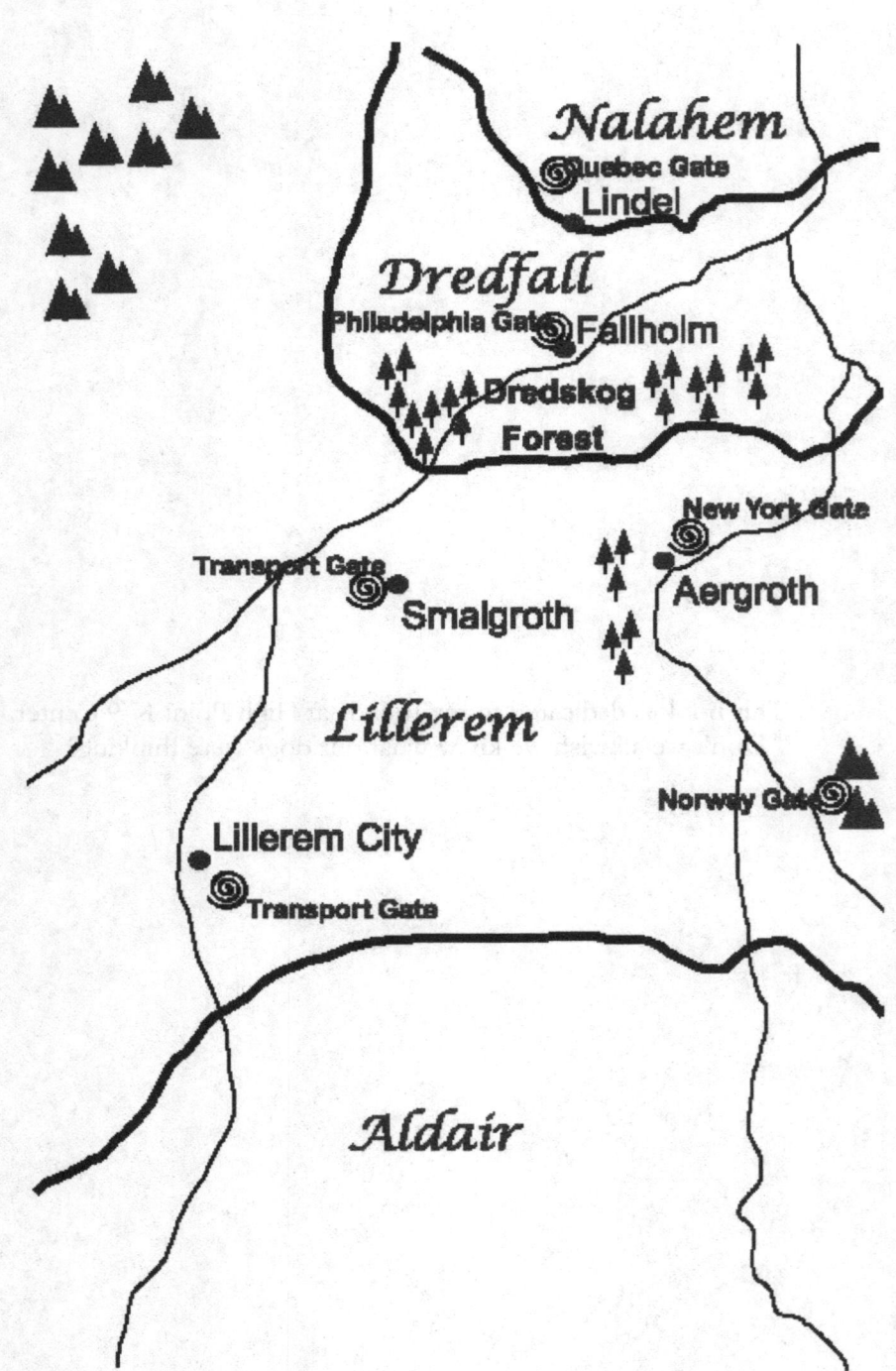

PROLOGUE

Ulford proudly sat in his saddle watching Castle Bindrell burn. He turned to the seeress beside him.

"With this stronghold conquered, I now control almost a quarter of Lillerem. Henceforth, this territory shall be known as Dredfall. I will be its King. Thank you, my love, for guiding me to this moment of glory."

The woman merely smiled. Today's battle had unfolded exactly as she had predicted.

Down in the mêlée, a different woman loaded her youngest boys into a cart. She kissed Leif, barely more than a toddler, on the head and then held him at arm's length. She memorized his features and those of his older brother Gunnar.

"You need to look after him, Gunnar. There is no exception to that duty. Leif must grow up away from all of this madness. The magic he carries is so strong. He will return when he is of age and set this right. My brother cannot be allowed to eclipse this idyllic land with slavery and fear."

Gunnar took the reins and slapped them against the backs of the ox that would pull them to the border of Aergroth. The cart moved off toward the gate, the portal to Norway, and the human realm. Gunnar's eyes remained fixed on his mother until they rounded the first bend in the road.

Voices came from behind Ekkelle and she turned to run back to the farmstead. She and Knut would make their stand there. Ekkelle knew her family would not prevail.

Syndral sat quietly in the brush. Her commander had deployed her battalion to this homestead while the remainder of the draw continued on to take Castle Bindrell. All the people within the house were dead at other soldiers' hands, but Syndral waited patiently for the real prize. Her reward would be commanding a draw of her own.

The female hastening up the path now was Ulford's sister. She was the last of King Bain's most powerful descendants. As Ekkelle rushed by Syndral's position toward the family she no longer had, Syndral silently moved in behind her. Before Ekkelle could turn, before any magic was exchanged, Syndral ran her blade across Ekkelle's throat and began her ascent through the ranks of the Dredfall army.

Vander stormed from Ulford's chambers. He angrily shoved several house slaves from his path as he went. Skalanis approached from the end of the hall. He turned when he reached Vander and matched his steps to those of the angry elf.

"What the hell just happened in there?"

"The King has lost his mind. That is what happened in there! It's our time! We are poised to take control of Lillerem. All that planning, all those dead soldiers, for nothing! Millspare's forces are depleted, Erik cowers behind the walls of Gulentine Palace, and the princes and that demi-princess bitch are off in the human realm. We should strike now!"

As the two soldiers exited the castle onto the parade grounds, one of Skalanis's pets joined their march. The foul creatures Skalanis kept in the kennels were not permitted within the castle walls. Skalanis stopped, forcing Vander to do the same. Skalanis faced Vander and held his stare for a moment before deciding to speak.

"What will the King have us do instead of continuing as planned?"

"Now that Ulford knows of the daughter of Leif, he thinks there are others in the human realm that stand between him and his rule over Alfheim. Since there is no way to determine how much power these half-breeds might hold, he's sending the entire First Draw into that realm to hunt and kill anyone with Elven blood."

"If Ulford wants to waste our talent on hunting humans, that is his prerogative. I see no reason why this interferes with his plans to take Lillerem. We already have a man on the inside at Gulentine. Erik can be removed from power at any time," Skalanis said as he scratched his beast between its ears.

"He refuses to leave Dredfall undefended since he has already taken the city of Lindel from Nalahem. Since he fears retaliation from Nalahem's forces in the north, Ulford is holding the majority of his forces here in Dredfall and he thinks sending a single draw into Lillerem will bring the return of the children of Ekkell to this realm. His warped mind no longer sees taking Lillerem as the priority. He has become infatuated with this half-breed princess and ridding the human realm of Elven blood."

"Hello?" Jess's mouth was dry from sleep.

"Hello, Ms. Bennett?"

"This is she,"

"My name is Larsen. I am trying to locate a Ms. Kindra Powers."

When Jess said nothing, Larsen went on, "I am an investigator with the Norwegian National Criminal Investigation Service."

Had Kindra committed any crimes? Unlikely, but did she really want to be found by a Norwegian investigator?

"I have made every effort to contact Kindra, but she is unreachable at the moment."

How was Jess going to explain to this man that he couldn't raise Kindra because there was no cell service in Alfheim?

"Please, Mr. Larsen, I need to know something," pleaded Jess. "Are Kindra's mother and sister ok?"

"I'd really feel more comfortable sharing this information with Ms. Powers herself. Are you able to have her call me if I leave my number with you?"

"No," Jess said. "That's just the thing. Kindra's off on a pilgrimage of sorts. It's like a self-discovery thing, and there's no way to reach her. She could be back next month, or she might not return until next year. Please, I need to know if Gretchen is hurt."

"I am sorry to have to share this news with you, but I need to share it with someone who knows the family." Jess's heart sank as Larsen spoke. "It appears Ms. Powers and Ms. Husland were victims of a gruesome attack perpetrated by unknown assailants. Neither of the women survived, and... frankly, there was not much left to use for identification of the victims."

Jess had known she was going to hear something similar from the man, even as early in the conversation as Odd Larsen giving his title. Several days ago, she received a call from Gretchen's cell number. The caller stated that Dredfall had come to the human realm and she should prepare to be the next to her grave.

"Sir, you say the assailants are unknown, but are there any leads? Is anything known about who did this?"

Larsen cleared his throat. "My department has been tracking a group of people who have been committing murders throughout southern Norway. Witnesses heard the group communicating about a man named Ulford as they evacuated a crime scene. We suspect the Ulford character is their leader."

Jess disconnected the call. Skipping a shower, Jess threw on a pair of jeans and a shirt. She grabbed an old pair of Adidas from the closet and ran to the kitchen. Spilling some food into the dogs' bowls, Jess quickly scrawled a note to Sean, saying she had to go find Kindra, and also that she did not know when she would be home.

Butch and Cassidy gave Jess confused looks as she let them outside to do their business. When the dogs were ready, Jess called them back inside. Neither dog complied. Jess felt her anger bubbling to the surface. The voice of the trainer sounded in her head to remind Jess that the dogs would not listen to her if she was angry. *The dogs will come when you call them, only if you give them a reason to come. If you're yelling and angry, what dog would want to go toward you?* Several deep breaths later, Jess used a cheery voice to call the dogs again. This time, Cassidy looked up for a moment, but continued to chase after his brother.

Thirty minutes later, Jess stood in Leif's basement. She was just outside of the semi-circle of discomfort created by the portal she knew was there, beyond the wall of the cellar. Jess felt the space out. Her skin began to crawl at the foot of the stairs, about four feet from the wall. Based on that measurement, Jess calculated almost twelve and one-half square feet of disquieting space. Though formulas and computation were calming for Jess, the result of the calculation did not help her figure out how to get near the door. The last time she faced it down, it had easily pushed her away.

Come on Jess. This is important. You need to reach Kindra. Jess backed half-way up the stairs and ran toward the wall. She threw her body against the stone and it slid inward. Her head throbbed as she entered the passageway. Jess did not take the time to look around or light a torch. She pushed herself blindly through the tunnel, colliding with the wall several times. The pressure in her head continued to build, and nausea overwhelmed her. Jess forged on, partially running, but mostly stumbling until she felt a sharp pain behind her eyes. There was light up ahead. Jess could see it through the tunnel vision that was encroaching on her sight. *I need to get to Kindra!*

Descendant Chart for Andril of Lillerem

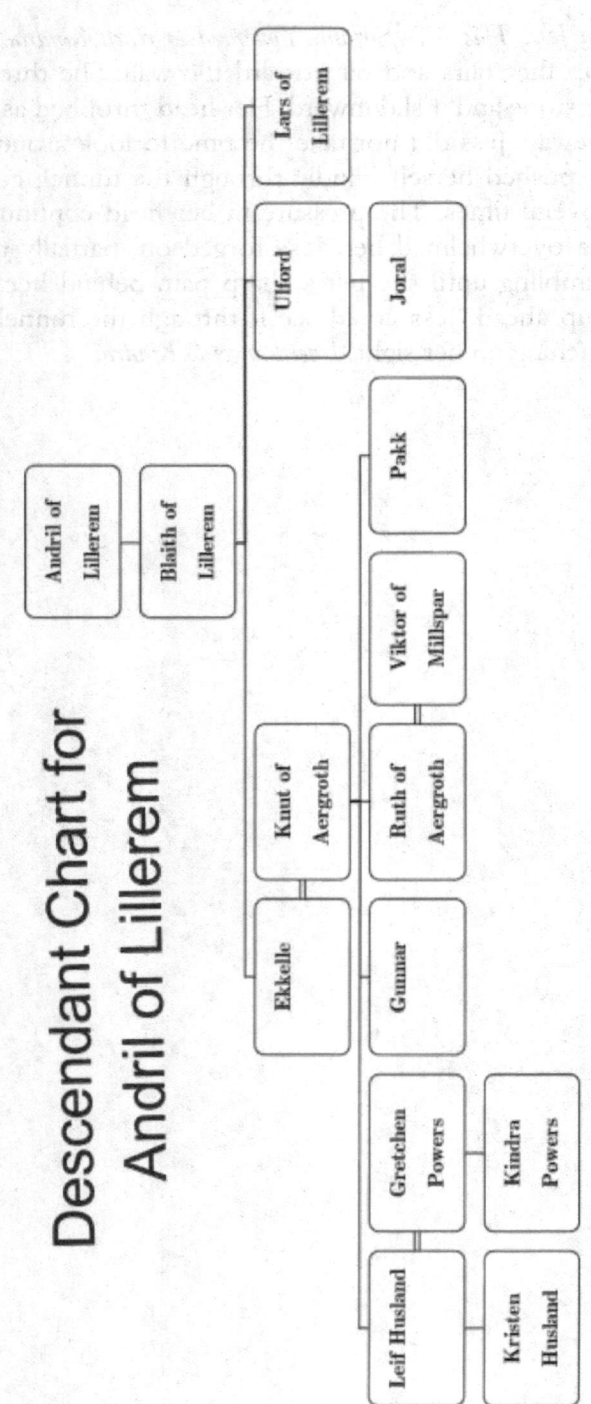

CHAPTER 1

Kindra stepped into the library in Mickelberg, hoping to find Robert this time. Her father, Leif felt Robert would be one of Dredfall's primary targets. Kindra's years of genealogy research made her an expert in using resources on the Internet to discover family connections people thought were long buried. Kindra had started her hunt when it was determined that Leif was not the only elf to father children in the human realm. Leif's brother, Pakk, had shared Leif's proclivities for sleeping around.

Mickelberg was one of the smallest towns Kindra had ever visited; two traffic lights, a gas station, a convenience store, Ed's Coffee House and a library. She had often driven through on her way to the State Park to swim in the lakes during her younger years, then later with her husband, Tom. She hadn't visited since her husband's tragic death, and learning the area outside of the park was designated as an actual town was surprising. Robert Bross had no known address and no listed phone number. A prior residence, discovered in one of Kindra's internet searches, belonged to Robert's ex-girlfriend. The woman thought Robert may have been living in Mickelberg and Kindra later found residents who knew him. They did not know where he lived, but they said he regularly spent time at the library.

Kindra's plan was the same as it had been for Leif's descendants, and now several descendants of Leif's brother, Pakk. She was to locate Robert, take him to Leif's cabin in Liberty, and then determine if he had enough Elven blood to make it through the gate to Alfheim. If he did, he could be looked after at Castle Millspare until the Kingdom of Dredfall no longer posed a threat in the human realm. If he was of lesser Elven blood, joining the growing camp outside of Leif's cabin might be Robert's only safe option.

Kindra smiled at the older woman manning the circulation desk. The woman immediately smiled back, recognizing Kindra by sight. It was a testament to the number of times Kindra had been here scouting for Robert in the last two weeks. Kindra moved past a blonde woman in a plush chair, reading a thick book. The woman was slim, but must have been a frequent flyer at the gym. The skinny jeans she had tucked into her boots failed to hide incredible muscle tone.

Kindra missed her Fae form at that moment. It wasn't much different from her human form, but in her Fae form, Kindra was noticeably more toned and had a lot more strength.

Despite the chill of the evening, the man browsing the science fiction section was wearing gray basketball shorts and ankle socks with his hoodie. Kindra walked past him and down the aisles at a leisurely pace, making her way toward the area in the back of the library where the study carrels stood silently waiting for people to actually come to the library to study. She did her best to forget about the man, but his infelicitous choice of attire wouldn't stop niggling at her.

Kindra stopped and perused some of the book titles on the back wall as a pretext for subtle glances into the carrels. No one was using them. Kindra plucked a book from the shelf and laughed to herself. A glance at the other books in front of her proved she had found her way to the Mathematics section. *Jess would die of delight if she knew I was even reading the titles of these books.*

Kindra's best friend, Jess, taught Math at the same middle school where Kindra worked as a school psychologist. Jess had stumbled through the portal to Alfheim two months ago, to deliver a warning that Kindra's evil Uncle Ulford had turned his sights toward the human realm. It had taken Jess as long to recover from her trip through the gate as it had taken Krish to determine how she had done it at all. As the son of Lillerem's King Erik, Krish had access to a collection of ancient scrolls at Gulentine Palace, describing the rules of the travel portals. It seemed the ability of humans to use the portal to travel between realms was determined by the strength of the Elven blood the human carried, not by the quantity. Jess was only one quarter elf, but Pakk, her Elven grandfather, had been extremely powerful. Travel between realms was possible for Jess, but not easy.

At this point, Jess should have as much training as Kindra had when she defended Aergroth from Dredfall. Each week, Gunnar claimed it would only be a little longer. Now that Jess's magic was coming to life, he was fairly confident she could make the return journey through the portal, but he was nervous. If Gunnar was wrong, and Jess did not have enough magic, she would die trying to return to the human realm.

Kindra was shelving the math book when movement drew her eye. An arm wrapped around Kindra's throat and pulled her back into a heavily muscled chest. Without a chance to react, Kindra found she was helpless. She couldn't move or cry out. The arm around her neck completely blocked her airway. Kindra willed her magic to throw her attacker backward, but she did not have enough power here in the human realm. Kindra was losing consciousness.

Could dying be this easy?

At that last moment, before the darkness grabbed her, Kindra's neck came free from her assailant's grasp. Her legs gave out, and she fell to the floor. The toned woman who had previously been reading near the front of the library had the man sporting the hoodie in a choke hold. The muscular woman was easily holding her own against the man. He was struggling to get free, but Kindra could see he was losing his own battle with consciousness.

The man sank to the floor, but the woman did not let go of her hold. She squatted to follow him to the ground, tightening her grip as she went. The looked dead, but the woman continued to squeeze his throat for another minute. Kindra did not move. When she released her grip, the woman pulled back the man's hood. The man was not a man at all. Kindra recognized the Elven male's face. This was Morthil, one of the Dredfall assassins.

Was I his intended target, or had he been here looking for Robert as well? The woman might have those answers.

Kindra left the elf on the library floor. She quickly exited the library. The poor lady at the circulation desk was going to be unhappy with the body in the math section. Kindra looked left and right as the cold hit her face and she darted into the parking lot. There were no cars pulling out, and no one was fleeing on foot. Kindra's rescuer had vanished.

Kindra pulled out her cell phone and called Leif. As she walked to her car, Kindra relayed the story of her failure to find Robert, as well as her brush with death. Leif had her describe, in as much detail as she could, the woman who had killed Morthil. Her description was similar to a blonde in a fitness competition, wearing jeans and a sweater instead of the typical bikini.

"I feel as if you might be a tad envious, Kindra. Your description was adequate, but the way you gave it made you sound as if you were describing your crush to high school friends in the girls' bathroom."

"Funny, pops. Your daughter was nearly murdered two minutes ago, yet you see fit to poke fun at her," Kindra sighed as she turned the key in the ignition. "I'll be back in about forty-five minutes and I'll communicate all the event's details to everyone at the same time."

Kindra disconnected the call and dropped her phone in one of the cup holders. She steered the car out onto the road and headed north.

Who the hell was that woman? Why had she been waiting at the library? No one goes to the library anymore!

Syndral watched the Honda Civic pull out of the parking lot. She waited for the car to turn left onto the highway before squeezing out from between the dumpster and the wall of the library. This encounter had not gone as planned. If Syndral could determine where her strategy had derailed, she might be able to decide how to proceed.

When Dredfall was defeated at the Battle of Millspare, Syndral had been badly wounded. As commander of the Second Draw, Syndral led her battalion cautiously to the gates of the castle. Her unease had been well-founded. her troops easily pushed to within several hundred yards of the castle wall. Millspare had hidden the greatest weapon within their arsenal, and she was not even from this realm.

Syndral crossed the street and climbed into her truck. She sank down in her seat and pressed her hand into her abdomen. She closed her eyes, thinking about the battle.

She pushed her horse to the front of her draw. Lieutenant Bakken and three other soldiers lowered the giant bridge, dragged for days through the forest roads, over the deep canyon between the Second Draw and the city of Aergroth. The bridge touched down on the far side and Syndral charged onto the wooden planks with the Second

Draw at her heels. She led her soldiers around the outskirts of the city instead of directly through the center. Though it was a longer route, it took less time because there were no people to block the path to the castle gate.

Reining in her horse thirty feet from the giant wooden doors, Syndral called for her ram team. A group of twenty soldiers ran up with a thick tree trunk carried between them. The log was dropped and twenty free soldiers took the place of those who had run with the battering ram until it was in position.

"Ready the ram!" shouted Syndral. "Charge!"

The team of twenty soldiers thundered for the doors to the castle. They drove the trunk of the tree into the double doors. The doors shook, but held firm.

"Reset the ram!" Syndral called to her soldiers as she circled back to the rest of the draw.

The first group of soldiers dropped the battering ram as soon as they returned to the line. The next group of twenty soldiers took up positions for the next charge.

Pain sliced through Syndral's left side. She dropped the reins of her horse to press her hand to the source of the agony, but she was thwarted by the shaft of an arrow. She turned her head, searching for Lieutenant Bakken. His eyes found hers. She toppled forward and the rocky ground flew up to meet her.

Syndral opened her eyes and turned the key in the ignition. Each time she exerted herself, the pain in her side forced the memories of the battle to rush back. The vivid images that often accompanied the pain were enough to drive Syndral mad. They were also inconvenient. Though Syndral knew Kindra had turned her car north, too much time had passed to follow her.

Syndral edged her truck into traffic, headed in the same direction as Kindra. She didn't have anywhere to be at the moment, and there was a chance that Kindra drove slowly enough for Syndral to catch up to her.

❧

Kindra reached for her coffee, but her hand met her cell phone instead. She groaned.

Nothing makes a solitary ride worse than not having coffee.

Kindra pulled into the next gas station. She jumped out of her car and jogged into the little bodega. She walked to the self-serve coffee station and grabbed a cup off the top of the pile. With luck, the coffee would be better than the dingy place suggested. She watched a Chevy Colorado pull into the lot as she filled her cup. Kindra was fairly sure that would be her next vehicle. It would be much easier to get up to Leif's cabin in a truck than the Civic. The coffee spilled over onto her hand and Kindra winced. She dumped some coffee out, added sugar and milk, and then headed to the counter to pay.

On her way out of the store, Kindra took in the lines of the Colorado. It was white, but it would look better in silver.

Since Kindra had been moonlighting as a detective, she hadn't been spending much money on entertainment. She was at school from 8am to 3pm, and then she headed straight for Leif's cabin or out to find one of Pakk's descendants. The only thing she really spent money on lately was gas. If she bought a Colorado, the amount she spent on fuel would increase.

Kindra's mind had always been prone to wandering. The only time she felt focused was when she was hunched over her computer trying to find the location of royal Elven descendants. Ulford was continuing his campaign to rid the realms of any elf with a stronger claim than his on the throne of Lillerem. Ulford's systematic cleansing of royal blood from Alfheim had resulted in the murder of hundreds of King Bain's descendants already, and now he was doing the same in this realm.

Ulford had sent men through the portal in Norway. The portal opened into the garage of Leif's childhood home. Kindra's mother, Gretchen, and half-sister, Kristen, had paid the price for being in the home at the time the Dredfall soldiers came through.

After the attacks in Norway, Kindra had been the one to recognize the connection between the victims Leif was not familiar with. She suspected they might all descend from a single elf. Krish had made the breakthrough when he found that Leif's eldest sibling, Pakk, had possessed the same proclivities as Leif. Pakk had enjoyed more time in the human realm than in Alfheim and had fathered hundreds of half-elf children. Those people with Elven blood, not descended from Leif, were likely descended from Pakk.

The next task had been to identify all of the people in the human realm, who were fathered by Pakk. That was Kindra's job. The descendants of Pakk, as well as Leif's descendants, could then enter Alfheim or stay under Leif's protection at the cabin. It was tedious work. On more than one occasion, Kindra had wondered how Ulford was locating these people. For every person Kindra found, and the princes protected, there were five who fell at the hands of Dredfall soldiers. The force of Dredfall soldiers in the human realm was small, but effective. Unlike the soldiers who had mounted the attack on Millspare, the soldiers in the human realm functioned more like assassins than a battalion.

Until tonight, Dredfall's assassins evaded eradication without fail. Kindra and the princes did not even know how many assassins were actually in the human realm. No soldiers had been seen entering or exiting the gates from Lillerem to the human realm since Dredfall started hunting humans.

Kindra pushed aside all concerns about buying a Colorado. She and the realms had bigger problems, and she needed to get back to Leif's cabin.

CHAPTER 2

Leif sat on the front steps of his cabin in Liberty and waited for Kindra. He took in the distant sounds of the Elven descendants training with Joral in the clearing behind his home. Some of those men were becoming soldiers. The sparring sessions and drills initially had been intended as a way to pass time for the men and for Joral. Those pastimes resulted in the beginning of a skilled force of soldiers. Some recruits were beyond the help of training, but others responded to it as if they had missed their calling in life.

Though Leif rarely participated in the training himself, he had taken to sitting outside and listening to the rhythm of the men moving through drills each morning and most evenings. He stared at the coffee in his mug. He was not sure he even liked the stuff. It was only recently that he started taking his coffee without a shot or two of whiskey in it. It dawned on Leif that his coffee had not been about the coffee at all. Having an acceptable mixer for his alcohol had been the motive. In the recent past, there had been days where he had abandoned all pretense of the coffee and simply put whiskey into a mug. It didn't seem to matter what was in the cup, but drinking from a mug in the morning seemed like it made it normal.

Leif missed the alcohol. He had been raised in the human realm and had always enjoyed the release from responsibility that alcohol afforded him. For most of his abnormally-long life, he had avoided reality and pain by staying drunk. Back among the humans after the attack on Millspare, obliged to make a conscious effort to work his magic, Leif found himself choosing sobriety, at considerable cost.

Leif was lucky. Many elves, even those strong enough to travel through the portal, were not able to wield their powers upon arrival. Those who could, found their magic greatly diminished. Meanwhile Ulford had hand-picked an elite team, so that the princes were facing only the strongest foes capable of using magic in the human realm.

Leif was the mightiest of elves, as befitted the the prince who had been expected to become the savior of his race. Lately though, he was beginning to wonder. Was Kindra even stronger than he was? He felt perplexed, yet immeasurably proud of his daughter.

The sounds from the camp ceased. The training session was over. Headlights shone as a car approached and Leif turned to go inside before Kindra got any notions about how much he had worried about her.

As Kindra turned her Civic into the narrow dirt lane that served as Leif's driveway, she was pondering possible methods Dredfall might employ to find those with Elven blood. It really bothered her that the assassins just seemed to know whom to target.

Kindra pulled the car up close to the front porch of the cabin. As she mounted the steps, Krish came through the door and met her outside. He swept her up into his arms and gave her a single spin before putting her down.

"I hear we came close to losing you," Krish said softly.

The worry in Krish's voice only irritated Kindra. "My recollection of pursuing the job of realm-saver must be cloudy. I believe it was you and your royal cousins who thought I should feel honored to carry that title. Since you played a part in putting me in danger, I'm not sure you can also reserve the right to be concerned for my safety."

"I suppose we will have to agree to disagree." Krish placed his hand on Kindra's shoulder and guided her through the door.

The expectant faces of Leif and Joral met them as they entered the living room. Kindra flopped down on the couch and gave the others a look that compelled them to take a seat.

"So, yes..." Kindra started. "I came very close to dying tonight. As you know, I traced Robert Bross, great-grandson of Pakk, to Mickelberg, about forty-five minutes north of New York City. I knew he lived in the town, and folks there said he often went to the library in the evenings. For days, I would drop in at the library to read after I left work. Most nights I would stay until the library closed. I didn't see Robert.

"Tonight was like any other night, except this time I ended up in a choke hold while inspecting the books in the math section. The cretin turned out to be Morthil! I don't know if he was also hunting Robert, or if he was there for me, but he came pretty close to finishing me off!"

A dark look came over Krish's face. Leif rose to his feet and commenced pacing. The mention of one of the few Dredfall assassins Kindra's party had identified changed the mood of the males in the room.

Kindra continued. "I wouldn't be here right now if some woman hadn't put her book down and pulled Morthil off of me. She strangled him, and did not release her grip until he fell to the floor. Even then, she kept squeezing, likely detaching his head from his neck. Then, she just stood up and walked away. I went right to the body and pulled back his hood. I was so shaken at first that it did not occur to me to go after the woman who killed him. When I finally got moving and went out to the parking lot, she was gone. I called you as I left to meet up with you and... here we are."

It was quiet for a moment as the princes processed the story and waited to ensure that Kindra had, indeed, finished her tale. Kindra relaxed her shoulders. She hadn't realized there were so many questions for which she had no answers.

"Who the hell was the woman?" Joral thought aloud.

Kindra felt the need to respond. "I don't know who she was, but she was well-trained and strong. I'm grateful to her for saving me, but it is extremely unsettling that she didn't say a word to me. She didn't even stop to ask if I was alright. She just killed Morthil, and then left."

"One more time," said Krish. "Describe every detail you can remember. Tell us exactly what she looked like."

"She looked exactly like me," said a female voice from near the front door.

Kindra's gaze swept toward the voice. It was the woman from Mickelberg Library. She was tall. Kindra was five feet and six inches in height, and this woman was definitely taller than her. The woman's skinny jeans gave the impression her legs composed most of her body. Her boots were black, and though they had a block heel, buckles and zippers adorned the leather; similar to motorcycle boots. The woman sported a plain black turtleneck that molded to her torso. Her shoulders were broad for a woman's, but what truly caught Kindra's eye were the woman's ears. With her hair tucked back, Kindra could see that this female was not a woman at all. She was an elf.

The sound of swords being drawn resounded around the room as the princes prepared to face the intruder. Krish, Joral and Leif all went to Kindra's side as she took to her feet and readied herself for a fight.

The female moved faster than any human ever could. She pulled a small Ruger from nowhere and pointed it toward Kindra and the males.

"Silly males!" The female had a huge smirk on her face. "You're in the human realm now. Why would you think a sword fight would ever be practical? Haven't you seen the statistics? Almost 4.5 million New Yorkers own guns. Your pretty swords are useless here. Now, how about you all sit back down and let me tell you why I am here? I don't want to hurt any of you. We are on the same side."

"The same side?" Leif sneered. "Why would someone on the same side sneak in here and be pointing a gun at us?"

"Show of good faith?" asked the woman as she slid her pistol back into the holster concealed at the small of her back.

Kindra lowered herself back into her seat. Joral and Leif lowered their swords and moved to sit on the couch. Krish looked unsure. Eventually, he sat on the arm of the couch and rested the flat of the sword across his thighs. Kindra was close enough to feel the tension radiating from Krish. She imagined the other two princes were also much more ready to strike than they appeared as well.

The female took a seat in the vacant rocking chair near the window. "My name is Syndral. I was born in the Kingdom of Nalahem, north of Dredfall. Lillerem is not the only land plagued by Ulford's attempts to control more and more. Though we have kept most of our land, Ulford took several small border towns and the City of Lindel over the last decade. My family was from Lindel."

Syndral's face showed tension as she spoke about her family. The use of the past tense had Kindra suspecting Syndral had lost some, or maybe all, of that family when the Dredfall soldiers sacked the city. It would explain how this elf, not from Lillerem, might find herself on the same side of the fight against Dredfall as the other occupants of the room. Kindra felt her heart go out to the woman and she knew her features softened. The tension to her left told her Syndral's words were not affecting Krish in the same way.

Kindra tried to bury some of the sympathy she was feeling, "So, you waltz in here, uninvited, after saying nothing to me at the library and you expect me to accept your offer of friendship?"

"I never said I was offering friendship," Syndral smirked. "Camaraderie and campfires are of no interest to me. I only want to team up against a common enemy."

Joral spoke to Kindra with his eyes. He told her to consider Syndral's offer. He wanted her to take a breath. Joral was trying to keep her from unleashing the hostility that he knew was bubbling under her skin. Kindra turned her eyes away from Joral. He was giving good advice, but Kindra was trying to pretend she hadn't noticed.

"You sprinted out of the library without a word. I appreciate you defending my life, but an explanation, or at least an introduction, would have made the proposal for an alliance more appealing. Right now, I feel as if some crazy psycho stalked me, killed my attacker, and then went right on stalking me. To ice the cake, that same psycho invited herself right into this living room as if we've all been pals since grade school!"

"I am sorry I did not explain myself at the library. You are correct, my disappearance and reappearance make me suspect, and I understand your hesitation." Syndral rested her elbows on her thighs and stretched her hands out, palms up, looking for forgiveness. "I couldn't risk being seen at the library, but I wanted to speak with you. When you pulled out of the parking lot, I followed you so I could explain. I wasn't even sure you knew Morthil, and I was not prepared to have a long conversation at the scene of a murder."

"Where is Robert?" Kindra asked.

"Already dead. It was you Morthil was waiting for at the library."

All the males were restless at these tidings, none more so than Leif. Syndral's words were eliciting strong protective instincts within them. Syndral continued. "I was going to approach you when you stopped for coffee, but I thought you would be more comfortable with your friends here." She gestured toward the princes in the room with her hands as she sat up straight.

Krish placed his hand on Kindra's thigh to keep her from speaking. "I'm willing to hear you out. What information can you give us about Dredfall's movements?"

"That's the thing," Syndral willingly began. "It isn't on behalf of Dredfall that Ulford is acting. It is common for Ulford to rally the people of Dredfall to a cause. When he sent the army to take Millspare, Ulford spent weeks garnering the support of the people and the troops. Ulford has made no public mention of his intent to kill the descendants of Blaith. Even the Dredfall troops are uninformed. Ulford quietly sent his personal guard into the human realm on this errand."

"Ulford is not an idiot," Krish spoke aloud, trying to understand. "He knows he needs to at least provide the illusion that he is working on behalf of his people. A move against humans has no bearing on the lives of the Dredfall citizens and would not aid him in gaining support for the conquest of Lillerem. The attack on Millspare was a smart move because the people would benefit from the acquisition of more land and resources, and also give Ulford the opportunity to eliminate Lady Ruth. Entering the human realm to kill half-breeds poses no immediate advantage to any of the elves living under Ulford's control."

Kindra stared ice at Krish. The term 'half-breed' was derogatory, but Kindra was even more offended because Krish, the male she would be marrying, had been the one to use it. Born of a human woman and a male elf, Kindra fell into the category Krish was describing so crassly. Krish dismissed Kindra's glare, which only served to further anger Kindra.

With Kindra's irritation redirected toward Krish, her tone with Syndral softened slightly. "How do you have this information? Where do your loyalties lie? What do you expect from us?"

Kindra was no longer using an accusatory tone with Syndral, but tossing the questions out in rapid succession had a similar effect. Syndral looked like she was struggling not to bite back at Kindra's questions with some venom of her own. Instead, Syndral took a slow breath and answered the questions in the order Kindra had thrown them toward her.

"I was a Dredfall soldier. I was commander of the Second Draw. I recognized Ulford as Dredfall's king and I collected my coin from his coffers, but I hail from a city he stole. The border between Dredfall and Nalahem ran through the southern tip of the city. Since a part of Lindel was in Dredfall, I could volunteer for the army that was stationed three hours from my home instead of the one that was stationed two days north. When Ulford took control of the Nalahem portion of Lindel and ordered the death of a quarter of my people, including my parents, I officially became a citizen of Dredfall. I have no love for Ulford; I chose life as one of his soldiers to avoid life as one of his slaves. Once under Dredfall's control, my people had few options, and none of them were ideal. I survived. I trained. I killed in the name of Dredfall, and I worked my way up to the rank of commander. Each promotion came with more coin for my purse, and I convinced myself I could continue to fight under Ulford's banner.

"I am no longer active; instead I train new recruits. I no longer go on campaigns, which gives me a lot of time to observe troop movements and assignments. Ulford was giving unusual orders to his guard, and he no longer had them operating as a draw. Instead, he tasked each member of the guard with a different mission. Some of these missions took several days, and the absence of the guard members was blatant. The disappearance of an entire draw, especially the most elite draw in the kingdom, is difficult to hide. Once I noticed none of the elite guard remained, I started asking casual questions."

Leif hit his limit on being patient. "Let me just interrupt your diatribe for a moment here. You were living happily in a city with your family. The evil king of a neighboring country invades your city and kills your parents. You join the same army that perpetrated crimes against your people, and decide to make a career of it. How am I doing so far?"

Syndral looked ready to object, but Leif plunged on. "You miss the power that comes with the title of Commander, so the discovery of a plot unfolding without your help offends you. Instead of soldiering on, you decide you want to be part of the important missions of the elite royal guard. You snoop around to figure out how you can get in on the action. Am I still on target?"

Syndral's voice was harsh. "Don't you know what happened in Norway? How could anyone think that was acceptable?"

Leif teleported from the far side of the room to stand before Syndral. He leaned down and placed his face inches from hers. "I damn well know what happened in Norway. Kindra's mother knows what happened in Norway. My daughter knows, exactly, what happened in Norway!" Leif was yelling by the time he mentioned his daughter, Kristen.

Syndral shrank back in her chair to avoid the spittle coming from Leif's mouth. With her head lowered, and in a softer voice, she continued. "A consort of Ulford's mentioned the departure of Morthil through one of the gates to the human realm. I checked the log book for the Dredfall Gate. There was no entry for the departure of any of the members of Ulford's Elite Draw. Since only Ulford and members of the First Draw are permitted the use of the Gate linking Dredfall to Philadelphia, there would be no reason not to log the excursions. I snuck over the border and into Lillerem. I climbed the cliffs to the gate leading to Norway. I'd never used that gate and I didn't know where I was when I exited the portal and found myself in a carriage house.

"The main home was blocked off by police tape. I wanted to know what crime had occurred at the site of a portal that should be watched from the side of the human realm. I went to the back of the house and entered through the bathroom window. The smell... There were bodies, both elven and human. I had to return to the carriage house. Do you know what Nissen are?"

Kindra sucked in a breath. The mention of Nissen brought back memories of Nils, the tiny old man who had encouraged her to take up Forsvarer. He and Kristen had been there at the start of her journey into Alfheim. She hoped Syndral's mention of Nissen, the creatures that guard the farms of Norway, was an indication that Nils had survived.

"Anyway," Syndral continued, "This little fellow Nils lives in the carriage house. He was there when the first assassin spilled into the human world and killed Gretchen and Kristen. After the initial discovery of those deaths, there were more. The assassins entered the human realm one at a time and they used Husland Farm as a boarding house. Any elf trying to enter Norway from Lillerem never left the farm. Likewise, any time curiosity led an unsuspecting soul near the outside of the home, the threat to the discovery of the assassins' location was... terminated.

"I ignored the wrongness of Dredfall's war crimes in Alfheim as long as my coin purse was full. I felt no remorse when the Second

Draw was sent to kill the residents of Millspare. I draw the line when the human realm is involved."

"What connection do you have with the human realm?" Leif shot back.

Syndral paused. It took her a beat to reply, and when she did, her demeanor turned haughty once again. "Leif Husland, you are not the only living elf that enjoys the pleasures offered in the human realm. I may not have littered the territory with the product of my seed as you have, but I have people here I care about. I would bet there are thousands of elves in the human realm right now. Not all of them are your spawn, and they don't deserve any less help than those who are."

Kindra felt ashamed. The revelation of her hubris for believing elves from her family would be the only ones to travel to the human realm burned her ego. Until this moment, Leif, Pakk, and Gunnar were the only elves Kindra knew to make the trip from Alfheim to the realm of humans. The gates in Lillerem were unguarded and rarely supervised. Travel was never prevented between realms, only watched. Elves could move between worlds freely, and as often as they wished, provided they possessed enough magic. The longer Kindra chewed on the information, the more she realized elves may have traveled to, or were currently traveling in, the human realm. *How many gates are there? Lillerem can't control them all. Just because I didn't know about elves and gates and magical swords doesn't mean that all of Alfheim is ignorant of humans and our realm.*

Kindra felt a squeeze on her thigh. Krish was trying, subtly, to pull her from her thoughts. Kindra looked at Krish. It wasn't he who had last spoken. Krish did not move his head as he directed Kindra's gaze to Syndral with his eyes. She had been the last to speak, and from the look on her face, Kindra guessed she was waiting for the answer to a question.

"Which gate do you usually use to travel to this realm?" Kindra asked.

"The Lindel Gate. I still have a cousin in Lindel. Each time I visit him, I also travel to this realm. I spend a week with cousin Darkel in Lindel, then a week here."

"Where in the human realm does the Lindel gate lead?" Kindra was onto something, but she wasn't exactly sure what.

"Saint-Raymond, Quebec, north of the Saint Lawrence River. It's about a two-hour flight from here."

"Flight? Then it's safe to assume you never used the gate outside Aergroth?" Kindra asked.

"The Aergroth gate would make travel to New York much faster. Unfortunately, I rarely find myself with an excuse to take leave in Lillerem, and even if I did, the Millspare Guard isn't very accepting of strangers. There are gates throughout Alfheim that are connected to this realm. The Lindel gate is my best option for travel to this area of your realm."

Joral spoke. "It is good that you did not attempt the New York Gate. We would have run a sword through your chest before you completely emerged from the tunnel."

Syndral's gaze was unfixed. "Knowing that, I am very glad I didn't attempt it. I'll admit, use of the gate here would have made my life simpler, but my death would have deprived you of the opportunity for an alliance with a skilled warrior whose enemy is your enemy."

CHAPTER 3

Syndral sat in the driver's seat of her truck watching the dark bedroom window in the upper left corner of a well-kept split level ranch. It was late and the little girl who occupied the bedroom was likely asleep. Syndral wanted nothing more than to ring the doorbell of the home and wake the little girl up. Unfortunately, that was not conducive to her plan to keep Riva safe.

She was the real reason Syndral did not sleep and needed no place to stay. Once Syndral determined that the assassins in Norway had made their way to the States, and to New York no less, Syndral had sat vigil outside of this house every night. She had not returned to Dredfall, and was now a deserter with no coin and nothing to go back to except the promise of execution. None of that mattered. Riva was the priority.

Syndral's decision to go to Kindra and the princes was not made lightly. Syndral was only one person, she had no magic in the human realm, and the assassins eventually would find their way to the quiet home she now watched in their search for Elven blood. The only other people with an interest in stopping Ulford's ceaseless and obsessive quest to rid the world of every descendant of King Andril had been in Leif's cabin tonight.

Syndral was not sure she had won them over. Syndral had not lied about any of the information she shared about herself tonight. She had left the little girl out though. Syndral did not intend to trust her recent enemies with information about someone so precious.

Syndral's white Chevrolet Colorado bumped down Leif's driveway, headed back to the road. As Kindra watched it depart, sh was not as enthralled with the vehicle as she once was. Maybe she wouldn't buy one after all.

"So, what are we thinking?" Krish addressed the room.

Kindra stepped back from the window once the truck was out of view. "I don't trust her."

Leif sighed. "I think that goes without saying. What we need to decide is if we want to work with her, despite the lack of trust."

Krish played with the edge of his sword. "She was correct about one thing. Our swords are nearly useless in this realm. The weapons here excel during ranged attacks. Unless we hold the element of surprise or desire secrecy, swords and daggers will be ineffective."

"I still have no plans to stash mine in the closet with Forsvarer!" Leif stated adamantly.

Kindra's eyes bored holes into Leif. She had carefully wrapped the family sword in a few of Leif's shirts and placed it in the back of his closet shortly after returning to the human realm. The sword was heavy and much more difficult to wield in her human form. Months ago, in Norway, Forsvarer had played Kindra a beautiful melody. That song was what led Kindra through the portal and into this fairy tale nightmare she now referred to as her life. Kindra found the sword only attracted unwanted attention in this realm. The only way it would look natural was if it were summer and Kindra dressed as if she were attending the local Renaissance Fair.

"So... guns it is?" asked Krish.

"This is New York," said Kindra. "It's not like we can just poke our heads into the local convenience store and order up a Glock at the deli. You need a permit, and a firearms safety course, and a background check, and..."

Leif rolled his eyes at Kindra. "Only people who follow the law do all those things. The criminals just buy guns from other criminals on the street. I am ashamed to have a daughter who is so naïve. You forget; not only are we elves not citizens of New York, we do not even exist as a people in this realm. Even if we wanted to obey your laws, we couldn't. I'll take care of the guns."

Leif glided from the living room and out the front door. Kindra heard her car start and the crunch of gravel as it backed out of its spot and headed down the driveway. Kindra checked her pockets. She did not have her key. She was never one to lock her doors and protect her vehicle. It wasn't because she thought she lived in a safe area; it was more because she believed if someone really wanted the car or the items inside, the person would find a way to take those things, anyway.

The problem was not that Kindra was now without a car. It was not even an issue that Leif went off on his own to gather the newly desired guns. The concern was that Leif had no license. When one is trying to keep a low profile, it is best to stay within the confines of the law. If Leif was pulled over in Kindra's vehicle, the police would impound the car, and Leif would go to jail. Unlike Krish and Joral, Leif had an identity in the human realm. Living with his extended life-span required altering that identity every decade, but he existed as a citizen of New York State. His current identity had enough DWI charges to keep him behind bars for multiple years if he was caught driving without a license tonight.

Joral, who had been quiet throughout the gun discussion, looked up when Kindra laughed aloud. "What is so funny?"

"I'm laughing because my first inclination was to worry about Leif not having a license when he took the car. When it occurred to me that he was using the car to purchase illegal firearms and probably driving across state-lines with those weapons, I realized I might be as naïve as Leif said I was."

Joral tried to put Kindra's mind at ease. "He'll be fine as long as he doesn't get caught."

"…said every criminal ever, right before they were caught and put in jail," Kindra concluded with an eye-roll and a slow shake of her head.

"What is our next move?" Krish posed the question to Kindra and Joral.

"I vote we continue as before," stated Joral. "Kindra has identified two other descendants of Pakk that have not yet turned into missing persons. Krish and I will each locate one of them and return them here to be assessed. Kindra, I suggest you continue to look for others."

"I can't tomorrow. I really need to see how Sean is holding up."

Sean Bennet was living alone because of Kindra. When Kindra's mother and sister were murdered in Norway, Kindra's best friend

Jess had pushed through the gate to Lillerem to inform Kindra of the terrible news. The portal had nearly drained Jess of her life. Until Jess built up enough strength to come back through the portal, Sean was stuck at home without his wife.

"I'm not sure that is a priority," said Joral. "If you have no inclination to hunt for more descendants, maybe you should spend some time trying to discern the means by which the assassins are tracking them down?"

Kindra was instantly defensive. "I have no idea how they do it! It takes me hours to trace unusual births on my ancestry site, and then days to verify that the result of each of those births is actually a living, breathing human with Elven blood. It's like the assassins have a magical device for picking up the scent they are after. I can't compete!"

Joral stuck his tongue against his cheek to stop himself from saying something he would regret. He raised his eyebrows in Kindra's direction and waited for her to simmer down.

"Sorry," she said. "I know that wasn't an attack on my work. The issue does need to be addressed. I'll get on it tomorrow."

Trying to ease the tension, Krish came up behind Kindra. "Does this mean I get to spend the evening with you?"

"It looks like I'm yours. I'm sure Leif will be back with my car eventually, but I'll certainly be here for some time." Kindra allowed Krish to swallow her in his embrace.

Joral cleared his throat. "Just to be clear, I am still in the room. I am heading out to check on the camp, though. You two should have a good hour together before I return. Please save me some stew. It's in the pot on the stove."

Kindra's face reddened as Joral left to look over the camp. Behind Leif's cabin, a tent city had formed. There were elves from the Lillerem army, as well as human descendants of elves camped out ther. The elves were here to support Kindra and the princes. Each elf, being powerful enough to travel to the human realm, had followed Kindra here to repay her for defending Aergroth when Millspare fell under attack. These elves took repaying debts seriously, and they proved indispensable in testing the humans brought to the camp.

The Elves examined each descendant for magical ability by bringing them near the portal. Depending on how the human reacted, he or she would be ushered through the tunnel to Aergroth or kept here among the Elven warriors. Those without enough magical ability to travel to Alfheim remained to train with the soldiers, and Kindra was discovering that many of them had a gift for swordsmanship. Even if a gun was more practical in the human realm, the sword training helped the humans think defensively and made them much better prepared to defend themselves.

At first, Kindra had been concerned the humans would feel as if they were captured and held hostage. This had not been the case. Most of the humans Kindra and the princes had identified as Elven descendants had already felt as if they were being followed or, in some cases, had already been victims of an attack. Those who were oblivious to there being any danger often felt the need for safety after being in the camp for a few hours and speaking to the other residents of the tent city.

Kindra cursed as she put a spoonful of the stew into her mouth. "My God, that is hot!"

Krish had just served Kindra a bowl of stew at the little kitchen table.

"I warned you to let it cool. As so often, your mind was elsewhere."

Kindra blushed. "I wonder how long it will take for you to find that cute quirk of mine less endearing than you find it now."

"When all of this is over and we are safe from Ulford's ruthlessness, I will contemplate each of your quirks and decide which I could stand to live without. Until then, I count each of your shortcomings as a reminder that you are a real person and not a woman from my fantasies."

"I think that was supposed to be sweet, so I will not take offense," Kindra replied as she spooned stew into her mouth.

Kindra didn't usually enjoy stew. This stew, however, was the nectar of the Gods, or if not exactly of the Gods then of elves like Einar, who could prepare food as well as a culinary school graduate. Joral must have picked up a few cooking tips while watching him. The stew placed in front of Kindra a minute ago disappeared only moments after Krish sat down with his own bowl.

"How is your palate?" asked Krish.

"What do you mean? It tasted good to me," said Kindra.

Krish laughed. "The roof of your mouth. Did you burn it as you gobbled down your stew?"

Kindra explored her mouth with her tongue and found she had some sensitive spots just behind her teeth. In one area, a blister was already forming.

Krish smiled. "I suppose some will pay a high price to have a magnificent stew warm them down to the belly."

As Kindra stood to bring her empty bowl to the sink, she saw the flash of headlights through the living room window. With a literal army living behind the cabin, Kindra felt foolish at first over the sense of worry that came over her with the approach of the car, then she quickly recalled Syndral's unexpected visit. *I guess I'm not as safe here as I thought.*

Gravel crunched as the vehicle came to a halt out front. The engine cut out and Kindra held her breath. It did not help her nerves to see Krish's hand resting on the hilt of his sword.

Leif pushed through the front door and walked straight into the kitchen. He placed a large bag on the table with a light thump. Krish and Kindra stared silently as Leif ladled some stew into a bowl, grabbed a beer from the refrigerator, and plopped down in one of the kitchen chairs. He went at the stew with the same fervor Kindra had shown. Kindra, still holding Krish's bowl and spoon, sat back down at the table.

Kindra broke the silence. "How the hell are you back so soon? You've been gone less than an hour."

"I got lucky. My guy was home."

Krish shook his head. "You have a guy. I should have known you'd have a guy. We were just talking about how difficult it is to buy a gun in New York and in less than an hour, you go see your guy and return with a bag full of guns."

"There's ammunition in the bag, too. If I recall, we were talking about how difficult it is to get a gun in New York legally. If one is willing to bypass the rules, he can be fully armed in under an hour. I just proved it," Leif said with satisfaction. "By the way, Kindra, you're nearly out of gas."

❦❦❦

The following day, Kindra brought a forged doctor's note to the school where both Kindra and Jess worked. The note would buy Jess another week or two. That had been as far ahead as Kindra could think. Kindra was floundering. The absence of her best friend left her feeling as if her logical side was missing.

On her lunch break, Kindra drove toward the deli where she and Jess used to eat together every day. She pulled into a spot on the far side of the lot and stepped from her car. She shut the door, and turned to find herself inches from Vander.

"I suppose you're here to talk about Morthil?" asked Kindra.

With remarkable speed, Vander swung his fist at her face. Kindra moved faster. She ducked under his arm and came up behind him. Vander spun to face Kindra and his nose met Kindra's hand as she used a backswing to meet him from the opposite direction. Kindra teleported to the inside of her car. She turned the key and lowered the window a half inch.

"Thanks for the chat!" Kindra said, plastering her left middle finger to the inside of the window and using her right hand to shift into reverse.

Cutting the wheel while the car rolled backward, Kindra clearly heard Vander's reply, "You and your friends can't hide! Ulford's hounds will be all over you before you know it!"

It seemed lunch was not an option today. Kindra zipped out of the parking lot. *Damn silent elves. I didn't even hear him coming. Ulford's hounds indeed... hopefully the assassins won't be locating me or the others any time soon.* She was fairly confident the strict security policies at the school made it a poor choice for the assassins to attack her there.

Leaving school three hours later, Kindra sent a text to Leif to let him know her plans. "Got a visit from Vander at lunch. Going to swing by Sean's to throw off anyone shadowing me, and then I'll head home to research methods for tracking blood."

Vander had referred to the assassins as Ulford's hounds. It had caused Kindra to form a theory. Bloodhounds are used to track scent. There are scent dogs that can detect explosives and drugs. Kindra even knew of a company that used a Beagle to sniff out bed bugs. It was a possibility that one of the assassins had the power to sniff out Elven blood. Maybe one of the elves was just walking the streets, nose in the air, trying to catch the right scent. It felt far-fetched, but Kindra still wanted to figure out a way to test the theory.

A few moments later, Kindra stood in Jess's living room. Butch, one of Jess's German Shepherd dogs, nuzzled Kindra's hand; at least,

Kindra was pretty sure it was Butch. She always had a difficult time telling the two dogs apart unless they were together. Jess trained with the dogs almost daily, and it was strange to see them without Jess to wrap themselves around.

"Cassidy, go lie down!" Sean reprimanded the dog.

Kindra had been wrong. This one was Cassidy. *Where is Butch?* Kindra glanced around the living room, but the dog wasn't in sight. Kindra stepped into the kitchen and heard scratching at the back door. She made her way past the pile of dishes in the sink and parted the curtains on the door. Butch's sad eyes looked at her from the back porch. Kindra opened the door and Butch made his way in. He did a lap of the living room, and not finding Jess, returned to Kindra.

"Hey Sean, I think Cassidy was just trying to tell me that Butch was locked outside."

"That makes sense. He hasn't left me alone for the last hour. I fed them and let them out. I must have let Cassidy in and forgotten Butch was still out there," Sean's gaze never left the television screen.

The first time Kindra visited Sean after Jess was trapped in Alfheim, the house had appeared normal. Kindra felt as if she had stopped in to see Jess and simply found she was not at home. Kindra tried to explain to Sean where Jess was, but hadn't made progress until she offered to take Sean to Leif's house. Upon arrival, introducing Sean to the pointy-eared duo of Leif and Krish, was not enough evidence for Sean. It had been the portal that finally convinced Sean that there was merit to Kindra's story.

Kindra had zero doubt that Sean possessed no Elven blood. He struggled to even climb down the steps to view the portal in Leif's basement. He couldn't adequately articulate it to Kindra, but kept saying he did not feel right going down the steps. He repeatedly told Kindra he did not belong down there. Sean had pushed through the discomfort long enough to get half-way down the steps and watch Kindra open and close the door to the tunnel. Sean now understood Kindra was telling the truth. It had not been viewing the tunnel itself; it had been the feeling he could not shake and could not explain. He said it was as unnatural as the story Kindra told.

"Earth to Kindra! Any news from Gunnar? Will my wife be home soon?"

"Last I spoke to Gunnar, he said Jess was very close. I came by today to let you know you should probably start getting this house in order. If Jess comes home and sees the place like this, she might turn around and leave again."

Kindra was trying to keep things light, but Sean didn't laugh. "If she misses me the way I miss her, she'll never leave again. She'll stay even if I stack every dish in the house on the coffee table and leave a trail of laundry down the hallway."

"I'm sure she will," said Kindra more seriously, but she couldn't help herself when she said, "Drips and drops in front of the toilet might be a deal-breaker, though."

Sean finally cracked a smile. He had not exactly managed to keep up with the housework, and Kindra could only hope he was caught up on the bills. Jess would have a lot of work to do to get the place back on its tight schedule and up to her organizational standards again, but Sean was still standing.

"Seriously," Kindra said. "I need to run, but you really need to clean this place up and make it look presentable. It wouldn't hurt to start reminding Butch and Cassidy that there were once rules under this roof and those rules will once again be enforced. Jess hasn't been on vacation. It has been a lot of hard work on her part to be able to get back here, and I'm sure it would be nice to avoid having her walk into more drudgery when she should just be enjoying being home."

Sean nodded his head. "Point taken. I'm on it. Go save elf-people and I'll start getting this place in order."

CHAPTER 4

Jess stood on a quaint walking path near the outskirts of Aergroth. She tried to draw succor from her beautiful surroundings to help calm her nerves. Only a few months ago, Kindra had stumbled on Jess, unconscious, in this very place. If not for Kindra finding Jess's limp form here on the path, Jess would not be here now. Once Jess was well enough to begin learning to use a sword, Jess and Kindra started sparing together. Joral trained Jess to use magic in the same way he had with Kindra. Jess's magic was far weaker than Kindra's, but that was unsurprising. Kindra was extremely powerful. She walked through the portal tunnel with almost no discomfort and could travel between realms with no adverse effects.

Months of training and strengthening her magic led Jess to where she stood now, three feet from the Aegroth portal to New York. Jess should, in theory, be able to walk through this portal without dying. As a mathematics teacher, Jess understood exactly what a theory was. It was an accepted truth; despite the fact no one had proved it was true for all situations. It was the thought that she might be an exception that had Jess standing at the entrance, instead of walking through the portal.

Jess drew on some of her magic. She called to a small songbird in the branches hanging over her head. The bird flew down and landed on Jess's shoulder.

"What do you think, my little friend?" Jess asked the bird. "Am I going to make it?"

The bird, unable to speak, pecked at Jess's shoulder gently and combed its beak through her blonde curls. Jess understood the encouragement. *Get out of your own head. You're starting to be worse than Kindra. Get moving. One foot in front of the other.* Jess moved her right foot, then the left. She approached a bush with beautiful flowers.

Pulling back on the branches, Jess revealed the face of a large rock. She pressed her hand on its cool surface and gave a little shove. A portion of the rock slid back and revealed a tunnel.

As Jess drew in a final breath to fortify herself, a hand fell on her shoulder. Jess pulled her sword from its scabbard and spun to face her assailant. She looked into the eyes of Kindra's uncle, Gunnar. If Jess understood correctly, Gunnar was also her uncle. To be precise, Gunnar was Jess's great uncle. Leif, Gunnar, and Jess's grandfather, Pakk, were brothers. The discovery that Jess was a descendant of Pakk meant that, to Jess's delight, she was also Kindra's cousin. The best friends now knew they shared a bond of blood, as well as the bond of friendship.

"Easy! It's just me," Gunnar said as he raised his hands in the air. "You didn't think I was going to let you take this journey alone, did you?"

Jess smiled. "No, I suppose I should have expected your arrival. I was just working up enough courage to step into the tunnel. Now that you're here, my confidence is soaring."

Gunnar picked up a pack he had dropped by his feet and slung it over his right shoulder. He checked the sword at his side and the dagger in the sheath he kept in the small of his back. Gunnar held out his hand to Jess, and she took it. The pair turned toward the tunnel and entered together. Gunnar struck flint to steel and ignited the torch near the door. As the torch illuminated a circle with a radius of about ten feet, the doorway slid closed.

"Do you feel anything?" Gunnar asked Jess.

"There's a slight tingle in the back of my head, but otherwise, no. I'm ok."

Gunnar let out a large puff of air. Before the giant sigh from Gunnar, Jess had thought he was full of assurance. She felt as if she should congratulate Gunnar on his ability to hide his fear that she had not built up enough magical strength to move through the portal.

Gunnar gave a small smile. "I knew you had this. I must say, I did not think you were this strong, though. Even I feel more than a tingle in my head. It borders on discomfort, and I will have a headache by the time we reach the other side."

Jess considered Gunnar's words. If the portal was any test of magical strength, her lack of discomfort meant that she was now stronger in magical ability than Gunnar. Though Gunnar was far from the strongest elf in the realm, he would not be considered weak. Jess did not possess many of the powers the other descendants of King Blaith could wield. She could not teleport or move things with her mind. Jess's body could heal itself, as could those of others in her family, and she had the added talent of communicating with animals. The animals understood her will and carried out her wishes. Gunnar and Joral had shown surprise at the revelation of Jess's unique talent. Neither elf had ever met someone with that ability, though both had heard legends of elves with connections to nature similar to hers. There had not been an elf with Jess's talents recorded in the scrolls in over five hundred years. All elves with the ability were female, the last of which had been the daughter of a blacksmith with no royal line.

Halfway along the tunnel, Jess felt the tops of her ears itch and her teeth throb dully. Jess knew from Kindra's experience with realm-traveling that those with a mix of human and Elven blood would display a form appropriate for the realm he or she entered. As Jess passed into the human realm, she felt her slightly elongated canine teeth retracting and the points at the tips of her ears rounding.

The torch's light picked up a wall at the end of the tunnel. The wall was ten feet away. Jess wasn't sure what had made her hesitate just before reentering the human realm, but the pause provided enough time for a wave of unwelcome thoughts. She focused on the circle of light around her and Gunnar. *The radius of my light circle is ten feet. I am standing in over 300 square feet of light.* Jess found that even math wasn't providing comfort. She had not seen Sean in months. She missed him, but there was trepidation where Jess thought there would be excitement. Everything and everyone in Jess's human life had continued on when Jess disappeared. There would be things that had changed. Jess knew she was not walking straight back into her old life. For one thing, her husband now knew there was at least one parallel realm and his wife partially belonged to it. Sean knew there were evil powers in play and that his wife was no longer just a math teacher with a penchant for keeping her house as if it were a museum. In the end, it was Butch and Cassidy that pushed Jess over the threshold and back into the human realm. She missed her babies terribly and could no longer put off the chance to bury her face in their fur.

Gunnar and Jess stepped through the portal door and made their way up the steps from Leif's basement as the gate slid shut behind them. At the top of the stairs, the bright lights of the kitchen greeted them. Leif was at the table with a bottle of whiskey and an empty glass. He looked up just in time to see Gunnar wipe the look of disappointment from his face.

"I haven't had any to drink. It's just me and an empty glass trying to convince this bottle that it looks better full than it will look empty," Leif offered.

"I can't say I'm surprised," said Gunnar.

Leif looked as if he were deciding if it was worth it to continue his explanation. "That's the strange part. In the past, I'd have finished this bottle several times over already. I've had the same one since coming back to this realm. Every day, I take this bottle out and sit down to have a drink, but each day, this is as far as I get. It isn't long before someone comes by or one of the descendants from the camp needs my help. Part of me misses a life of nothingness and lack of responsibility, but I fear my newfound obligations might be providing a healthy change in my habits."

Gunnar nodded. "Whatever works, I suppose."

"Enough about me," said Leif. "I see Jess did not die a painful death coming through the portal. How was the journey?" Leif's demeanor switched noticeably, from pensive, to one more fitting of his reputation for being overly obnoxious.

Jess knew better than to challenge Leif's flippancy. "Uneventful; just the way we like it. I'm still not sure I'm ready to leave my magic wardrobe behind, but I miss my dogs. I'm here."

"The wardrobes are wonderful aren't they?" mused Leif. "Kindra asked if it was possible to bring at least one back to the human realm. Unfortunately, the small amount of magic charming them is not enough to work here. You would just own a very heavy, stunningly beautiful piece of bedroom furniture. It would not read your mind or pick out the perfect outfit in this realm."

It surprised Jess how disappointed she was by Leif's wardrobe report. Somewhere in the back of her mind, she had really been hoping transporting one of the magical devices to her home would be the big payoff for having lost so much time in her real life. *There I go again. This is still my real life. It's just that my new life is not like my old life. Both lives are real.* She shook her head and decidedly stopped mourning the loss of the wardrobe dream.

"So, what do you need me to do first, Captain?" Jess asked.

When Jess reintroduced herself to Leif at Millspare, she hadn't known what to call him. As her best friend's father, Leif should simply have been called Dad by Jess. Considering Kindra had known Leif for less than a year, and Kindra did not even refer to Leif as Dad, Jess was uncomfortable using the name herself. Instead, Jess had taken to referring to Leif as Captain. She really wasn't sure why the name stuck for her. Leif liked to give orders, though he really had no command over the other princes, or even over Kindra. One day, after Leif spit out a string of commands, Kindra had replied by saying, "Aye, Aye, Captain!" and Jess had nearly wet her pants, laughing at the look on Leif's face.

"The first thing you need to do, my little computation connoisseur, is go home to your husband and dogs," Leif said with no uncertainty. "You've been away long enough. Go get a little love and some snuggles. When you're finished with that, say hello to Sean and then head back over here."

"Cute," said Jess. "The joke is on you, though. Butch and Cassidy are better snugglers than Sean will ever be."

Jess turned and stalked from the room. She carefully wrapped her sword in some of Leif's discarded clothing and placed it beside Forsvarer in the back of Leif's closet. A balled-up flannel shirt tumbled to the floor with a clunk. Jess picked up the clothing ball and unwrapped it. Inside the bundle was one of the smallest guns she had ever seen. Jess grabbed the pistol and strode back to the kitchen.

"So, Kindra is resorting to guns now? How bad is it here that she feels the need to carry this around?"

Leif turned to look at the tiny gun in the open palm of Jess's hand. "Apparently, Kindra does not feel the need to carry it around, as you found it in the back of my closet, along with the sword she also does not carry. That girl does everything she can to leave herself open to harm."

Jess tossed the gun on the table. "So, it wasn't her that picked this pocket pistol up? I assume that means this was your doing, Leif? Are you trying to get her killed? What is this tiny little thing going to do?"

"That," Leif said, "is a Baby Browning chambered in .25 ACP. At close range, it is just as deadly as any full-sized handgun and it has the added advantage of being able to fit in those minuscule compartments, masquerading as pockets, which seem to be a staple of women's clothing. I picked up guns for all of us. I felt that model would be best for Kindra."

Jess rolled her eyes. "Let's ignore the fact that, at close range, Kindra is more deadly with a dagger than she would ever be with this thing. Let's, instead, focus on the reason for the guns in the first place."

Jess sat down at the table. Leif relayed the story of Syndral's visit to the cabin to both Jess and Gunnar. Gunnar had to put his hand on Jess's arm several times to keep her from interrupting with one outburst or another, but Leif eventually succeeded in explaining Syndral's willingness to team up against Dredfall and the princes' inability to get close to her during her surprise visit due to the gun she possessed. Toward the end of the story, some understanding was dawning in Jess's eyes.

"If I have this straight," started Jess, "Dredfall has enemies to its north, as well as an enemy in Lillerem. A high-ranking soldier of the Dredfall army, having seen her family massacred by Dredfall, has decided it is now time to fight back because Ulford has set his sights on innocent humans. She fought for Dredfall loyally, despite the butchering of most of her family, but she can't stand the idea of humans being hunted. Yeah, I'm not buying it. There is more to this story."

Gunnar turned to Jess. "Your conclusion is logical, as expected. Unfortunately, though there may be more to the story, this is the only part of the tale we currently have to work with."

Jess sighed and gave her head a quick shake. She pushed back from the table and headed for the front door. She nearly collided with a young boy carrying a large metal tin with a red cross on it. The sandy haired boy smiled up at Jess as he slid by her. He looked about six.

"Hey Timmy, Did Joral have any luck with your father's finger?" Leif asked the boy.

"Nah, he tried real hard though! Prince Joral feels so bad he couldn't get it to stay attached. It looks like me and Bobby aren't the only ones that are not allowed to use the throwing axes anymore!"

Leif laughed harder than the situation called for. "Maybe you should keep that first aid kit up at the camp for a while?"

The boy shook his head in affirmation, nodded goodbye to Jess and Gunnar, then hustled back out the door, heading in the direction of the tent city behind Leif's cabin.

"Which one of these vehicles can I take back to my house?" Jess asked as she stared out into the driveway.

"They all have keys in them. Take care of whatever one you choose. They each belong to people up in camp. Hey, do you want me to get you a gun too?" Leif called after Jess.

"I'm married to a cop. I already have a gun of my own," Jess called back as she stepped outside.

Jess stood on the porch and surveyed the multitude of vehicles parked in the driveway and on the grassy areas surrounding Leif's cabin. It made sense that all would be available for use. The men and women here in the camp were not leaving while Dredfall was hunting them.

A dark blue Subaru caught Jess's eye. She walked toward the practical sedan and climbed into the driver seat. The car was perfect for getting her from Leif's cabin to her own house, under the radar, and using as little gas as possible. The sensibleness of the choice relaxed Jess slightly. It felt as if it had been a long time since she had made any choices for herself, let alone a choice that was concrete. Nothing, since Kindra's discovery of Alfheim, had been logical or predictable in Jess's life, and it was more than unsettling for her.

Jess put the bland Subaru in drive and took solace in the completely average and sobering sound of its little engine. It had been months since Jess drove a car. She spent hours on horseback in Alfheim, but there were no gas engines there. As the car bounced down the dirt driveway, Jess took time to re-familiarize herself with the functions of an automobile. *All this time, and all these people coming here, and they still haven't fixed this driveway.* At the end of the drive, Jess pulled the car onto the paved road and pointed the little Subaru toward home.

❦

As Kindra climbed into her car outside Jess's house, her phone went off. The screen displayed the word, Asshole. Kindra pressed the red button to decline the call. She started the car and backed out of the driveway. Kindra only made it to the end of the block before the phone rang again. This time Kindra pressed the green button.

"Yes, father dearest?" Kindra's eye-roll was evident in her greeting.

Leif's voice came through the speaker. "Why don't you ever pick up the first time I call?"

"Sorry Pop," said Kindra. "I truly enjoy testing your patience."

"And here I was, thinking I missed out on those cherished teen years of your life," said Leif with even more sarcasm than Kindra was exuding.

Kindra had many of Leif's qualities. Her magic was potent, and her green eyes and copper hair were only shades paler than Leif's. Most importantly, though, was that both father and daughter were masters of the art of acerbity.

"Listen, are you done with your visit with Sean?"

"I am," Kindra replied succinctly.

"Good. Jess is back. She's on her way home now and said she'd meet you back here later. Until then, I have an adventure for you. I'll text you an address. Joral found another one."

Leif disconnected the call as soon as he said the last word. Kindra's phone buzzed a moment later. She brought the message up on the screen and jumped in her seat as a car horn honked behind her. She had been sitting at the stop sign at the end of the road for over a minute and the driver behind her had hit his limit on patience. Kindra pulled through the intersection and drew her car up to the curb on the next street. She put the car in park and read Leif's text. The address on the screen was in a town about half-way between her current location and Leif's cabin. It would take twenty minutes to get there. Kindra entered the address into her GPS and put the car back in drive.

As Kindra pulled back into the street, the questions started swirling in her mind. Who was this new person of Elven blood? Was the person male or female? Were they young or older? Most of the family members Kindra helped to ferret away at Millspare did not know they held magic within them before the testing at Leif's cabin. They denied any abilities right until they stepped into Alfheim.

As soon as they entered the realm, the descendants were made to climb the cliff outside Aegroth. Many of the test-subjects fell from the cliff, as Kindra had when she had taken her first leaps in her

Elven form. Each recovered from what should have been life-ending injuries in varying amounts of time. At that point, most became believers in their own magic, and Kindra concluded that healing powers might be the only magic these elves possessed. It would explain why Leif had not bothered to ship them to Alfheim earlier in their lives. Healing abilities are not exactly the most formidable powers when you are trying to create an army from your own brood.

Those who made it to the top of the cliff without injury were harder to convince. In one case, it took Leif slicing a man's leg with his sword so the man could watch his own flesh knit back together. Leif had then taken to shoving people off the cliff when they were about half-way up to avoid the need to pull a sword. The man Leif had cut would probably never trust Leif, and it was not helpful to instill wariness in those that were already difficult to sway. Leif used his own gifted power to push the future magic wielders off the rocks. The invisible shove felt as if they had simply lost their balance and any trust remained intact. It seemed ridiculous, but Kindra continuously reminded herself that she was unaware of her own powers until she was faced with avoiding a fall. Of course, her fall had been into a stream; these elves were falling off of a cliff.

Kindra's GPS announced she had reached her destination. There were no houses in the vicinity. She rolled the car by a bar with a tattoo parlor above it before parking on the side of the road in front of a chain-link fence. Garbage littered the street. There was a gas station that looked as if it had last been in operation when Kindra had just learned to drive. Boards coved several of the windows in the small shop behind the pumps. A single car sat in the lot, but no one was at the wheel. Kindra exited her Civic and stepped into the street. She kicked a broken beer bottle out from under her front tire so she wouldn't crunch over it when she left later, and then headed across the street toward the car parked at the gas station.

As Kindra stepped up onto the curb on the other side of the street, an arm locked with hers and steered her toward the right. Joral held her close as if they were two lovers out for a stroll. He picked up his pace and pulled Kindra along with him.

"Just keep walking," he said into Kindra's ear. "Pretend we're in love and out for a date."

"This is hardly the type of neighborhood I would visit for a date. What's going on?" Kindra tried to keep up with Joral as she spoke.

"That car has been here for about fifteen minutes. I was waiting for you when it pulled in. Two people in hoodies left the car, crossed the street, and hopped the fence. You parked exactly where they entered the lot. From the build on the driver, I would guess he is male, and the one that rode as a passenger is likely female, but I did not see either of their faces. The grace with which they mounted that fence indicated they were probably elves. I see no reason for two elves to hop a fence and enter a property owned by an identified descendant unless they are Dredfall assassins who beat us to the location."

Joral finally slowed as he guided Kindra back to the other side of the street. The pair turned the corner. The property in question was now to their right. No sound came from the lot. Tall bushes planted on the other side of the fence obscured the view. The shrubs seemed to enclose the entire property. Joral stopped and turned to face Kindra.

"This lot is owned by Patty Tully. There was once a house on this lot, but it burned to the ground twenty years ago. Patty's husband, Willie, died in that fire. They had no children. Patty buried her husband on a Wednesday and purchased a double-wide trailer on Thursday. That Friday, the trailer was placed at the back of this lot and Patty has been here since. She receives deliveries, but does not leave the property. The entire neighborhood disappeared around her. Shops closed and vagrants moved in. The only reason we know she is still alive is because she regularly reports trespassers to the local police. I envision a little old lady sitting on a laptop watching footage from security cameras around her property all day until there is something to report."

Kindra scrunched up her face. "That is incredibly sad."

"Yes," Joral said. "I cannot imagine my life being reduced to that."

"No," said Kindra. "It's sad that you think she sits around and watches security footage all day just because she complains about trespassers. You need to make fewer assumptions."

Joral shook his head and started walking again. Kindra kept pace as they approached the middle of the block where there was a break in the fence. A metal gate ran the width of the opening. A chunky chain and even heftier padlock secured the gate on the left side. The gate would keep vehicles out, but it only rose to Kindra's hip, making it much easier to climb than the fence that surrounded the rest of the property.

As she and Joral stepped onto, and then over, the gate, Kindra noted the silence pressing on her. No birds were chirping, and there were no rustles in the leaves. There was no traffic outside of the fence. Kindra knew Joral noticed the lack of sound as well. He stood frozen, in a slight crouch next to Kindra, listening and trying to decide on a next move. Kindra scanned the immediate vicinity and saw no movement. She swiveled her head back an inch when her eyes caught a glimmer in the trees to her left. Attached to the trunk of a slim walnut tree was a game camera. Whatever Joral and Kindra's next move, someone would be watching.

CHAPTER 5

Jess stood in front of the toilet, alternating between lifting her right and left foot from the ground. She simultaneously felt that her feet were sticking to the floor and listened to the sound of her sneaker soles peeling from the tile. She was in the bathroom of the home she and Sean shared. Jess ran her fingers over the sink and felt the grittiness of whatever was on the quartz top. She sighed. *It's so good to be home.* Jess shuffled out of the bathroom as well as she could with two German Shepherd dogs glued to her sides. Butch and Cassidy had practically knocked Jess over when she arrived at the house and walked through the front door. All licks, sniffs and initial rubs complete, the two dogs had assumed positions as close to Jess as possible and remained there in case she tried to disappear again.

About two years ago, when Butch was about three and Cassidy was almost a year old, Jess had started attending a dog training class. Each dog went on a separate day, but the same instructor ran both sessions. Lynn, the trainer, found the difference in the two dogs especially amusing. Working closely with Jess and each dog, Lynn had noticed immediately that Butch was the people-pleaser. Butch excelled at all things relating to obedience. In less than a year, Butch had earned his Canine Good Citizen title. A year after that, Butch earned his Advanced Canine Good Citizen. In the same amount of time, Cassidy had learned commands for 'sit' and 'stay' but would still choose to ignore Jess if he wasn't in the mood to train.

It wasn't that Cassidy was a bad dog; it was just the opposite. Cassidy was such a good dog, that Jess never worked him as hard as she should. He made good choices on his own and was happier on the couch watching television than chasing squirrels in the yard. The one commonality between the dogs' personalities was the desire to protect Jess at all costs. Butch took the job more seriously and had always been more alert, but Cassidy would spring into action within seconds if Butch sensed a threat. Butch never really left his protective mode. She was a little concerned that Butch might be missing out on being a dog because he was so concerned about protecting Jess.

As much as Jess complained about the neediness of her Velcro-dogs, she enjoyed being the center of the dogs' world and knowing they would do anything to defend her. Butch and Cassidy allowed Jess to move back into the living room, where Sean sat on the couch. There was a bottle of glass cleaner and a roll of paper towels on the coffee table, and a damp mop leaned against the wall of the kitchen, just outside of the living room. At least Sean had tried. According to Sean, Kindra was at the house about thirty minutes earlier. Jess had just missed her. She knew the miniscule amount of cleaning Sean was so proud of completing had only happened because Kindra had suggested it.

Jess's chest had been filled with love and longing for her husband as she entered the house. She had dropped her things at the door and walked straight into his arms. The warmth radiating from him had made Jess feel as if she, at no time, wanted to move from his embrace again. Seconds later, two fluffy canines had barreled in from the kitchen and jumped, repetitively, on Sean and Jess. Jess had relinquished her hold on her husband and willingly fell to the floor to roll around with Butch and Cassidy. The sense of warmth and family had flowed through Jess as she reacquainted herself with three of her favorite individuals.

The feeling had not lasted long. As Jess moved about the house and had the opportunity to observe the state of disarray, she fought to keep herself from turning around and leaving again. Her orderly home was now more akin to a filthy bachelor's loft. There were dishes piled in the sink. The caked-on food looked as if it had enough time to sprout little science experiments. The dishwasher was full of the same clean dishes she had meant to put away the night she heard of Gretchen's death. Sean knew how to use the dishwasher, but maybe Jess should have offered him a class to learn to put dishes away.

Standing in front of her husband now, Jess waited for Sean to say something about the state of the house. She just wanted to hear him admit that he had let it go and then promise he would clean it all up. Even if he never did, it would be nice to hear he acknowledged there was work to be done. None of those words came from Sean's mouth.

"I'm going to shower and get changed," said Jess.

Jess entered the bedroom she and Sean shared to change her clothes, and she felt the need to close her eyes. No surface of the furniture was visible. *What's the point of spending money on a beautiful bedroom set if it's only going to be covered by clothing?* She opened her eyes and dug a pair of jeans and a t-shirt from her, still clean and still neatly folded, clothing and put them on the bed with a bra and fresh pair of underwear. Jess stripped down and went to the shower.

In the private bath, off of the primary bedroom, Jess was greeted with more sticky floors. She ignored the scum of the shower curtain as she slid into the stall and let the hot water run over her skin. *At least the water is clean. Maybe I can just stay in here forever.* Jess was in the middle of seriously contemplating leaving the house and returning to her magic wardrobe in Alfheim when two noses poked into the tub enclosure from outside of the curtain to tell her she had been in the shower long enough.

Jess toweled off and walked to the bedroom. Shrugging into the clothes she had neatly placed on the bed before her shower, she took in the bedroom's disorderly state. Jess made the decision that she would not be staying here right now. She would call a cleaning service if she had to, but she had too much pride to come home and immediately clean up after her husband. Jess pulled on socks and her sneakers and went to deliver the news to Sean. Sean was still lounging on the couch, watching soccer, when Jess entered the living room.

"I'm heading back out. I can't handle this mess right now," Jess told him.

"I know," Sean replied.

"What do you mean, you know? I just decided for myself seconds ago."

Sean pointed toward the front door. "The boys already got the memo."

It was not unusual for one or both dogs to sit at the exit, leash in his maw, begging to go for a walk, but the sight at the door now was comical. Butch had both leashes in his mouth, waiting patiently beside his brother. Cassidy was holding the strap to Jess's handbag, waiting for her to grab it and head outside. The dogs had always picked up on Jess's emotions and been a comfort when required, or gave her space when she demanded it, but this level of understanding was novel. Sean did not seem like anything surprised him at this point. When Jess looked at him, as if to ask if he had anything to do with these shenanigans, Sean simply shrugged.

"I'll be sure to have this place cleaned up for her highness when she returns. For now, the boys demand your attention. Send a text to let me know if you'll be disappearing for another month or even a few weeks."

Jess was about to argue that she was not royalty and Sean was an ass, but stopped herself. She was, technically, a princess. All descendants of the last true king of Lillerem were given the title prince or princess. Also, Sean had just recognized the house was a mess. Jess chose, instead, to ignore Sean's comments. Without a word, she turned and opened the front door. She walked to her RAV4 with Butch on her left side and Cassidy on her right. The dogs sat and waited for Jess to open the back door and then hopped into their respective spots on the blanket-covered back seat. Cassidy dropped Jess's bag into the spot behind the passenger seat as Jess took her place in the driver's seat in front of Butch.

With the car backed out of its spot and ready to head off down the road, it occurred to Jess that she did not know where she was going. Her only thought was of being out of that disgusting house until it looked more like the home she left behind months ago. Cassidy stuck his head between the two front seats and nuzzled Jess's elbow. She rubbed his head and smiled down into his soulful brown eyes.

"You're right, boy. We're outside. The sun is out and we can go wherever we want. How does the park sound?"

Butch and Cassidy each gave a clipped bark of agreement. Jess turned her eyes back to the road and drove off toward the wide open area in town referred to as the park. It was a communal space that some used to sit and read outdoors, while others walked or jogged the paths that wove through the area. Jess often brought the dogs to the space to train and get exercise, but she rarely brought the two of them together unless she was only planning on a walk.

When Jess pulled her car through the park entrance, she was glad to see the lot was nearly empty. The fewer people in the park, the easier it was to enjoy time with the dogs without distractions of which to be wary. All it took was a teenager on a skateboard or a dog with the wrong smell, and Jess could find herself embroiled in the chore of controlling her dogs and safely exiting the park. Jess had worked very hard, training for long hours with each dog separately to break countless poor habits, but they were German Shepherd dogs. If either dog perceived a threat, even if the threat was a baby being pushed in a stroller, Jess still lost the dogs' attention sometimes.

Jess opened her car door and gave the wait command. She walked around to the back door and held up her hand as she opened it. Neither dog moved. This was new. The dogs knew the wait command and did not jump out of the car until they were told they could, but they usually crouched in the open door, ready to spring forward, as she leashed them up. Today, the dogs lounged in the back seat as Jess attached leads to each of their collars. Jess called the dogs to exit the car, and they hopped out and immediately flanked Jess. Jess reached into the back seat, grabbed two tennis balls, and stuffed them in her pocket. She slammed the back door and walked toward the grassy field on the other side of the lot.

With Butch on her left and Cassidy on her right, Jess knew she looked like a woman to be left to herself. Some of Jess's friends complained of other dog owners at the park asking if it would be ok for their dog to "say hello" to theirs. Jess agreed. There was no need for two dogs that did not live together and would likely never see each other again to be friendly. If you want your dog to have friends, take it to doggie day-care. Of course, Jess had never experienced this need for a meet and greet at the park herself. The two goofy Shepherds were intimidating enough to eliminate that issue.

Jess always felt safe when she walked with her dogs. She was well aware the dogs possessed inherent instincts to protect her. Today, as the trio walked onto the grass together, Jess could actually feel the protective drive emanating from them. She somehow knew Butch was concerned with the lone bush off to the left. She knew he felt the presence of something within the bush and was watching closely to see if anything chose to emerge. Jess sensed Cassidy's desire to reach the other side of the field to check that the woods beyond were safe for all of them. *Is this my magic? Could I have done this before I went to Alfheim?* Jess walked the dogs around the entire field, permitting them to sniff and assure themselves that all was safe in the area.

At last, Jess unclipped the leashes and took out the two tennis balls. "Ok kids, it's time to take a break and have some fun. Ready to run?"

Anticipating the madness that was about to ensue, Jess found herself wishing, unrealistically, for dogs who knew how to take turns. Instead, strangest game of fetch Jess had ever directed commenced. One dog would retrieve the ball, and the other would lie down in the grass and wait. There was no longer doubt in her mind. This was her magical ability manifesting, here in the human realm. Jess knew from Gretchen and Kindra's kitchen table conversations that only elves with substantial power could use magic in the human realm, and even then, it was often diminished. The ease with which Jess had passed through the portal today was an indication that Jess had built her magic up significantly, but here in the park was proof. Jess's dogs were obeying her commands. More than obeying commands, her dogs were listening to her thoughts and interpreting them. The dogs were then carrying out her wishes, though there had been no prior training for the actions.

Jess felt excited by this new prospect. Her dogs were doing whatever she wanted. It was every dog owner's dream. A creepy feeling came over Jess as she thought about it some more. Her dogs knew all of her thoughts and desires. They might not have the ability to share the information with other people, but getting used to knowing that her mind was not her own anymore would still take time. The German Shepherd dogs rubbed against her legs. They knew her discovery was making her uncomfortable, and they were soothing her.

Jess threw the ball one last time. Cassidy grabbed the ball and ran back to Jess with his prize and tossed the slobber-coated ball into Jess's hands. The precision ball toss, Cassidy's signature move, was often cute but sometimes resulted in a ball landing on your dinner plate when least expected. The dog had amazing accuracy. She scooped up the leashes and slung them over her shoulder. She was certain she would not need them anytime soon. Butch took his place at Jess's left, and Cassidy put himself on Jess's right side. The dogs escorted her back to the Toyota and hopped into the back seat without issue.

Jess pulled from the lot and steered the car in the direction of Leif's cabin. She was sure the house was not yet clean and it would be a good idea to let the princes see her magical connection to her dogs. With no threats inside the vehicle, Butch and Cassidy snoozed in the back as Jess flipped through the radio stations. Nothing on the radio held Jess's interest for long, and she eventually clicked it off. Driving in silence, Jess watched the world go by and noted all the slight changes since she'd last traveled through the area.

It had been several years since Jess had driven the back roads to go upstate. Some neighborhoods, including the one she currently drove through, had seen better days. There were many boarded-up businesses, and the homes appeared run down or vacant. Many lots stood empty, and the streets contained more than a little trash. Suddenly, the dogs sat straight to attention and started whining. It was the same whine they used when trying to dispel the anxiety of a vet trip or a new situation. The dogs stared through the passenger side window and Jess felt them urging her to go in that direction. Jess turned the car right at the next road and continued to follow the press in her mind from the dogs guiding her through left and right turns.

After a right turn, Jess pulled in a sharp breath. Ahead on the right side of the road was Kindra's Honda Civic. The 'Coexist' bumper sticker in the rear window was all the assurance Jess needed that this was her friend's car. *What on earth are you doing out here, Kindra?* There were no houses and no open stores in the area. Jess pulled up behind the Civic and turned off the engine. She looked up and down the street, but there was no way to tell where Kindra might be. Jess took out her cell phone and dialed Leif's number. A loud belch sounded in Jess's ear, and then there was a pause before the recording continued.

"Well, that was nasty. Leave a message."

Jess ended the call, then immediately redialed. This time, Leif picked up.

"Why are you calling? You're supposed to be home getting it on with your long-lost husband."

"The welcome home party didn't meet my expectations. I'm out with the dogs. Anyway, the strangest thing happened. The dogs took me to Kindra's car. I'm parked behind it right now, and it is not in a very nice neighborhood." Jess's voice was full of concern as she spilled out the information as quickly as she could.

Leif's response came in a less perturbed manner. "Relax. Kindra went to meet Joral. They're going to bring in another of Pakk's lineage. She's probably inside one of the houses right now, trying to convince the woman she is in danger and needs to leave."

"That's the thing," Jess said with worry in her voice. "There are no houses around here."

"Give me a moment. Let me think about this." Leif's moment was barely a few seconds. "I remember now. The women they're going to retrieve lives in a trailer on an abandoned lot. There is no house. If you're so concerned, you can go join them. The lady is almost seventy years old, so I'm pretty sure Kindra and Joral can handle her, but if you're desperate to have something to do, then be my guest. I'm sure those dogs of yours will persuade the woman to jump right into the car with you." The sarcasm dripped from Leif's lips as he spoke.

Jess pressed the red button on her phone to end the call. She looked at Butch and Cassidy through the rear-view mirror of the car.

"What do you think, boys? Want to give Aunt Kindra a hand?"

The dogs let out little whimpers of excitement. Jess opened her car door and walked around to the passenger side to let the dogs out onto the sidewalk. Prepared to yell at the canines if they tried to dash off, Jess opened the door. The dogs jumped out of the car and took up positions at Jess's side. Butch stood on her left, and Cassidy on her right. Jess shut the door, and the dogs took a few steps. They stopped and simultaneously swung their heads to look at Jess. Jess understood this to be Butch and Cassidy hurrying her along. She obliged and broke into a trot.

The two dogs stayed only slightly in front of her as they led Jess to the end of the block and turned right. The trio took the turn and continued at the same pace until the dogs stopped in front of a low metal gate. Butch and Cassidy sat on either side of the gate like lions at the entry to the driveway of an expensive home. Jess peered into the property. There was nothing to see but overgrown gardens and some woods. Closer inspection showed there might be a structure toward the rear of the lot. Jess stepped over the gate and entered the property. The dogs hopped over, following right behind her.

Syndral watched Riva come through the front door. She carried a backpack, hugged to her chest instead of using the straps in the usual manner. Her dirty blonde hair hung thin and straight at the sides of her face. The girl was tiny. She could pass for a child in fourth grade, though Syndral knew the girl was in her third year at the local middle school. The same school, Syndral had recently discovered, where Jess and Kindra worked.

A vibration in Syndral's pocket sent her squirming to free her phone. The task was hampered by her seated position behind the wheel. Freeing the phone at last, Syndral answered when she saw Leif's name on her screen.

"Hey, Leif. What do you have?"

"I need a favor."

"A favor?" Syndral exclaimed. "I'm sorry we ever swapped numbers."

"It's nothing you won't enjoy. Kindra is meeting Joral in a rough area to bring in a new descendant. I let Jess know, but I'm really not sure how long it will take her to get there. I just...I just have a bad feeling about this one," said Leif.

"This really is cute," said Syndral. "Who knew you were such a concerned father?" Syndral's tone was not pleasant.

"It's not like that. It's just a bad feeling. I thought you might want to prove your worth to the team... you know, show them you are on our side?"

Syndral decided to let Leif pretend his call was about her worth to the others, and not about his worry for Kindra.

"Fine. Text me the address."

CHAPTER 6

Kindra was standing on a platform constructed from Joral's hands, peering into the window of the trailer. Joral had laced his fingers together to make a little basket for Kindra to use as a step. The window looked in on the bedroom. The lights were off, and Kindra could see nothing. She hopped down to the ground, shaking her head. She and Joral had slowly explored the entire property before approaching the trailer.

"There's no sign of Patty, or the people from that other car," Kindra said. "I'm going to go around to the right, you try the left side. We'll meet in the back. If we haven't found anyone at that point, we'll enter through the back door."

Joral didn't reply. He turned and walked off, following the perimeter of the trailer. Kindra turned to her right and mirrored Joral's movements. She reached the end of the trailer and turned left to walk the short end of the building. A twig snapped to her right and instinct forced Kindra to duck into a forward roll. A figure soared over her and hit the side of the trailer. Aiming for Kindra's torso, the assailant had not anticipated Kindra's movement. Kindra was up in an instant and mounting a counterattack. The assailant had landed face-down and Kindra drove a boot into the person's kidney. The figure grunted and rolled away from Kindra. Kindra scrambled after him.

Kindra grabbed one of the assailant's legs as he tried to rise and tugged. The male sprawled back onto his stomach. He rolled to the right and was able to find his feet. At the same time, Kindra also planted her feet beneath her body. As the attacker turned to meet Kindra head-on, she verified the male was an elf. He did not have a weapon, but Kindra was certain he would not need one to cause harm. The male was not tall. He might have been two or three inches taller than Kindra, but he outweighed her by over a hundred pounds. His arms and legs were thick, and his movements were nearly feline in grace and speed. Even if Kindra hadn't left Forsvarer in Leif's closet, the balance would not have leaned in Kindra's favor.

Kindra wished the tiny pistol Leif had gifted her was in her pocket instead of wrapped up with her sword. She wasn't even sure the bullet would pierce this male's skin, but at least she could have fired at him and run. Kindra summoned her magic and hurled a stone from the ground at the elf's head. He held up his hand and the stone dropped into the grass harmlessly. His smirk made Kindra want to punch him in the face, but Kindra was not sure what kind of powers this elf wielded, and kept her distance. Her eyes picked up a fallen log several feet away. Kindra summoned her magic again and pictured the tree trunk flying toward her attacker. The log did not move. Either she was too worked up to focus, or her magic wasn't as strong in the human realm as she had thought it was.

"Who are you?" Kindra asked as she circled the male.

The male smiled. His canines glistened with saliva. He attempted to lunge for Kindra's arm, but she teleported backward and out of his reach. He resumed circling with her as if they were a pair of boxers in a ring, each afraid to throw a punch. Kindra acknowledged that the strength of her magic must not be the issue. Teleportation took a lot of magical strength, but very little concentration when it was used as an option for self-preservation. Kindra had been circling to her left, but now she abruptly lunged to the right, hoping to catch the male off-guard. He easily ducked under Kindra's swing and came up behind her. She turned to face him and the circling commenced anew.

"My name is Ruith. I assume you are here for the half-breed? No need to worry. We took care of her already."

The term half-breed boiled Kindra's blood. She wasn't sure if Patty was a half, a quarter or an eighth Elven, but Kindra still detested the phrase. Fueled by rage, Kindra dove for the elf's legs, attempting to drive him to the ground. Ruith stepped gracefully to the side, causing Kindra to land with her arms stretched above her head and her face in the dirt. A knee pushed into Kindra's spine as Ruith kneeled down and wrapped his fingers around Kindra's neck. He pulled on her hair to yank her head back for a better grip and then squeezed her throat, cutting off Kindra's airway. For the second time in as many days, Kindra couldn't breathe. She tried to remain calm so she could focus on her magic. She frantically searched within herself but could not feel the familiar hum. Kindra closed her eyes.

Kindra heard galloping steps and a ferocious growl. The weight lifted from her back and then Ruith's hands slipped from around her neck. Kindra rolled onto her side in time to see the elf crash to the ground beneath a snarling German Shepherd. The dog landed with its front paws on Ruith's chest and immediately bit down on the elf's throat. The canine thrashed his head back and forth and tore away a chunk of meat. Blood sprayed from the artery the dog had severed with its teeth. Ruith thrashed and choked as the dog ripped more flesh from his neck, shoulders, and arms. It was less than a minute before the elf stilled, though the dog remained clamped on the elf's throat for several minutes longer.

Kindra took a sharp breath after realizing she had not been breathing while she watched the bloody assault. The dog's head snapped up to look in Kindra's direction. *This is where I die. It figures Patty Tully had a crazed Shepherd roaming her lot. It wasn't able to save the old woman, but it's going to be sure to avenge her death.* Kindra pulled her knees under her body slowly, trying not to spook the dog. She held her hands forward as if the dog would understand she did not intend to cause it any harm. It stepped toward her and she froze. Kindra looked into the dog's eyes.

"Cassidy?" Kindra asked tentatively.

The dog whined, tilted its head and then licked its bloody lips.

"Butch?" Kindra tried again.

The dog's ears perked up and its tail started to wag. Kindra, half-way to standing, plopped back down on the ground and sat with her legs crossed.

"Come here Butch."

The dog trotted over to Kindra and proceeded to stretch the front half of his body over Kindra's lap. Kindra smoothed the bloody fur around the dog's ears and neck.

"I'm so happy you're here, boy. You saved me. Did you follow me here? Did Sean let you out and forget about you again?"

Butch licked Kindra's face. She could feel the blood from his muzzle transferring to her skin, but Kindra didn't care. The dog was currently her savior and he could do anything he wished. Butch looked Kindra in the eyes once more, made a noise somewhere between a bark and a snuffle, then jumped up and ran around to the front of the trailer. Kindra moved onto her hands and knees, then pushed herself up to her feet. She started dusting the dirt off of her clothes but gave up when she considered how insignificant her clothing was when compared to her bloody face. As she turned toward the back of the trailer to find Joral, a voice came from behind her.

"The blood is a good look for you. Definitely makes you even more badass!"

Kindra whirled. Standing ten feet from her, with a dog at either hip, was Jess. Her blonde curls were pulled back from the front of her face in a thick, loose braid that came around to the front, passing over her left shoulder. Jess had never been lean, but she was now solid. Muscles showed through her black jeans and her arms were tanned and toned. She exuded confidence and strength, with Butch and Cassidy at her sides.

Kindra ran to her friend. The women threw their arms around each other and Jess lifted Kindra from the ground. Kindra had always been the smaller of the two friends, but the muscle Jess had developed while training at Millspare let Jess pull her friend from the ground with ease.

"Butch saved me, Jess! He tore that elf to shreds!" Kindra gestured to the bloody mess behind her.

Jess stepped back from her friend, a look of genuine surprise on her face.

"What's wrong?" Kindra asked.

"Nothing's wrong," said Jess. "I just can't believe you got his name right. You always mix the two dogs up!"

"Well, you'll be happy to know things have not changed. I got it wrong on my first attempt. Butch corrected me. Speaking of Butch, how did he end up in the position to rescue me?"

"There's a lot to tell," replied Jess. "Joral's out front. He had an altercation with an elf, too. That one was smarter. She got one look at Cassidy charging toward her and then she took off running. Cassidy chased her to the fence. The elf easily hopped over and Cassidy gave up the pursuit."

Joral was exiting the trailer through the front door as the girls turned the corner. He winced when he saw Kindra.

"Don't worry. Most of the blood isn't mine. I'll be ok."

"Good," said Joral. "Imra was not lying. The elves killed Patty before we arrived. We were too late, again."

"Who is Imra?" asked Kindra.

"Imra, was the name Cassidy's would-be prey gave before fleeing for her life. She informed me we were too late; that Dredfall had already removed Patty from the equation. She then told me we were to die next. I did not have the opportunity to find out if that was truly a possibility. Cassidy charged from out of nowhere and prevented the altercation."

Jess rubbed Cassidy's head. "Kindra's assailant acted more quickly. It's either that, or Butch is slower than his brother," Jess cupped her hands over Butch's ears, "and we wouldn't want to accuse Butch of being slow."

Joral took in the drying gore covering Butch's muzzle and much of the fur around his neck and paws. Kindra stepped over to the bloody dog and squatted down in front of him. She put her hands out for Butch to lick, but Butch planted a slobbery kiss on her cheek instead.

"Fast or slow," Kindra said to the dog, "you are my hero. I still don't love your slobbery kisses, though."

"Did you ride together?" Jess asked.

Joral answered. "I parked a car I took from the cabin several blocks away. We have three cars here. Are you heading home to Sean?"

"I saw Sean already. Why don't we all head to the cabin?" Jess replied. "We can share what happened here, and I have some things to show everyone as well."

Jess turned to walk back to her car, and the dogs stuck to her hips like glue. On her left, Butch walked proudly, wearing the blood of his enemy like a badge of honor. Cassidy, on Jess's right, seemed to prance as he walked. He acted as if the recent, life-threatening situation was an event from long ago. Though the two dogs had almost identical black and tan markings, Kindra had never taken the time to notice the very different personalities they possessed. The differences were obvious to her now, as the trio walked away.

Joral placed his hand on Kindra's shoulder and squeezed. "Are you ok? Is any of that blood yours?"

Kindra smiled weakly. "If any of it is mine, it's not much. I am only bruised, for the most part. In any event, I'm in much better shape than the elf on the ground over there."

"Butch may have ended that fight, but I suspect you were holding your own before he arrived."

"I'm glad he was here. I might not have been able to fight my way out of that one. I still have little ability to call on my magic when I panic," admitted Kindra.

"That is the trick of it. You need to keep the panic at bay. The more times you come close to death, the less you will panic when someone tries to kill you. I hate to say it, Kindra, but I suspect you will have more opportunities to practice. I'll see you back at the cabin."

Joral turned off the path that had once been a driveway and stepped silently into the woods. A moment later, Jess heard a very faint metallic tinkle as Joral climbed the fence and exited the property. Kindra continued to the gate at the front side of the lot and stepped over it. As she exited into the street, she caught a glimpse of a ragged looking mutt turning the corner off to her right. *Maybe Patty did have a dog, but the thing had the same inclination to run as Imra had when it saw Jess's furry weapons.* Kindra laughed to herself, turned left, walked to the end of the block, and turned left again.

Kindra's car waited for her at the curb where she left it. The well-built, blonde female elf leaning on the hood of the car had not been there then. The attack at the trailer, and the inability to wield her magic well, had left Kindra tired and frustrated. She was not in the frame of mind for the conversation that was about to transpire. Kindra took a deep breath and started for her vehicle.

"Get your ass off my hood, Syndral. I'm not in the mood," Kindra greeted the unwelcome female.

"Kindra, wait. I wish I'd been here sooner. You should have called me and I would have come out with you. I could have helped."

"Speaking of coming out here," Kindra started, "how the hell did you know where we were? We didn't call you. No one asked for your help, late or otherwise."

"Actually," Syndral finally stood up straight and removed herself from Kindra's car hood, "Leif called me. He knew you were all converging here and thought I might be able to help keep you safe."

"Great, just great! My loving father sends a former Dredfall soldier to rescue his daughter in her time of need. He's so considerate."

"If he had called even a little earlier, I could have prevented you from injury. I know each of the Dredfall assassins. Remember, they are all from Ulford's First Draw. I spent years in their company. Who was here tonight? Which elves did he send for this job?"

Kindra pointed at the fence. "Ruith is a pile of torn meat on the right side of the trailer. Imra ran at the first sign she might have to face a dog instead of another elf."

Syndral's expression changed for just a moment when Kindra said Imra's name. At least, Kindra thought it had changed. There had been no reaction from the female at the mention of Ruith's demise, but Kindra thought there was a flash of something in Syndral's eyes when she had spoken of Imra.

"I can't tell if you're happy or upset that Imra escaped," said Kindra.

"Neither," Syndral came back quickly. "I guess I'm just surprised she was here at all. Imra is more of an advisor to Ulford than a soldier. She is a member of Ulford's Guard, but she is not known for her fighting prowess. Her talents are more those of words and the mind."

"It explains why she was so quick to run when Cassidy charged toward her. She must have hoped to surprise Joral and take him out quickly. As soon as she realized there would be a fight, she disengaged," Kindra acknowledged. "Listen, we're all heading to the cabin to regroup. Why don't you meet us there?"

Syndral snorted. "Does this mean we're friends now?"

"Definitely not," Kindra said as she moved past Syndral. "I suspect your knowledge of the assassins could be very helpful to our cause. You tell Jess and the princes what you know about the Royal Guard members and, in exchange, you can listen to our debrief of the things we discovered today."

Syndral chuckled. "Princes...For a moment, I forgot you are all royalty."

"You find that amusing?" asked Kindra.

"The fact that the future of Lillerem isn't even in Lillerem? Yes, I find it very amusing. It seems to me that Ulford's decision to mount attacks in the human realm makes more sense than I had initially thought."

"Dredfall's attacks on humans started while the princes and I were still at Millspare. If Ulford wanted us dead, there was no reason for him to leave the realm to find us."

"He didn't. Ulford stayed in Dredfall. He sent his assassins here to get your attention. You aren't exceptionally bright, are you? He failed in his attempt to erase the royal line while in Alfheim. Attacking the humans brought you all here. Elven magic is not a significant concern when fighting in the human realm. He drew you all here to take your magic off the table. Mark my words, Ulford is getting exactly what he wants by having you all here in this realm."

"Thankfully, we're not all here. Bane remains at Millspare to ensure the people of Aergroth are safe," said Kindra.

"Similar to Ulford, I am not a fool," Syndral said. "Bane stayed in Alfheim because he is not strong enough to travel through the portal. I have never met him, and he is likely a powerful fighter, but he wields little magic. Millspare is vulnerable."

"Regardless," Kindra said, as she climbed into her car. "Come to the cabin. Tell us what you know and we will all try to find a way to end this madness."

Kindra turned the key in the ignition and pulled on her seat belt. Syndral stepped away from the car and a few feet into the road. Kindra put the car in drive and pulled away from the curb, watching Syndral in her rear-view mirror as she departed. Turning her eyes forward, Kindra saw the familiar Chevy Colorado ahead on the next block. Kindra's disgust for Syndral melded with her feelings about the white truck parked up ahead. Kindra no longer wanted a truck at all. *When all of this is over, I'll look into an SUV.*

As Syndral walked back to her truck, she removed her phone from her pocket and sent a quick text to Leif.

"I got here after the scuffle. No men were lost, but the descendant is dead. We're all coming to your cabin."

Climbing into the truck, Syndral felt a surge of satisfaction. Acts of kindness were new for Syndral, but she found she liked the way putting Leif at ease made her feel. If there were someone who could assure Syndral that the girl would be safe, she would welcome it.

Since no one had stepped up to do that yet, Syndral would continue to sit outside of that house. It was the best she could do on her own.

CHAPTER 7

Jess pulled up the long dirt road leading to Leif's cabin. She parked near the front porch and climbed out of her car. She opened the rear door of the SUV and Butch hopped out. When he didn't immediately take off, Jess looked at Cassidy and tilted her head. Cassidy, understanding the silent question, stood up and made his way across the back seat to hop out of the vehicle.

Jess headed for the stairs, Butch on her left and Cassidy on her right, with purposeful steps. She climbed to the small landing outside of the cabin. When Jess paused to pull open the door, the dogs automatically sat at her sides.

"Well, children, we're not all going to fit through the doorway at the same time, so you're going to need a change of plan," Jess told the dogs.

Jess pushed open the door. Butch and Cassidy rushed inside and took up positions on either side of the doorway, waiting for Jess to enter. It was like having her own Royal Guard. The dogs stormed in and cleared the room, making sure it was safe before Jess entered. Sure enough, as Jess entered the living room, she saw Krish sitting straight up on the edge of the couch with his hand on the pommel of his sword. His hand fell from his sword, and he relaxed when he saw Jess walk into the room.

"I see you've formed your own army! I will fight the urge to send soldiers to your defense in the future. Those hounds of yours have the job under control. Come, sit."

Jess smiled and stepped over to the seating area, Butch and Cassidy escorting her the entire distance. She took the place next to Krish on the couch and leaned back. Jess permitted herself to feel the stressful events of the day. She had entered a portal to leave Alfheim, not knowing if she could survive the journey, this morning. Since then, she had visited with Sean, left her filthy home with her pets in tow, and discovered she now had a mental tether to them. Jess could feel Butch and Cassidy's emotions as she relaxed into the cushions of the couch. Cassidy was enjoying a break, using only his ears to remain alert to danger. Butch, always more serious, sat at Jess's side, facing the door. He used all his senses to ensure Jess's safety.

Krish broke the silence. "Are Kindra and Joral returning?"

"Yeah," Jess said. "They should be here any moment. There is a story to tell, of course. We'll need to wait for Gunnar and Leif as well. There is no sense saying everything more than once."

Butch's ears pricked, and his head whipped in the direction of the kitchen. The sound of the back door opening sent both dogs sprinting from the room. There was a lot of growling, and then a loud thud as someone hit the ground. Jess stood from the couch and hurried into the kitchen. The door was wide open. Cassidy stood in the doorway, preventing anyone from entering. Butch stood growling with his front paws on Leif's chest. Leif sported a petrified look as he lay back, frozen. He saw Jess from the corner of his eye and realization dawned in his emerald eyes.

"Dammit Jess! Get this beast off of me!"

Jess sent soothing thoughts to the dogs. Cassidy drew back from the doorway and took his position on Jess's right side. Butch turned to look at Jess, as if to ask if she was sure that the angry elf on the floor should be released.

"It's ok boy. That mean male is Aunt Kindra's dad. Even if we want to kill him, we can't."

Butch yawned to calm himself and removed his paws from Leif's chest. He took a tentative step away from Leif, watching to be sure the elf wasn't going to spring back up and attack. Jess continued to send soothing thoughts to Butch until he turned and took his position on her left. With the two dogs entrenched beside Jess, Gunnar and Joral safely spilled through the back door, laughing. Leif glared at his brother and cousin as he dragged himself to his feet.

"I'm glad you two find this so amusing. I could've hit my head and been killed! Killed in my own house by Jess's crazy mutts; and you're both laughing about it!"

Leif was shaking his head and muttering as he walked by the dogs and Jess into the living room. He squinted his eyes at Butch as he went past him. Butch, to his credit, did not acknowledge Leif's negative attention. The dog continued to stand sentry at Jess's side. Gunnar dropped to one knee and threw his arms open wide.

"Come here, boys!"

The Shepherds, sensing no fear or anxiety from Jess, left Jess's side and bounded over to Gunnar. They knocked him backward onto his ass and proceeded to lick his face, fighting over the lap that was created when he fell backward. Gunnar scratched behind their ears and rolled around on the floor with them playfully.

To say Jess was surprised, would be a serious understatement. Aside from Bane, Gunnar was the most stoic of all the princes. She had rarely seen him smile, let alone laugh and carry on the way he was doing now. Jess knew some individuals liked dogs more than people. Truthfully, Jess liked dogs more than people. Gunnar's reaction to Butch and Cassidy showed he was one of the same clan.

Gunnar stood and went into the living room. The dogs ignored Jess and followed the elf, hopping like puppies as they went. Gunnar sat next to Krish on the couch and the dogs jumped up beside him, impolitely pushing Krish up against the armrest. Leif sat in the rocking chair, still staring daggers at Butch. Jess dragged two chairs from the kitchen into the living room and set them on either side of an empty recliner. Joral remained in the doorway to the kitchen. The male liked to stand. Jess, remembering she was exhausted, collapsed into the recliner. Turning about thirty degrees toward the window, Jess could see a set of headlights coming up the drive.

"Headlights," she said, "Probably Kindra."

Jess watched the lights jerk up and down as her friend's Civic navigated the ruts in the driveway. A second set of lights appeared behind the first car.

"We've got company. There are two vehicles," announced Jess.

The room was silent as gravel crunched outside, and the two cars parked. Jess wordlessly sent Butch and Cassidy to either side of the front door. Footsteps fell on the front porch. Cassidy started whining. He was excited. Jess knew Kindra was on the other side of the door based on Cassidy's enthusiasm, but who was the second person? Cassidy, sensing Jess's concern, stopped wagging his tail and waited to see who walked into the cabin.

The door opened and Kindra came into the small entryway adjoining the living room. Butch and Cassidy closed ranks behind Kindra and started growling at the person still outside. The hackles of both dogs rose. The remnants of the blood on Butch's muzzle from earlier that day made him look even more menacing than usual. Kindra, surprised by the dogs' reactions, spun and tried to grab the dogs by the collar. Both dogs swiveled their heads and gave her a little snap in the air to tell her to back off.

"Who's with you, Kindra?" Jess asked over the noise of the growling dogs.

A female voice from the outside exclaimed, "It's Syndral! I come in peace. Please call off the hounds!"

Jess mentally backed the dogs up, but did not ask them to relax. Syndral walked slowly into the cabin with her hands in the air. For each step she took toward the group, Butch and Cassidy relinquished the same space, keeping themselves between the party in the living room and Syndral. Kindra motioned for Syndral to take one of the vacant chairs. As Syndral moved for the chair, Jess called the dogs back to her. Neither dog relaxed, but they did return to Jess and sit at attention, facing Jess and the adjacent chair that Syndral was lowering herself into. The dogs seemed not to blink as they watched the female.

Safely seated, Syndral tried to speak casually as she said, "The new security upgrades are impressive. If they had been installed when I was here last, I never would have made it into the cabin."

Gunnar chuckled and threw a look at Leif. Leif gave Gunnar the same evil squint he had bestowed on Butch after Butch's welcome at the back door. Watching the exchange, Syndral cracked a slight smile.

"I take it I am not the first one to get such a warm greeting this evening?" she asked Leif.

"The hounds from hell seem to have a difficult time telling friend from foe," Leif replied.

Kindra pushed a spiral of copper hair behind her ear and leaned forward. "Now that we are all here, we can catch up. Syndral is agreeable to sharing all she knows of the Dredfall assassins with us. In exchange, she will get an update on our intelligence."

"I know we agreed to aid each other, but I don't recall deciding to trust her," said Leif.

"You don't have to trust her," said Kindra, "but her knowledge of Ulford's Royal Guard may prove invaluable. I think it's worth the exchange of information to learn who we are up against."

Leif sat back and resumed glaring at the back of Butch's head. He did not like the idea of giving information to someone outside of the family. Joral leaned against the frame of the doorway, between the kitchen and living room. Gunnar had resumed his introverted silence, and Krish sat tall in his seat. The princes waited for Syndral to share.

Syndral, on the other hand, was in no rush to be the first to give up valuable facts. She, too, sat waiting for someone to speak. Each person in the room looked to another until all eyes eventually alighted on Kindra. Kindra let her breath out slowly. She supposed things were going about as well as they could. No one had drawn blood yet, and they had all made a verbal agreement to share. Kindra acknowledged that she would likely need to start the ball rolling by telling of what happened earlier at Patty Tully's lot. She drew in some air to begin the story, but before she emitted a sound, Jess stood and stepped to the center of the circle.

"You are all acquainted with Butch and Cassidy, to varying degrees. I suppose I could share my discovery with all of you."

The dogs stood and went to Jess's sides. Butch took his place on the left, and Cassidy stood at Jess's right hip. Jess gave each dog a scratch behind the ears. She left her hands on the tops of the dogs' heads as she continued speaking.

"Butch and Cassidy can read my mind."

Jess waited for someone to comment, but no one spoke. She was expecting a shocked exclamation or two, at least. She continued, deciding to start from the beginning.

"I came home today and discovered the disaster area my home has become in my absence. Butch and Cassidy knew I was going to turn and leave before I'd said anything out loud. Cassidy was even kind enough to have my purse waiting for me at the door. I took the dogs for an outing at the park. Both dogs executed verbal commands with such precision; it was as if they were reading my mind.

"The real shocker came when we were playing fetch and I found myself wishing the dogs would take turns going to get the ball so there would be less rough-housing between them and I could ensure they both were getting exercised. The dogs started taking turns. I have never even tried to get them to do this. They innately understood what it meant to take turns, and one would rest behind me in the grass while I threw the ball for the other. Anyone watching would have thought I had simply worked my dogs since puppyhood to play fetch in this way. Until that moment, there had only ever been chaos during games of fetch."

"So," Leif interrupted, "Your big news is that your dogs are suddenly well-behaved? You wanted them to do something, and they did it. Isn't that what dogs are supposed to do for their owners? Congratulations."

"I don't know if well-behaved is the correct descriptor," Syndral chimed in. "I'm pretty sure their socialization skills leave a lot to be desired. Do you agree, Leif?"

Leif shifted his dagger-eyes from Butch to Syndral, then back to Butch again. Butch ignored Leif and continued to stare down Syndral. Neither he nor Cassidy had taken their eyes off the female since she arrived at the cabin. Jess may have decided to give the woman a reprieve, but the dogs were not as easily swayed.

Jess continued, "It's more than them doing what I say. They do things before I say them and they do it exactly as I envision it happening. I think they can see inside my thoughts."

It was Kindra's turn to show disbelief, though her words were kinder than Leif's had been. "Are you sure it isn't just that you and your dogs have been training together long enough for them to know your thoughts? Maybe they aren't seeing inside your head, but simply looking to please you because they missed you so much?"

"Unlikely," said Jess. "The things they are doing are not things we have trained for. Basic commands are not an issue for them. The dogs can sit, stay, and come. They understand that when they are told to wait, they should stop where they are until they are released or given another command. When walking, they heel, and do not pull on a leash, but even those commands are not perfect. All it takes is one squirrel or kid on a skateboard to break their attention and they are off and running. At least, those are the dogs I left back here in this realm when I traveled to Alfheim. Since I've returned, it is as if they went to doggie boot camp."

Krish spoke. "Sean has been alone for quite some time. Is it possible he has been training with the dogs while you have been away?"

Both Jess and Kindra burst out laughing. The women looked at each other and each saw the tears in each other's eyes. This caused another set of chortles. Kindra covered her eyes and started taking quick breaths, trying to get a hold of herself. Her mirth was close to extinguished when she found the air to speak at last.

"I think it's safe to say," Kindra spoke through her giggles, "that Sean is more of the self-preservation type. Jess is lucky Sean fed the dogs and gave them water. There is no way he would spend the energy on keeping up with the training they already have, let alone pushing the dogs farther. Likely, there were days Sean forgot the dogs were even there."

"You don't need to be that harsh, Kindra. She is correct, though. Sean has never been known for self-directed productivity. Besides, I haven't told you the strangest part yet. I can feel Butch and Cassidy's emotions. I know what they are thinking and feeling."

The last part caused the room to go silent. There was no quick explanation for why Jess could now read her dogs' minds. Every dog owner likes to think they can read their dog's thoughts, but Jess was serious. Everyone in the room eyed Butch and Cassidy. The dogs continued to stare at Syndral. For her part, Syndral didn't seem disturbed by the attention. Most people would not be comfortable with two large German Shepherd Dogs directing their full focus toward them.

"Prove it," Syndral said as she stood from her chair. "They won't take their eyes off of me, anyway. I'll take them into the kitchen and you can tell everyone what they are thinking. Joral can continue to hold up the wall while he reconciles the description you give with the actual real-time activities in the kitchen."

Syndral walked into the kitchen. Jess looked down at the dogs and nodded in Syndral's direction. The dogs followed Syndral and disappeared around the corner. Joral positioned himself in the doorway so he could see Syndral and the dogs, as well as the occupants of the living room. Jess closed her eyes. Without waiting for Syndral to say she was ready, Jess started giving the play-by-play as she saw it through the dogs' eyes.

"Cassidy is trying to tell you to forget the bread and to look for meat in the refrigerator. Butch is waiting for you to turn your back so he can nip at you and put you in your place. Cassidy is hoping you'll be leaving out water if you are going to feed him those crackers. Butch is upset that I gave away his plan because now you're moving around the kitchen without turning your back on him."

Joral was convinced. "That's enough. It's evident that Jess sees through the dogs' eyes at the very least. If that is the case, it is not a stretch to imagine she can also feel the dogs' intentions and read their thoughts. It is then, very likely, that the dogs can do the same with Jess and that is why they seem so perfectly trained."

Gunnar broke his pensive silence. "Your communication with the wildlife in Alfheim was impressive. It was exciting to see such a rare gift return to us. Some, like Leif, are able to understand animals better than others. His ability to persuade them to act on his will is faint, though present. Your strength with the skill was superior to Leif's from the start, but your connection to your own animals has magnified your abilities, even here, in the realm of humans, where your magic should be minimal."

Leif defended his magic. "I don't know if I'd call my power over animals faint. I can make birds land on my shoulders or fly in a certain path. I can keep predators away from a camp or a home."

Gunnar smiled at his brother. "You always found delight in bringing animals in close so you could pet them. It was adorable when you were a young one. I think mother hoped you had the gift. If you are honest with yourself, Leif, you must know your abilities are only an echo of a greater power."

Leif looked over at Butch. He and Cassidy had resumed protection detail at Jess's sides in the middle of the room. Leif knew, if his control of animals had been even close to Jess's power, he would not have been on his back on the kitchen floor. Though Leif felt as if the dog was laughing at him right now, he could not actually feel it the way Jess was describing. Leif was never able to see through the eyes of an animal the way Jess demonstrated with Butch and Cassidy. Gunnar spoke the truth. Leif felt magic flowing through him, even sitting here in the living room of his cabin, but the full power of the beasts was not his to wield. That gift ran in Jess's veins.

Kindra threw a wink at Jess; a silent acknowledgement of her thanks for getting things rolling. Jess nodded back and returned to her seat. The dogs remained in the center of the circle of furniture, facing Syndral.

"Well," Syndral said. "It looks like these two are reminding me it is my turn to speak."

Butch and Cassidy had yet to look away from Syndral for more than a few seconds. Her continued references to the dogs looking at her or expecting behaviors from her was the only outward evidence that Butch and Cassidy were making Syndral nervous. Jess felt an invisible slime oozing from this female. She felt it through the dogs' senses, as well as her own. Her dislike for Syndral amplified the dogs' distrust. Likewise, Jess found it hard to ignore her negative feelings about the elf with Butch and Cassidy's adverse thoughts rumbling in her head.

When Syndral stood to take the floor, Jess encouraged the dogs to keep her movements hampered and slow by virtue of their proximity. Syndral managed to stand and walk to the center of the room without watching the dogs. Jess was sure Syndral had planned a captivating presentation of her knowledge about the Dredfall assassins, but Jess would have Butch and Cassidy keep Syndral's movements to a minimum. Syndral should have just spoken from her seat. As she started talking, Syndral looked ridiculous standing in the center of the room, only able to turn in a small circle to speak to everyone. Jess allowed herself a little smile.

Syndral faced Jess as she started her speech. "The assassins you are facing in the human realm are members of Ulford's personal draw. They are similar to Lillerem's Royal Guard and it makes sense for you to refer to this draw as such. Do not make the mistake of thinking the Elite Draw, as it is called in Dredfall, is synonymous with your Royal Guard, though. Members of the Elite Draw perform all the tasks of a Lillerem Royal Guard, and then more.

"The Elite Draw is the first draw of Ulford's army. They are the smallest of the draws, partly because of the training and skill required to become a part of it. To become a member of the Elite Draw, one trains from childhood. Elves showing an aptitude for weapon skills, stealth, strength, and strategy are removed from their family homes and raised by the current Elite Draw. I use the term 'raised' loosely. They are not loved. They are simply provided with food, water and shelter. Their bodies and minds are trained. Members of the Elite

Draw sever all ties to family, and any relationships that go beyond satisfying physical need are prohibited."

Krish, always interested in war strategy, interrupted. "You've told us you commanded the Second Draw. Who commands the First?"

Syndral turned to look at Krish. "The commander of the Elite Draw, officially named the First Draw, is Vander. He has held command of the First Draw for over sixty years. Members of the First Draw have no desires of their own. Their only will is that of Ulford."

Jess could not shake the feeling that Syndral was speaking of this special squad of killers with reverence. She wanted to call Syndral out on it. Syndral may have told the group she was no longer a Dredfall soldier, but the way she spoke of the First Draw made Jess feel as if the female would join back up in a heartbeat if there were a chance she could join the elite group. The more Syndral spoke, the less Jess trusted that Syndral had severed ties with Dredfall.

"You need to understand," Syndral was still speaking, "soldiers of Dredfall are paid well. The amount of coin they earn ensures loyalty. The Elite Draw is the only unpaid draw in the entire army. For the members of the First, the draw is their life. They know nothing else. If they were to be paid, there would be nothing to spend their coin on, anyway. Everything they need is provided by Ulford. In a way, members of the First Draw are more like pets than employees. They are closer to slaves than people."

Butch and Cassidy growled at the comparison between slaves and pets. Syndral did not notice, but Jess sent soothing thoughts to the dogs. She didn't want them thinking she felt like their master, though she could see the comparison. The thoughts made Jess uncomfortable, and she felt she should change the direction of the conversation.

"Syndral," Jess interrupted, "Who was the other elf from today? She said her name was Imra."

CHAPTER 8

Syndral's description of each of the Dredfall assassins had been detailed, but lengthy. Jess and Kindra had opted to spend the rest of the night at the cabin. Kindra, Jess, Butch and Cassidy commandeered Leif's bedroom and spent the night sharing the room's enormous bed. Kindra woke first and stared at the ceiling. Cassidy, sensing that Kindra was awake, wiggled a little closer so Kindra could scratch behind his ears as she pondered all the new information.

Kindra replayed Syndral's extensive presentation in her mind. The woman had been so calm under pressure. She had not seemed to notice the stares from Butch and Cassidy, not to mention the untrusting faces of the princes. Syndral was in a hostile environment, but her demeanor was that of a person attending a gathering of close friends. Kindra was envious of Syndral's poise. She wanted to get to know the female. She felt she could learn more from her than just the details of Dredfall's evil workings.

After last night, Kindra felt more prepared to face the remaining assassins. Two of them were already dead. Of those still in the human realm, Imra would be the least powerful. Syndral's description had not explicitly spelled out the relationship between Ulford and Imra, but it felt as if the two might be lovers, or at least more than friends. According to Syndral, Imra fancied herself as some kind of mastermind. She could be credited with many of the ideas Ulford brought to fruition. If this was the case, then Imra must also be ruthless.

It seemed Imra acted as Ulford's right hand. She was an advisor and a soldier, though Syndral had hinted that Imra's military prowess fell more on the side of strategy than actual battle. As Kindra had seen at Patty's trailer, Imra was more likely to run than to fight, especially if she calculated the odds were not in her favor. If Kindra were to do a threat assessment of the assassins, and list them in order from greatest to least, she would place Imra at the bottom of the list. Well, nearly at the bottom. She mentally added Morthil and Ruith under Imra's name. Dead assassins were less threatening than any assassin still roaming the human realm.

"You have a mind full of assassins, don't you?"

Jess's voice made Kindra sit up, startled. Poor Cassidy was unceremoniously dumped to the floor. Kindra turned to look at Jess and saw she was laughing.

"It's good to be back. I missed how easy it is to sneak up on you when you're off in your own head. You really should consider working on that. I can't imagine you'll stay alive long if you're always so closed off to what's going on around you," chided Jess.

Kindra sighed. "I'm glad you're amused by my weaknesses. I enjoy being in my own mind. It's the perfect time for it, anyway. I'm snuggled in bed with two ferocious, furry friends, and Cassidy is here too."

Jess pulled the pillow from beneath Kindra's head and hit her with it. Butch jumped to the floor, sensing that the time to relax was at an end. Between swings of the pillow, Jess extracted herself from the bed. Kindra grabbed the pillow on its final blow and pulled it from Jess's hands. She scrunched it up and placed it back under her head.

"There is good news," Kindra said. "It seems we are down to three assassins. Syndral said the Elite Guard had five soldiers. Ruith and Morthil have been eliminated. Of the remaining three, we know the least about Skalanis. It concerns me that even Syndral, who knew him for several decades, has little to share about him."

"Granted, Syndral told us there were five of them. She told us she doesn't know much about Skalanis," said Jess. "It doesn't mean she really doesn't have the information. Until a day ago, we considered her an enemy. It is very likely she was part of the attack on Millspare. You probably killed many soldiers that had been under her command. I find it difficult to believe she is ready to walk in here and be your new best friend."

Kindra sat up. "Come on Jess. She has as much reason to hate Ulford as we do. The man conquered Southern Nalahem and took over Lindel. Syndral's family is from Lindel. She told us Ulford had her family killed or enslaved in the process. She said she wants revenge. Revenge is a powerful motivator."

"She *told* us Ulford murdered and enslaved her family members. Everything we know about her came from her mouth. How do we know she isn't lying? Remember, she was happy to earn her living in Dredfall's army until recently. Syndral took no issue with slaughtering the Royal Family of Lillerem. Do you really believe she is abashed by the thought of taking the lives of humans? She doesn't know any humans. They are of no consequence to her."

Kindra went to challenge Jess's allegations against Syndral, but Jess held up her hand. Jess's face softened. She was not trying to start a fight with her friend.

"Let me guess," said Jess in a softer tone. "Syndral told us she has connections here in the human realm, too. She has an interest in protecting them."

Kindra fell back against her pillow. Jess's point was made. Everything they knew about Syndral and the Dredfall assassins had come from Syndral. Once again, Jess was proving why she and Kindra needed each other. Kindra was willing to believe everything Syndral had shared. Jess was taking none of the information as fact. Kindra was impulsive. Jess was far more cautious, clinical even.

Jess, knowing she had planted a seed of doubt in Kindra's mind, finished lacing her boots and turned to the door. Butch and Cassidy scrambled to her sides. Jess stopped with her hand on the doorknob.

"There is a Russian proverb that Ronald Reagan became very fond of during the Cold War. When the proverb is translated into English, it tells us to trust, but verify. I'm sure it was a lot cooler-sounding in Russian because the words rhymed, but the meaning behind it is a sentiment we should always consider when taking information from people outside of the family. Leif gets it. I'm sure that was why he asked her to go follow up with that Pakk descendant in New Jersey. It's like a test."

Kindra nodded, but didn't say anything. Jess opened the door, and she and the dogs left the bedroom. Kindra threw off the covers and found her jeans on the floor near the bed. She pulled them on and then sat on the bed again to lace up her boots. Opening the closet door, Kindra looked at the pile of wrapped clothing in the back corner. There was a part of her that knew she should be carrying some kind of weapon. The sword was a bit ostentatious for walking around during the day, but the small handgun might not be the worst idea. Kindra groped around in the wrapped clothes until she found the tiny Browning pistol. She slid it into her pocket and was surprised to find it was completely concealed as she dropped the hem of her t-shirt down.

Kindra stopped in the bathroom to empty her bladder and rinse her face before stumbling to the kitchen. Krish, Leif, and Gunnar sat at the table. A mug of coffee waited on the table in front of the only empty chair. Kindra slid the seat out and sat in front of the mug. She took a sip. It was perfect. Kindra divined Krish had prepared the coffee when she saw that he was waiting for acknowledgement. She inclined her head to him and gave him a smile of thanks.

Leif wasted no time and said, "Gunnar and Krish are returning to Alfheim. We need to look into the information Syndral gave us on the assassins and there is no better place to do so than the Royal library."

Kindra lifted her head from her mug. "I guess Jess gave you her 'verify the people you should trust' speech as well?"

Leif continued, "I believe the term was 'trust but verify' and President Reagan was very fond of the expression."

Jess had, indeed, spoken with the princes, but Leif had probably heard Reagan use the expression in speeches on television at the time he actually said it. Kindra nodded her head slowly in agreement.

"I agree. We need to validate the information we now have, but I want to go with Krish. It will be nice to spend some time together, and we've been a good match when it comes to research. Why don't I go with him and the rest of you can stay here to try to find more of King Andril's descendants? We've been focused on those from King Blaith's line, but Andril must have had other children."

Leif replied, "Andril's only child was Blaith. Even if there were others, it's Blaith's line that would interest Ulford. Since Blaith took the throne after Andril, it is his descendants that can lay claim to the throne of Lillerem. Ulford, himself has a better claim to the throne than King Erik does now. Erik, as an adopted son of King Lars, does not have a direct bloodline to Blaith. By blood, Ulford is the rightful heir to the throne of Lillerem. Once his sister Ekkelle's descendants are gone, Ulford can depose King Erik by claiming he is the single living elf with that right."

"It's time we admit there are likely few descendants of Ekkel left for us to find," added Gunnar. "This means Ulford will be focused on us."

"Maybe it would make sense to investigate the descendants of any other children of King Andril as well. We only know of Blaith, but this family seems to collect bastards. There could be others we don't yet know about. I'd like to have knowledge of all of Andril's blood relations," said Leif.

Jess came through the back door with Butch and Cassidy. She filled a large bowl with water at the sink and set it on the floor for the dogs. The dogs slurped and slobbered greedily. More water was soaking the floor than hydrating the canines. Leif got up to grab a dish towel from the counter and tossed it on the floor near the bowl. Jess bent guiltily to use it to sop up the mess.

"It's settled then?" asked Krish. "We'll leave in a few hours. We'll have a little breakfast and be on our way."

Jess looked up from her position on the floor. She stood, threw the rag in the sink, and gave Krish a hard look.

"What is settled, exactly? Who's leaving and why? I just got back to my friend, and now you're taking her away? Wherever you're sending her, we're going, too."

"Jess," Kindra said. "We're going back to Alfheim. You just came back to the human realm. Do you really want to leave Sean and the dogs again so soon?"

Jess's eyes blazed. "First, I'll decide if I'm happy to be back in the human realm or not. Second, I don't see a reason Butch and Cassidy can't come too. Third, regarding Sean, I told him I would return when our house no longer looks like a landfill. I'm pretty sure he'll need a few days to make that happen."

"Ok then," said Leif. "I am not leaving this realm again until someone drags me from it, so I'll be staying here. Brother?"

Leif turned to Gunnar. Gunnar looked from Krish to Leif. He let his eyes fall to Butch and Cassidy. The dogs tilted their heads at him and he smiled. Leif sighed in resignation.

"Let me guess," said Leif, "you intend to go where the dogs go. Fine. Joral will want to stay here and mind the camp. There are some half-decent soldiers out there at this point as a result of his training.

We might use some of them to help with surveillance, or at the very least, use them for bait."

Kindra shot Leif a stern look.

"Relax, darling daughter. I won't be throwing any of them off any cliffs. I promise to keep them from harm."

Kindra was not sure she believed Leif, but his word was all she had. She looked at Jess.

"You're sure you want to go back?"

"Sure?" asked Jess. "I'm already having trouble deciding what to wear. I need to get back to my wardrobe at Millspare. We'll take a ride over to Sean's so I can change, then we'll head back here for the trip."

Kindra understood the feelings about the magic wardrobes of Alfheim. She had never been particularly fashionable and would never have been dressed appropriately at Millspare if not for the furniture having the power to pick out her clothing. She did not want to be the one to explain to Jess that there would be no time to visit with the furniture at Millspare Castle. Likely, that would have no bearing on Jess's desire to leave the human realm anyway. Kindra had picked up on Jess calling her home 'Sean's house,' as if it were no longer hers. She chose to let those words slide and stood to lead the way outside.

About half-way down Leif's bumpy driveway, a deer darted out in front of the car. Jess stopped in time to avoid it, but took a few breaths before starting the car forward again.

"That was close," Jess said. "I hate that feeling when something like that happens and your heart goes all crazy in your chest. It makes you want to pull over and stop driving for a little while until you feel normal again."

"Want me to drive?" Kindra asked.

"I want my heart to slow, Kindra. I'm not looking to give myself a heart attack. One, one, two, three, five, eight, thirteen..."

Kindra rolled her eyes, but laughed. Jess was the better driver by far, with or without suicidal deer. She gave her friend a moment to count out her number sequence and calm down. Jess's voice faded as her heart slowed and she put the car back in drive. At the end of the driveway, Jess turned left and picked up speed. As the car turned, Kindra thought she saw a wolf standing just inside the tree line at the bottom of the driveway. She spun in her seat to get a better look as the car headed down the road. It wasn't a wolf. It was the biggest dog she had ever seen.

"That's not something you see every day," Kindra said.

"What?" asked Jess.

"Someone's dog was on the side of the road. If it's still around when we get back, we should call animal control."

Jess looked at Kindra incredulously. "What did the dog look like?"

"It was gray, with hair a little longer than these guys," Kindra pointed her thumb at the back seat. "It had a slim body with very long legs. Its fur looked more like hair. Yeah, it kinda had an old man's beard for a coat. I just can't get over how tall it was."

"It sounds like you're describing a wolf hound. That's probably what scared that deer into running in front of the car," said Jess.

Kindra Googled 'wolf hound' on her phone. She looked at the images and found one that looked similar to the dog she had seen. She read through the description of the breed.

"You are likely correct, Jess," said Kindra. "It appears that I saw an Irish Wolfhound. Besides the description of its coat and body, it's probably the only breed big enough to be the animal I saw. Even the dog in this description seems too small, though. The dog I just saw may have rivaled the size of a small horse."

"People don't just misplace a wolfhound. It must live in one of the houses in this area. If it's still there when we get back, we'll ask the neighbors. There's no reason to call animal control."

"Point taken," said Kindra. "There are a lot of long driveways off this road. The dog probably lives in one of those houses back in the woods. I just hope his owners don't go looking for him and stumble on the camp behind Leif's cabin."

"What difference would it make?" asked Jess. "Even if they see the camp, they'll just chalk it up to a bunch of weirdos getting together to reenact some Civil War battle and camping out."

Kindra laughed. "Yeah, I can't imagine what some of the people in this area are up to on their properties. They probably wouldn't even blink an eye at a bunch of canvas tents and people practicing with swords."

About thirty minutes later, the RAV4 pulled into the driveway where Sean's truck should have been. Jess's spot was occupied by an old Subaru. As Kindra let the dogs out of the back seat, she gestured toward the little car.

"Yeah, I borrowed it from Leif's cabin," explained Jess. "Maybe you can drive it back when we go? I had to choose between my own car and that one when I went out earlier. I didn't think the owner would appreciate a back seat covered in dog hair."

Kindra nodded and Jess threw her the Subaru key. Butch and Cassidy were already waiting on the front stoop when the women got to the door. Jess unlocked it and the dogs bounded in. Now that they were home, they were back to acting like the dogs Kindra knew. She supposed the dogs were now off duty since they were in a comfortable place.

Jess went to the pail of dog food and filled Butch and Cassidy's bowls. It wasn't going to be possible to bring a huge bag of kibble through the portal, so she fed the boys well. Kindra snickered at the measuring cup Jess used to dole out the dogs' meal. Jess filled a few plastic storage bags with extra dog food and treats. She refrained from precise measuring of the food portions to avoid provoking Kindra into teasing her relentlessly. The food wouldn't last long, but it was something. As an afterthought, she grabbed an unopened bag of trail mix for Kindra and herself.

Jess let Butch and Cassidy out into the backyard and returned to the living room. The coffee table was clear of debris, but the end tables were piled with magazines, used cups and plates, and empty potato chip bags. The glass cleaner and roll of paper towels were gone. It did not seem that the products had been used on any new surfaces. The light streaming through the front window, as the sun dipped out of the sky, put the layers of dust on full display. Jess looked for the mop that was leaning against the wall when she was last here. It was still standing guard in the doorway to the kitchen. Jess's stomach turned. She had to get out of this house.

"Kindra, you ready?" Jess called loudly so her voice might find her friend.

Kindra's voice came from behind the closed door of the bathroom. "I'd love to leave; unfortunately, I think I'm stuck to the floor. This place is absolutely disgusting. I think I understand why you refused to stay."

Jess went to the back door and let the dogs in. She grabbed a pen from the junk drawer and scribbled a quick note on the pad attached via a magnet to the refrigerator. She heard the door to the bathroom open and Kindra's steps coming down the short hall. Jess turned and met her friend in the living room.

"Let's get out of here before I set the place on fire. Maybe Sean will hire someone to clean and the next time I am here, I'll feel better about staying."

Kindra obliged Jess by opening the front door. The dogs bounded out into the front yard as if they couldn't stand the filth they were leaving behind, either. Jess didn't bother locking the door. Maybe someone would rob the place and Sean would feel the need to clean, just to perform an inventory of any items that were taken.

Kindra climbed into the little Subaru and started the engine. She backed down the driveway and onto the road. She rolled down the window to speak to Jess.

"Are you going to swing by the police station and see Sean at work? Shouldn't you say goodbye?"

"Nah," said Jess. "I left him a note."

"You left him a note? That's a little abrupt, don't you think?"

Jess cocked an eyebrow. "Should I also send him a text?"

Kindra shook her head and rolled up the window. Jess walked to her SUV as Kindra pulled away in the Subaru. She had a twinge of regret that she would not be seeing Sean before she left. She truly loved him, but it was evident that he did not care enough about her to keep their home presentable. Jess prided herself on caring for her home. She could no longer see evidence of herself behind that front door.

The note Jess left on the fridge simply read, "The place is still disgusting. The dogs and I will be in Alfheim for a while. I love you, but I can't stay in this filth."

Jess decided the note was appropriate. She had written to Sean saying she loved him, and this was true. She had also said she could not remain in the house. Given the state of the place, this was also true. The note was abrupt, but it was honest. Jess wanted to believe that she would return to the human realm and find her house reverted to its previous state of cleanliness, but the logical part of her knew she would be required to clean it herself if she ever planned to live there again.

CHAPTER 9

The entire party stood in Leif's basement. Krish and Kindra stood inches from the place in the wall where the portal would open. Kindra could feel the smallest sensation at the back of her skull, letting her know magic was near. Behind them stood Jess and Gunnar. Butch stood to Jess's left, and Cassidy was squeezed between her and Gunnar.

Jess was far enough from the portal to feel nothing, but the dogs were uneasy. She could feel anxiety in Cassidy's mind and Butch was completely alert, as if a stranger were approaching. Gunnar and Jess spent thirty minutes of the journey's preparation time deciding if this trip would be safe for the canines. Jess had reasoned that they would be able to tell if the portal was rejecting their presence, both from the behavior of the animals and Jess's mental connection with them. Gunnar was concerned that the same determination that had pushed Jess on through the portal the first time she had crossed would encourage the dogs to push too far. He was also worried that the dogs' desire to please Jess and stay at her side would keep them from heeding any warnings about their well-being and might push them too far. Jess had assured Gunnar she would keep only a light grip on the dogs.

Jess consciously released her connection to Butch and Cassidy. As she did, a feeling of discomfort, close to loneliness, overwhelmed her. Jess was startled by how much she felt like she needed to connect with the hounds. They looked up at her, looking for reassurance. It was as if they were wondering why she had left, even though she was still standing right next to them. Jess gave them a reassuring smile and rubbed the tops of their heads, the way she did in the past when the dogs were unsure of trying something new. Jess reminded herself that she could not force the dogs to enter the gate. If they felt threatened, they would need to stay in the human realm. Jess was not coaxing them to walk down a flight of stairs. The exploit the dogs were about to attempt could kill them. The doubt and insecurity they felt while learning this trick was much more founded than during the preparation for any other stunt they had ever learned while training with Jess.

"They look good," Gunnar said to Jess. "Just stay out of their heads. We'll watch them closely for signs of distress. If they look uncomfortable, we'll just turn around and go back."

Jess nodded. It comforted her to know Gunnar was thinking about the dogs as much as she was. It was also nice to know that she would not be the only one turning back if the dogs proved unable to make the journey between realms. She unclipped the dogs' leashes. Putting the leashes in the pouch of her gray hoodie, she scratched Butch and Cassidy behind their left and right ears, respectively.

Kindra placed her hand on the wall before her. The stones parted and revealed the darkness beyond the barrier. Krish stepped into the darkness. A moment later, a match flared and then the opening was lit by torchlight. Kindra entered the tunnel. Gunnar gestured to Jess that she should precede him into the void. She only hesitated for a moment. Jess gave Butch and Cassidy one last reassuring scratch behind the ears and started forward. The dogs remained at her sides. The trio disappeared into the tunnel and Gunnar followed. The wall slid shut behind him as he joined the rest of the party in the circle of firelight at the beginning of the tunnel that served as a portal to Aegroth.

"So far, so good," said Jess.

Butch and Cassidy were looking up at her expectantly. They seemed ready for whatever adventure was asked of them. Jess started off into the darkness. Krish, holding the torch high, followed after her and the dogs to keep Jess from finding herself blinded to what was in front of her. Gunnar and Kindra took up the rear, walking adjacent to each other. No one spoke. Everyone watched Butch and Cassidy as the group walked through the tunnel. As they neared the half-way point, Butch started panting. The tunnel was not warm, so the dog was likely experiencing some kind of discomfort. Cassidy did not seem to be affected.

Jess had not considered what she would do if only one dog was able to make it safely through the tunnel. Butch and Cassidy had never been separated. Jess watched Butch closely and made the decision that she would turn back with both dogs if Butch's demeanor changed any more than the small amount it had changed already.

Kindra was the first to comment on Butch's panting. "Cassidy seems fine, but I can't tell if Butch is just nervous about being in a new place or if he is experiencing some pain."

"I know," said Jess. "Without being connected to his mind, I have no idea if there is a genuine issue, or if he is just unsure of his surroundings."

Jess turned to look at Kindra as she spoke. In the torchlight, she could see that Kindra's ears had tapered to slight points. If Kindra was in her Fae form, or close to it, then they were already closer to Alfheim than the human realm. Even as Jess took another step, the slight pressure she was feeling at the base of her skull abated. Jess glanced back down at Butch and saw that he was no longer panting.

Gunnar had seen the change as well. "It is possible that Butch was only experiencing anxiety, caused by the change he felt as we passed through the portal center. He seems fine now."

Jess, feeling some relief, let a small laugh escape. "What does it say about Cassidy that he didn't even seem to notice we walked into another realm?"

Jess scratched Cassidy's head and smiled at the dog. Butch looked up at her as if to ask where his head scratch was. Jess gave Butch a scratch as well, and was happy to see the dog seemed absolutely fine. Jess recalled her first trip through this tunnel. She had not even known she had possessed any kind of magic. The doorway had opened for her, but the portal had pushed against her the entire period she was walking its length. By the time Jess had reached the middle of the tunnel, she had been dizzy, disoriented, and nauseous. Jess could not recall her final steps through the tunnel or exiting into the lush land just outside of the city of Aergroth. Her next memories were waking up in a plush bed covered in more pillows than were necessary for any person to sleep comfortably.

It seemed Butch and Cassidy did not need to fight the portal the way Jess had that first time. Other than Butch noticing an unsettling change, the dogs were fine as the group approached the end of the tunnel. Kindra placed her hand on the stone, and sunlight spilled into the passage. Krish extinguished the torch and hung it in its place on the wall. Gunnar dropped to one knee, and the dogs went to him. He rubbed each of them all over and the dogs made little excited circles. Cassidy gave Gunnar's face a lick. Jess broke out in a huge smile. It warmed her heart to see Gunnar release the tension he must have felt over the dogs' wellbeing. Covering his worry must have been stressful, and this bit of play with the dogs provided an instant release of his disquiet. Jess watched the feeling pour from Gunnar's face before he stood and walked out of the tunnel. The dogs looked as if they might follow Gunnar, but then glanced up at Jess and went back to her sides instead. They sensed that the brief respite was over and it was time to return to work.

As the sunlight touched her skin, Jess allowed her mind to join with the minds of her dogs once again. It was her turn to feel an immediate sense of calm. Jess marveled, not for the first time, at the power dogs had to sway human emotions. She truly felt that any problem could be solved by a dog, in some way. Cassidy's mind was on fire with curiosity. It was taking some effort for him to refrain from bounding off to explore all the fresh smells. Butch, on the other hand, felt nothing but a powerful urge to remain close to Jess and protect her in this unfamiliar place. Jess gave Butch a scratch of appreciation and sent reassuring thoughts to him.

The path running near the portal entrance had no one on it as the troop stepped out of the brush. Kindra turned toward Millspare and they all started walking. A peddler, driving his cart of wares, came toward them from around a bend. The group stepped off the path to let him drive by. The man tipped his hat, even as Butch and Cassidy eyed the horse that was pulling the cart. Hundreds of pounds heavier than the dogs, the horse continued to clop along, looking straight ahead. Jess scratched the tops of the dogs' heads to thank them for abstaining from causing a scene.

Gunnar turned to Jess, "How much of that was your will, as opposed to the dogs' restraint?"

Jess smiled. "They are good babies, but I did send them a little reminder that we are guests in this land. Since the place isn't teeming with German Shepherds, I feel it is prudent we try to be on our best behavior. They are representing the breed and there is no need to incur the wrath of the locals from the start of the journey."

Kindra, having been away from Millspare the longest, took in the sights and allowed the memories to flood over her. As Krish led the group down the winding path to Millspare, Kindra remembered the night the Dredfall army marched for the castle. She saw herself emerge from the portal and onto this path. She was sneaking up on the guards stationed just outside of Aergroth again. Her heart picked up pace as she remembered blinking into the castle office, then riding out into the town on Branka's back. Kindra saw herself leaping from rooftop to rooftop to reach the edge of the town, and then blinking into the fray to burn Dredfall's artillery.

It became difficult for Kindra to breathe as she remembered being caught in that net. She was, once again, feeling as she had in those moments that could have been her last. They were not her last moments, though. Leif was there. Leif rescued Kindra and spirited her back to the rooftops of town. Together, she and Leif returned to Millspare to defend the people there, making a last stand. Many lives, on both sides, were lost, but Kindra had frozen time itself to burn the enemy from the gates. All those lives lost...

Krish cleared his throat. Kindra looked up from her feet and she stopped walking. When Krish came to terms with the fact Kindra had not heard a word he said, he sighed.

"Welcome back. I said, I wonder if Branka missed you."

"Sorry," said Kindra. "Funny you should ask, though. I was just thinking about her. She really is a brave horse."

Krish looked at Kindra knowingly and said, "I'm sure you were only thinking about Branka."

The corner of Kindra's mouth turned up. She knew Krish's lighthearted sarcasm was his way of telling her to let the past go. The number of souls Kindra sent to the afterlife on the day of the attack was a burden Kindra was slowly releasing. Being back in Alfheim was forcing that weight to the front of Kindra's mind again. Kindra knew her actions were a result of a war she had not started. The blood on her hands had been necessary to protect her Elven family and all the inhabitants of Aergroth. Still, Kindra knew she would never feel clean again.

The sounds of stomping hooves greeted the group as they approached the stables of Millspare. Krish, who had spent years caring for Millspare's horses, picked up his pace. It made Kindra smile to think how doing the job of an ordinary stable boy made her Elven Prince so happy. Kindra caught up to Krish as he approached Branka's stall. He opened the gate and Branka happily trotted out. She trotted right past Krish and went straight to Kindra. Kindra put her forehead to the horse's muzzle and stroked the side of Branka's face. Krish, looking only slightly unhappy at being jilted, smiled at his fiancée, and shook his head.

Gunnar's voice came from the stable entrance. "Leave it to Krish to bypass the main entrance and fanfare for the barn and the manure. We could be in Einar's kitchen enjoying a warm meal right now."

Jess's eyes darted between the horses in the stalls and the dogs at her sides. "Yeah, maybe we can leave Kindra and Krish to their equine reunion and Gunnar and I will go grab some food?"

Gunnar picked up on Jess's request and nodded in agreement. He strode off toward the castle. Jess and the dogs followed behind. Kindra grabbed a brush off the wall and used it to pamper Branka, while Krish checked to be sure the other horses were healthy and happy in his absence. After a few more strokes of the brush, Kindra stopped and turned to Krish. Branka nuzzled Kindra's cheek over her shoulder.

"Is everything up to par?" Kindra asked Krish.

"It seems so. No one is lame, sick, or filthy, so I am satisfied."

"Admit it," Kindra said. "Part of you was hoping the horses would be neglected so you could pat yourself on the back for being the best male qualified to care for them."

Krish blushed. He didn't respond to Kindra's statement, but turned toward the castle and walked away. Kindra returned the brush to the wall and gave Branka one last rub as she walked the horse into her stall. She wore a satisfied grin on her face as she started off after her proud male. Kindra teleported to Krish's side and entered the kitchen with her hand in his.

Gunnar and Jess were at the large table, already enjoying bowls of something hot. Butch and Cassidy lay under the table, licking their lips. An empty bowl sat next to each dog's head. Einar stepped back from the serving counter and wiped his hands on a rag. He scooped up two new steaming bowls and walked them over to the table. The bowls were set down and Einar added a wooden soup spoon to each. As Krish and Kindra took seats in front of the steaming bowls, Mildred whisked through the doorway and into the kitchen. The woman carried the light of the sun on her face as she tried to contain her excitement over the kitchen guests' presence.

The often dour woman said brightly, "Kindra! It has been a while! I'm so happy Millspare's savior has returned! Krish, it is always a pleasure to have your handsome face at our table. Gunnar, it's lovely to have you back as well. Jess! I did not expect to see you so soon!"

Mildred inhaled a deep breath and plopped down on the end of one of the two benches. The poor woman had probably sprinted from the other side of the castle to greet them. Once in the kitchen, she spilled all of her hellos into one giant greeting without taking time to catch her breath. Kindra laughed and reached to put her hand on top of Mildred's wrist. She gave the old female a squeeze.

"So, Krish gets the addition of 'handsome face,' and I just get a 'good to see you?' I see how it is," Gunnar said to Mildred good naturedly.

For just a moment, Mildred looked upset. She hadn't meant it that way. She recovered quickly and doubled down instead.

"Sorry Gunnar. There just isn't a world where you measure up to the golden-haired heir to a kingdom."

Gunnar bowed his head slightly in acknowledgement. Mildred had played off her unintentional slight well. Mildred looked as if she might go on, or maybe she had intended to change the topic of conversation entirely, but she did not get the chance. The old female sprung out of her seat and backed away from the table. She dropped to all fours and gazed into Butch's steady, piercing eyes.

"This must be Butch and Cassidy," Mildred said.

The woman held Butch's stare, but she directed the statement to Jess. Jess didn't bother to answer. Unquestionably, there was not a resident in the castle who would not recognize the canines at first sight.

"You can really see the ancient relationship to wolves," Mildred wondered aloud.

Mildred had not dropped Butch's stare. Gunnar was fairly certain the dog may have backed up an inch. Mildred may have been an older elf, but she was one of the most imposing and feared females in Aergroth. Not only did she pack a prickly personality, but she was once a commander in Lillerem's army and a fierce warrior. Many dark elves had fallen on Mildred's blade in past years, and more recently, she had sent hundreds of Dredfall soldiers to their deaths.

Cassidy finally deigned to lift himself from the floor and plod over to Butch's side. Unlike his distrusting brother, Cassidy felt no threat from Mildred. He leaned his head forward to sniff the female and then licked her from her chin to her temple. Cassidy promptly spun around and returned to his place on the floor beneath the table. Einar threw his wife the rag he had used earlier for his hands. After wiping her face, Mildred sat back and smiled at Jess.

"You weren't kidding when you described the differences in their personalities. I think Cassidy likes me, but the relationship between Butch and I might need a little work."

Kindra tried not to laugh. "That is nothing. You should see the way Butch watches Leif. It is as if the dog is waiting for the perfect opportunity to eat the bastard. Aside from Jess, the only one Butch really seems to like is Gunnar."

At Gunnar's name, Butch retreated to the male's side. Gunnar reached down and scratched the shepherd's head. Mildred stood and reclaimed her seat on the bench. Einar grabbed the towel from his wife's hands and threw it onto the counter. He came to the table with a bowl for Mildred and one for himself. Through slurps of soup, the group caught each other up on the events and gossip of both worlds. When spoons started to scrape the bottoms of bowls, Mildred and Einar stood to clear the table.

Mildred started for the door, but called over her shoulder, "I'm sure you'll want to rest. I'm going to go make up your rooms."

"There will be no need for that, Mildred," Krish called after her. "Come back over here and say your farewells. It is imperative that we waste no time. Einar has fueled us and we will now be heading to Gulentine. Likely, we will stay overnight there until we find what we need in the royal library."

Mildred looked disappointed. "You'd rather stay at your father's home than here? I thought the reason you were here so often was to avoid your father."

Krish smiled. "Usually, yes. It has worked since I was a boy. I love the man, but it can be difficult to wiggle out from under his thumb. If not for our need of the the library, we would not have ventured to Alfheim at all."

CHAPTER 10

"Do we ride, or do we walk?" Gunnar asked Jess as he eyed Butch and Cassidy in the stable.

The plan was to ride to Smalgroth and use the gate there to travel to Lillerem City. Unlike the gates that housed the portals to the human realm, the Smalgroth gate was one of a few public gates used for travel throughout the kingdom. Butch and Cassidy were watching Krish prepare four horses for the task and did not appear to deem the horses trustworthy, nor did they seem likely to sanction equine travel.

Jess was shaking her head slowly. She could feel the distrust and fear the horses were causing in the dogs. Her heart was telling her to admit defeat. She had never socialized the dogs with horses. She did not think there would ever be a need for them to be familiar with the mammoth animals. It was starting to look as if Jess would be spending a lot of time on her feet over the next few days, and she was already beginning to feel tired.

Movement from across the main aisle of the barn swung the heads of the dogs away from Krish, who was saddling a dark gray mare. A chestnut colored horse with a dark, flowing mane was walking toward Butch and Cassidy. Jess watched in amazement as the horse approached the dogs backwards. The horse was slowly placing one hoof behind the last to move toward Butch and Cassidy in the least threatening manner possible. Had Jess thought it through, she might have come up with the idea herself, but the horse thought faster than she did.

"I knew Branka was a good listener," said Krish, "but it seems human words are not the only language she understands. She felt their trepidation. She is trying to show them there is nothing to fear."

Branka continued her slow approach in reverse until she was standing directly in front of Jess and the two canines. The horse presented her flank, still not looking at the dogs. Cassidy was the first to stretch his head forward to take in Branka's scent. After a moment, he took a tentative step forward so he could smell closer to the horse's rear end. Jess kept him from stepping behind the horse, but Cassidy seemed satisfied with the access he currently had. Butch started to lean in to smell the horse as well, once Cassidy was more relaxed. Branka took a small step forward. The dogs pulled back a few inches, but did not flinch or attack the horse. Branka took a few more steps away from the dogs and the dogs trotted off to explore more of the stable.

"I think we just got clearance to add horses to our traveling party," said Jess. "It is a good thing, too. I really do not think my feet would have carried me the ten miles to Smalgroth."

Butch and Cassidy were now making circles around Branka. Butch was keeping some distance between him and the mare, but Cassidy was throwing his forelegs to the ground, offering repetitive little play bows to the horse. It was safe to say Cassidy had made a new friend and Butch was working toward tolerating the gentle animal. Butch's attempt was exponentially stronger than any he had ever made for Leif, so Jess was feeling confident about the coming trek on horseback.

Krish stepped over to Jess. "I think Branka would understand if you were to take her reins for the journey. I know Kindra and Branka have formed an affinity for each other, but I think the dogs' comfort should take priority over my intended's desires."

Kindra sent a brush flying from the wall toward Krish's head. He easily deflected her half-hearted magical attack, and the brush dropped harmlessly to the floor. She turned her back on Krish and mounted a horse with spots on its rear. The type of horse started with the letter A, but Kindra hadn't retained the name of the breed. She did recall the horse's name, though. The horse was called Bob, and Kindra found it amusing that a horse with such decorative paint would have such a plain, human name. She steered Bob toward the sunlight and the others readied themselves to follow.

Jess left the stable, with Butch on her left and Cassidy on her right. Branka did not seem to mind inheriting the small bodyguards. Atop the horse, and flanked by her dogs, Jess couldn't help but feel nearly invincible. She followed Gunnar, who was riding a horse of jet black. The mane and tail of the horse were long and absolutely beautiful.

Jess was jealous. She fingered her frizzy blonde hair, noting the numerous split ends, and laughed to herself as she wondered if she should ask Gunnar's horse what kind of shampoo he used. The horse sent back emotions to Jess to convey that he knew he was beautiful and that there would be no way to tame her unruly locks and make them resemble his luscious mane. Jess, not meaning to communicate with the horse, was startled as she realized the horse had been listening to her thoughts. That was part of it, anyway; the other part was the realization that the horse was a bit of a snob. Gunnar, far from snobbish, would be mortified to learn this about his mount.

Jess strategically blocked her thoughts from the horse in front of her. The last thing she needed was to give Butch and Cassidy a reason to spite the animal. They were just beginning to accept horses, and Jess did not want to taint that progress with any animosity. She pushed her envy aside and took in the beautiful countryside instead of perseverating on her desire for nicer hair. It would be about three hours before the group reached Smalgroth, and Jess wanted to enjoy the peacefulness of Lillerem as they traveled.

Kindra relinquished the lead to Krish, since this was her first trip out of Aergroth. She had a fair idea about the correct direction in which to travel, but Krish traveled to Gulentine Palace via the Smalgroth gate regularly. She followed behind the blonde male, watching his broad shoulders flex with the movements of his horse. Soon, they would be getting married. It was not exactly her choice, but it was the expectation.

Kindra enjoyed her time with Krish. They found few moments alone, but she looked forward to each minute they stole for themselves. Kindra was attracted to this male, but that was no surprise. The surprise would be if a female could be found who was not attracted to Krish. He was the kind of handsome that only graced the covers of romance novels. Those looks did not belong to people in the real world, regardless of the realm they inhabited. Kindra closed her eyes to better picture Krish. She saw his hair framing his perfect face. His kind eyes, that supernatural shade of green, were speaking to her; even in her reverie. Kindra knew she cared for Krish, but did she love him? Was Krish truly her mate? If he was, would she be asking herself these questions? As she did whenever these doubts penetrated her thoughts, Kindra told herself the thoughts were not caused by Krish at all.

After the loss of her first husband, Tom, remarrying had never crossed Kindra's mind. At least, it hadn't been a thought until her Aunt Ruth caught wind of Krish's feelings for Kindra and had seen the perfect union of family and the throne on the horizon. Kindra had a history of carrying out the will of others under the guise of her own desires. Truthfully, Kindra rarely followed her own heart. It wasn't because she didn't want to do so; it was simply that often, even Kindra couldn't separate her needs from the wants of others.

"Are you with us?" Krish, turning to face Kindra, asked.

"Yes, sorry," Kindra blushed. "I'm just concentrating on convincing Speckle Butt to keep moving."

Kindra gestured to her horse as she offered up the laughable nickname. She exaggerated her attempts to urge the horse on, but she was not fooling Krish.

"Appaloosas can be stubborn, but there is something else. You look genuinely concerned."

As the breed of horse rolled from Krish's tongue, Kindra made a note to try harder to file the word away this time. She made a show of nodding her head in agreement while she scrounged for a better explanation for her most recent disassociation from the present. She snatched at a thread of an idea.

"I guess I am a little concerned. It isn't just Bob's stubbornness, though that isn't helping. There was a dog outside Leif's this morning. Jess and I were going to try to find its owners if it was still there when we got back, but we forgot to look for it. I feel bad about it."

"What kind of dog was it?" Krish didn't seem convinced this was the problem, but he was playing along.

"I Googled it, you know, looked it up online? I'm pretty sure it was an Irish Wolfhound. The picture wasn't exactly right, but it was the only breed that might have even been close to matching the size of the thing."

"Bigger than a Wolfhound?" Krish showed more interest. "What made you feel it didn't match the images you saw?"

"The dog I saw had muscles that were much more defined. His head was wider. The ones online had long, thin heads. Also, the dog I saw had ears that stuck up like Butch and Cassidy have. The Irish Wolfhounds online all had ears that flopped over."

Krish was pale. His already light skin was so drained of color; it was now a greenish gray. He stopped his horse and stared down at his saddle. Kindra stopped, with Bob facing Krish's gelding. Gunnar continued up the trail with Jess and the dogs behind him. Several moments dragged by with Krish remaining silent. When he went to speak, he failed on the first attempt because his mouth was now dry. Krish took a sip of water from his skin and replaced it on his belt before trying again.

"That was no Wolfhound. I fear the thing you saw was a hundespor."

Kindra knew Krish didn't expect her to comprehend the grand meaning behind his revelation. She waited patiently as he collected himself and plunged on with an explanation.

"The hundespor are a type of Svartålfar. They do loosely resemble wolfhounds in coat texture and shape, but they are not dogs."

"Ok... So, why do you look as if I just told you I have a deadly disease?" asked Kindra.

"It would be impossible for one to cross to the human realm accidentally."

Kindra's eyes opened wide. Krish's pallor made more sense now. A hundespor was scary, but someone transporting them for use as weapons was worse. There was no way to warn Leif and Joral without returning to the human realm. With luck, the beast Kindra had seen was simply running some kind of reconnaissance. They could discuss it together when they returned to Leif's cabin in a few days.

Up ahead, Gunnar and Jess waited at the top of the rise that the group had been climbing steadily. Butch was staring into the brambles on the left, and Jess had an amused look in her eyes. As Krish and Kindra drew closer, a long twig poked slowly from the brush and bopped Butch on the nose. The dog jumped back and lowered his head, snarling at the bush. Gunnar and Jess were now laughing openly.

"It seems the Little Folk have taken a liking to teasing Grumpy over here." Gunnar gestured to Butch. "They've been taunting him for the last ten minutes. Jess and I are trying to decide how long it will take Butch to jump into the bushes and go after the poor creatures."

"Poor creatures!" Jess exclaimed. "The little heathens are driving Butch crazy!"

Krish smiled. "Butch will get to relax now. We've hit the edge of the forest."

The group looked down over the grassy slope before them. At the base of the hill, the town of Smalgroth was in sight. The town was a brownish square, standing in a field of green. The farming village was home to fewer than five hundred elves. Buildings were clustered in the town's center, which was little more than a mile or two square. Surrounding the town were fields. Ninety percent of Smalgroth's land was employed for farming. Instead of a defensive wall, like other towns might have, there were large storage towers between the fields and homes of the village.

"How is it that such a small community is home to a gate to Lillerem City?" asked Jess.

Krish explained. "My father has never enjoyed the taste of the local produce found in the forests and fields of Lillerem. Many years ago, he commissioned an excursion to the human realm to obtain seeds from all over your world. The king built Smalgroth for the families of Lillerem, who wished to live a simpler life away from the city farming foods from the human realm. Though Smalgroth governs itself for the most part, it is actually an arm of Lillerem proper, under direct service to Gulentine Palace. The land outside of the palace was not suitable for growing fruits and vegetables. My father found land with rich soil and built his farmers a town. The gate at the center of town allows for easy transport of food, but also provides weary travelers quick access to the Capital City."

"So these people are little more than a pet project of your father's creation?" asked Jess.

"Do not think the situation is so terrible. The people of Smalgroth would be doing the same or similar work in Lillerem City. Out here, they get to live their own lives while avoiding the commotion of armies and the business of the marketplace. It's a peaceful life. Are there not people in the human realm who prefer to live far from cities?"

Jess thought about it. It was difficult to make the comparison between Alfheim and the present-day human realm. Instead, she imagined the serfs of old Europe being permitted to travel far from the kings they served. They would still earn their keep, providing for the kingdom, but the difference would be the illusion of being free from their ruler. Jess smiled to herself. Maybe it was more like letting the kids go off to college and feel as if they were living their own lives even though mom and dad would always be just a call away. Jess decided this analogy was a better fit.

Butch and Cassidy tore up and down the slope, as the horses carefully picked their way down toward the village. Jess was pretty sure the dogs were celebrating the end of their relentless torment by the Little Folk. There was nothing in the canines' minds but a sense of freedom and happiness. Jess searched Branka's thoughts and found the horse too, was happy to be approaching this quaint town. There was warmth and familiarity in Branka's memories of Smalgroth, and Jess was looking forward to seeing the place. Jess was just starting to think of this visit as a miniature vacation when Krish spoke again.

"We're not sight-seeing. We'll leave the horses at the stable and grab something to eat. After that, we'll need to leave for the palace. We need to gather what information we can from the archives, and then get back to Leif and Joral."

Jess sighed. The peace in Smalgroth had fooled her into thinking she might get to benefit from the serene atmosphere. Unfortunately, she was forced to acknowledge that the horses would be the only ones taking a break from the fast pace of life. It was no wonder Branka had fond feelings for this place. This was a spa trip for horses. They were pampered in the stables while their riders went on to Lillerem City.

Having left the horses at the spa, Krish led the group to a small cottage on the other side of the lane. He climbed the three steps to stand on the large front porch and raised his arm to knock on the door. Before his skin made contact with the wood, the door swung open and a figure encompassed the entire doorway. Krish looked surprised, but immediately shook the hand of the giant figure.

In the street, Kindra, Jess and Gunnar waited to see who had come to the door. In answer, the hulking form of Bane stepped out onto the porch. He motioned for the group to follow him into the cottage. When Butch and Cassidy attempted to follow Jess inside, Bane threw them a hard stare and blocked them from entering. The dogs did not raise their hackles or feel threatened. Instead, Butch and Cassidy were giving Bane the sad eyes of chastised puppies. Bane's stony heart seemed not to notice. He pointed to the corner of the porch where bowls of water and some blankets had been left out. The dogs got the hint and skulked over to their temporary pallet.

Inside the cottage, a male elf motioned for the group to take seats at an enormous wooden table. The table and its chairs were the only furnishings. It spanned half of the kitchen area and the entire living space into which the group had entered. There was a dark hall to the right that likely led to the male's sleeping quarters.

Before sitting, Krish made introductions. "Kindra, Jess, this is Kanin Gundersen. He is retired from the Lillerem army and has provided sustenance to weary travelers for the last fifty years."

Kindra turned to Kanin. "Retired? I didn't know soldiers could retire. I just figured they all…" Kindra let her words drop.

"Died?" picked up Kanin. "Yes, most soldiers serve for life. Not runners, though. We lose our usefulness as we lose our speed. When the army needs to send a message, it needs to be done immediately, not after the runner has worked the pain of old age from his joints."

"Old age?" Jess was amazed. "If you've been retired for fifty years, you were likely a teenager when you retired."

Kanin blushed. "I retired after seeing eighty-five summers. The job of a runner is reserved for the young."

"Don't let him fool you," said Gunnar. "Kanin may not be as swift as he once was, but he can still outrun all those at this table."

Kanin's blush deepened. "Enough about me. Eat your fill."

Kanin gestured to the bounty spread before them on the table. Jess recognized many of the fruits and vegetables. There were slices of pear and apple, as well as carrots and celery sticks. She spooned a mixture of broccoli and cauliflower, that smelled of the vinaigrette in which it was bathed, onto the plate before her. Kindra procured corn on the cob from the center of the table and placed it next to the berry mixture already sitting on her plate. Krish had piled his plate with leafy greens and was now topping it with nuts and berries. Gunnar and Bane were already diving into the mound of bean salad each had added to their plates. Jess couldn't help but feel as if she had been invited to a party at the home of a vegetarian friend.

"Do you not eat any meat?" Jess asked Kanin.

"Oh, I do," he replied. "So much of what we eat here in Alfheim is hunted from the forest. It is a treat for most travelers to have so many fruits and vegetables to choose from. I do have meat, if you're interested."

"Oh no!" Jess felt as if she may have offended the male. "Everything here is wonderful. It just seemed odd. I have come to expect that mostly meat is provided at meals, and there was none. I should've thought about the reason. This is probably the only place where food like this is found."

Kindra saved her friend from her rambling. "I have to say, as someone who has had the pleasure of sampling most of these delicacies before, the flavor of each food is so rich. I'm not sure if it is the soil or those who tend the land, but I can understand why people would come here for just a taste."

Kanin smiled happily. "Precisely. This is exactly why people come to visit Smalgroth."

Jess did not want to further hurt the male's feelings, but she was pretty sure he was missing the mark. The food did taste amazing, but it seemed much more logical that travelers would be in Smalgroth to use the gate to the palace in Lillerem. She kept her thoughts to herself to allow Kanin pride in his production. Instead, Jess heaped more food onto her plate and continued her feast.

CHAPTER 11

Leif sat in his favorite spot on the cabin steps enjoying the early morning camp sounds in the distance. It was cool for the time of year, especially since the sun was barely above the horizon. Leif was seriously considering heading up to the camp to join the training session that had recently commenced. Then again, that would require standing. It would also require speaking to people. Leif was friendly with the camp residents, but he had no desire to form any bonds with them. It was one of Leif's new responsibilities to supply a safe place for the descendants to live, but there was no expectation that he share life with them.

Something pulled Leif from his thoughts. He looked into the woods and listened carefully for what had disturbed him. There were no abnormal sounds. Wait. That was the problem. There were no normal sounds. The men could still be heard training behind the cabins, but there was nothing else. Leif could hear no birds or rustling in the leaves.

As if waiting for the moment when Leif noticed her presence, Syndral stepped directly in front of Leif. "Where's Kindra?"

"I'm sorry, Syndral. Kindra's not at home right now. Shall I tell her you stopped by and maybe you girls can have a playdate another time?"

"Always a pleasure to see you," Syndral said as she rolled her eyes. "I have news, and I need to speak to her. Where is she?"

"I told you, she's not here. She went to go meet her future in-laws."

"Kindra left the human realm? Krish is with her?"

Leif let out an exasperated sigh. "Yeah, yeah, yeah. She and Krish are gone. Gunnar and Jess went with them, too. Why don't you just tell me the news and Joral and I can decide what to do with it?"

"No," said Syndral. "This is something I want to share with Kindra."

"Why Kindra?" asked Leif. "If I recall, I sent you to go retrieve a descendant from the New Jersey border and I see you standing here alone. If something went wrong on your mission, I would think you would be reporting to me."

Syndral glanced into the woods as if she were waiting for someone to materialize from its depths. She was considering something. Leif could tell she had not intended to find Kindra absent upon her arrival at the cabin. Syndral turned back toward Leif, still looking over her shoulder at the woods.

"I think you, I mean we, well, all of us could be in more trouble than we thought," Syndral admitted to Leif as she finally turned to look at him again.

"Go on," said Leif.

"You might want to get Joral. This will certainly be something he would want to hear."

As if hearing his name, Joral strode from inside the cabin and out onto the porch. Likely, Joral had entered the house through the back door around the same time Syndral appeared. He gave Syndral an icy stare. Joral dipped his head in acknowledgement more than as a greeting to Syndral.

"Ok. I think I solved our biggest problem," started Syndral. "I may have figured out how the assassins are locating Elven descendants."

Leif replied dryly, "Amazing. The Dredfall soldier figured out how other Dredfall soldiers operate."

Syndral looked toward the front door of the cabin.

"It's a nice morning. We can sit here on the steps and talk," said Leif.

Syndral did not take a seat next to Leif. Instead, she dragged a lawn chair from several feet away to the area in front of the steps. She tested the chair and lowered herself into it once she made the decision that it was worthy of bearing her weight. Syndral leaned forward in the chair as Joral took a seat on the step above Leif.

"I may have left out some information about one of the assassins," Syndral admitted. "It wasn't intentional or part of some plot or anything. I just didn't really think about it at the time."

Leif and Joral exchanged a look. Neither male was surprised that Syndral chose to leave out some details. Syndral read their faces as Joral and Leif turned back to her and her look became determined.

"I kept nothing from you intentionally. It is only that Skalanis is so quiet and seemingly unimportant. He stays in the background and rarely acts of his own accord."

"And you've changed your mind about his importance, why?" urged Joral..

"I was following up on Leif's lead. He found a male descendant of Pakk in Bergen County, New Jersey. He runs a mechanic shop near old route 17, just inside the border with New York," Syndral replied to Joral.

Leif made a circling motion with his hand. "Get to the part that is a threat to us all."

"I went to the shop to find the man, and I saw a hundespor."

Syndral looked at the males on the porch expectantly. Leif, having lived most of his life in the human realm, stared back blankly. Joral, on the other hand, was deep in thought. Leif turned to his cousin for an explanation. When Joral did not notice the unspoken question, Leif turned back to Syndral.

Syndral offered some details. "Hundespor roam Alfheim in small numbers. They look like giant dogs, but they are far from canine. They are Dark Elves. Some say they were brought to Alfheim through a portal from another world."

Leif shrugged. "What's the big deal? If they've traveled through portals before, why is it such a surprise that you saw one in the human realm?"

Joral answered. "Dark elves cannot operate the portals. It would take someone with the Elven blood of the Ljósálfar to open the portal and allow them through. I'm guessing Syndral has reason to believe the light elf who opened the portal is Skalanis."

"It's not just that he opened the portal for the hundespor to enter," continued Syndral. "I'm afraid it is far worse. Skalanis keeps a pack of hundespor like pets in Alfheim. He can speak to them in a manner similar to the way Jess communicates with Butch and

Cassidy. I fear he has let one or more hundespor enter the human realm and is in control of their actions."

"Ok, that's a bit unsettling," said Leif, "but I am still failing to see why this has you two so upset."

"Hundespor hunt by smell. Some believe they can scent the souls of Ljósálfar. They are known to enjoy devouring the flesh of an elf while simultaneously reveling in the act of tormenting the person's soul," said Joral.

"That all sounds very unpleasant," said Leif. "I am still missing why this kind of evil is so much more terrible than the evil we have faced before."

"It's not that the evil is any more terrible," said Syndral. "You might say the evil is more specialized. It is very likely that Skalanis is using the hundespor as bloodhounds. He sends them out to uncover the location of anyone with Elven blood living in the human realm. The part I do not understand is why he would not simply have the dark elves dispatch the descendant once he or she was located. I don't understand why Skalanis has been notifying the assassins and having them kill the humans instead."

"Ok," acknowledged Leif. "These hundespor are likely able to just stroll through the streets of an area and follow the scent of Elven blood to the next target. It is a rapid method for locating people and explains why the assassins are one step ahead of us at every turn. You bring up an excellent question though about why Skalanis isn't just having his dogs kill the descendants once they are located."

Syndral said, "I am sure Skalanis has his reasons. If we can find Skalanis, and take him out of the equation, then the hundespor will have no directive. It will remove the majority of the threat from those with Elven Blood, but other humans will then become targets. The Hundespor are not solitary hunters. Each enjoys devouring flesh and soul. Every human in this realm would become prey once the hundespor are set free from Skalanis."

"So, we have two terrible options?" asked Joral. "We can let the hundespor hunt the Pakk descendants, or we can kill Skalanis to take the pressure off of those with Elven blood. The problem with the former plan is that it would make every human in the realm an unsuspecting target. The latter plan might be impossible for only three people to accomplish."

Syndral replied, "There might be a third option. We could just hunt down the hundespor."

"Yeah…I can see it now," said Leif sarcastically. "We'll head off into the countryside like the old French trappers. We'll just put out some snares and wait for the oblivious hundespor to wander into the area."

"Well," said Syndral, "your thoughts are closer to what I have in mind than you think."

Joral and Leif both looked at Syndral expectantly. It took a moment, but Joral caught on to her plan first.

"You want us to bait them?" asked Joral incredulously. "You're going to put innocent lives at risk?"

"We'll be there to protect them. All we need to do is locate a Pakk descendant the assassins have not targeted and wait for the hundespor to find that person," said Syndral.

"That could take days, or even months!" Leif said. "How could we even begin to know where the hundespor are hunting? Even if we had a suitable location, how would we know they are going to target our bait?"

"Of course you are not disturbed by a plan that uses people as bait. You are concerned about the timeline." Joral shook his head disgustedly. "Locating a Pakk descendant is not a problem for us. We have a camp full of them, training to defend each other. If we were a little less secretive about them, the hundespor and the assassins would come straight to us."

"How do you keep a camp full of people so quiet?" asked Syndral.

Joral took in a breath to answer, but stopped. He cocked his head and listened. Though his Fae hearing was lessened by his presence in the human realm, he should still be able to hear the soldiers. Right now, Joral was hearing silence. There was no sound of birds, voices, or sword strikes. The lack of noise sounded very wrong.

"We may have a problem," said Joral.

He turned and headed back into the house. Leif heard the back door open, and then slam shut before he realized what the problem was. When Syndral had appeared before him earlier, Leif felt confident that her presence was the reason for the silence in the forest. The sounds of the forest had not returned. Engrossed in conversation, Leif had not noticed. He sprang from his seat on the steps and sprinted after Joral.

Leif ran out of the back door and immediately teleported to the center of the camp. His eyes beheld the devastating scene before him. There were no bodies. There was sinew and bone. Everything was covered in blood, but there were no corpses to remind Leif of the men who recently slept, ate and trained in this camp.

Joral came into the small clearing and dropped to his knees. He did not speak. He met Leif's eyes and Leif's heart clenched for the male before him. Joral worked closely with the people of this camp. He was their trainer, savior, and friend. Joral knew every member of the camp by name and knew of their families. Those people were now memories.

Syndral entered the camp and started picking through the remains. She lifted a sword and rolled her eyes at the severed hand attached to the hilt. Joral watched Syndral with distaste. Joral climbed to his feet and purposefully made his way through the destruction to stand before Syndral.

"Have you no heart? These were people. They had families. Some of them were children. These are the humans you claim to be here to help save and you toss them aside as if they are grime from your boots."

"At this point, that is exactly what they are," Syndral sneered as she scraped one of her boots on a rock to remove the gore stuck in the treads.

Joral was dumbstruck. He had no words for the cruelty Syndral used to meet his accusation. He looked to Leif for support, but the male was also picking through the remnants of the camp. Leif took more care to show a modicum of respect as he did so, but it still made Joral's stomach turn.

"What I want to know," said Leif as he approached Syndral and Joral, "is why we didn't hear anything. I sit on the steps and listen to the men spar throughout the day. An attack such as this would have caused screaming that should have been heard for miles. The three of us were just chatting away while this happened. I admit, the conversation was engaging, but not so much that this attack should have gone unheard."

"I'm not sure," admitted Syndral. "Not much is known of hundespor attacks. No one has ever witnessed one."

"When did we decide this was the work of the hundespor?" asked Leif.

Syndral held up the sword she still had in her hand. She held the blade to keep the blood from the wrist of the mangled hand from touching her clothes. Leif looked closely at the hand. It had been torn from its owner's arm with force, not severed cleanly by a blade. Marring the skin of the hand were bite marks; deep punctures from canine teeth, as well as smaller tears. The animal that had gripped this hand was large. The punctures were several inches from each other and the force of the bite had crushed the bones of the hand enough to deform it.

Nearly an hour later, Syndral pulled up in front of the girl's home. She had not stayed to help Joral and Leif clean up the remains of the camp. As soon as she had made the connection between the wounds on that hand and the creatures Skalanis had with him at all times, Syndral had come to check on the girl.

If the hundespor had found the camp of descendants tucked away upstate, there was no question the girl was in danger. Syndral had to assume it was bling luck that had shielded the girl from being scented before now, and Syndral was completely at a loss for what to do.

Leif was not the most pleasant person she had ever met, but Syndral was starting to think he might understand the girl's predicament. He spoke as if he were blind to the needs of others, but Syndral had seen the cracks in his armor. The male behaved as if he hated all those around him and was only doing his best to tolerate their existence in his world. Truthfully, Syndral suspected the only person Leif hated was himself.

Syndral turned the key in the ignition as the girl exited the home. This would be the first time Syndral followed the girl. On other mornings, Syndral had left the street outside the girl's home early, likely before the girl had even risen from bed, and parked outside of the middle school. Once the girl arrived safely, Syndral would go about her day. Today, Syndral's concern for the girl was great enough that the girl would need to remain in Syndral sight the entire time.

The first beast made an appearance two blocks from the building where the girl attended her classes. It prowled across a lawn, angling to head the girl off before she reached the school. Syndral was about to pull the truck over and attack the beast when she noticed a second and third hundespor flanking the girl from the left. There was no way Syndral could take them all on at once.

Syndral pressed the accelerator and pulled up parallel to the girl. The hundespor froze upon Syndral's arrival. Syndral rolled down the window of the truck and offered the girl a ride to school.

"No thank you," the girl said simply.

"It's no trouble," replied Syndral. "I'm headed there anyway."

The little girl had suspicion in her eyes and Syndral was happy to see it. If the girl had just hopped into the truck with her, she would have had to have a discussion with the girl's parents.

"It's just up there. I don't need a ride. Besides, I can cut across the grass and you have to pull into the parking lot. It's actually a lot faster if I walk. Bye!"

The little girl left the sidewalk and cut her way across the lawn of the school toward the front entrance. Syndral drove the truck at a crawl while watching the girl until she reached the building. She no longer cared if someone thought she looked suspicious. Syndral would need to return later to make sure the girl got home from school safely.

CHAPTER 12

Jess, Gunnar, Krish and Kindra stood at the entrance to the Smalgroth portal. Krish took Kindra's hand and squeezed gently. Kindra appreciated the act of solidarity, knowing she would meet her future in-laws in moments. On the other side of this portal, was her future. Krish would one day inherit the Kingdom of Lillerem and Kindra would rule beside him as his queen.

As she and Krish stepped into the portal, Kindra contemplated her life before Alfheim. She did not think she would miss her students and their petty problems. With an entire kingdom to guide and look after, Kindra felt sure that part of her soul would be content. There was no way to compare the love she had for Tom with her feelings for Krish. She and Tom were young and thought they knew all there was to know about love when they were married. Tom was the only man Kindra had ever wanted, but she could now see that her view of the future was tainted by her lack of life experience. There had been nothing wrong with her husband, but there was so much more for Kindra than a life of taking care of a home and children. Tom had been the personification of a normal life. Krish represented every adventure Kindra could summon from her imagination.

It was not lost on Kindra that she was not comparing two people, but the two lives those people represented. The respective mates in those lives could easily be replaced by others. Kindra tightened her grip on Krish's hand as a sour feeling crept through her thoughts. She struggled to find her love for Krish in her heart. Kindra enjoyed his company, but she did not feel a sense that life would not go on without him. She was attracted to him physically, but there was not a female in any realm who would not be attracted to an elf with his looks.

As the group neared the end of the tunnel, Kindra pushed her feelings to the back of her mind and brought forward thoughts of her purpose here in Lillerem City. She would meet the king and the rest of Krish's family. She would visit the palace archives and research the history of each Dredfall assassin. Kindra would find a strategy for removing the threat Ulford posed to the human realm. She stepped out of the dark tunnel, still holding Krish's hand, and into a garden of stone and greenery.

Kindra stopped short as she took in the beauty of her surroundings, causing Jess to stumble into Krish's back.

"Sorry," Jess said.

"Think nothing of it," Krish replied.

Kindra released Krish's hand and turned to draw Jess up beside her. The four of them stood in a line, in front of the portal's exit. Butch was entrenched between Kindra and Jess, and Cassidy sat to Jess's right with Gunnar beside him. Krish maintained his place on the far left of the line. Bright surroundings froze Jess and Kindra in place as they looked upon the sights of the garden. To them, it looked as if there were glitter on the stones and foliage. Gunnar and Krish, having seen the sight many times, watched the females instead. It was entertaining to see the look on the faces of first-time visitors to Lillerem City.

Butch and Cassidy sniffed the air. Jess knew the dogs were not impressed with the sights of the allotment, but they were captivated by the smells of honeysuckle and lilac. To them, the place they were entering smelled of peace and happiness. The canines sensed no threats and felt completely relaxed. Jess gave the dogs a silent command to be free and explore, and the dogs happily loped forward to discover the scents of the area.

A bird, similar to a peacock, strutted from right to left before the group. As Jess followed the bird's trajectory beyond Krish, she saw several figures entering the garden through an archway. The arch was constructed from green vines and sparkling white flowers. Jess knew there was likely a frame under the vines to shape the arch, but the foliage was so dense that none was visible. The welcome party strode down a path of glittering white stone, flanked by evergreen shrubs, speckled with small purple flowers.

The party stopped in front of Krish. A tall male, dressed completely in black except for his cloak, stepped forward. The cloak was a deep purple and trimmed with gold thread. As Krish stepped forward to embrace the male, Jess saw the similar light green eyes. Though the tall male in the cloak had wrinkles rimming his eyes, the parallels between him and the Crown Prince were glaring. There was no doubt this man was Krish's father.

King Erik had long white hair, pulled back from his face and tied with a leather cord. The hair on the back of Erik's head remained unbound and flowed straight down his back, some falling to the front of his shoulders. Jess attempted to stifle a smile as she noticed how similar this male looked to a Jedi from one of the earlier Star Wars movies. She reined in her thoughts as she realized Kindra stood rigid beside her.

Jess subtly touched her friend's hand to reassure her as King Erik stepped in front of Kindra. Kindra did not know what to say. The male scrutinized her, looking her over from her toes, up her body and back to her face. His light eyes bore into hers as if he were examining her thoughts as well. Finally, he smiled warmly and Kindra felt as if her legs were about to give out in relief. Erik pulled her into an embrace that kept her weak legs from dragging Kindra to the ground, and then Erik held her at arm's length.

"Daughter!" he bellowed in a powerful voice. "Krish has not exaggerated your beauty, or your strength. Forgive my close examination, but I felt for sure he must have overlooked some flaw. On the contrary, I find that his analysis was spot-on! You are perfect!"

Kindra blushed and let out the breath she had been holding. She was relieved to have the male's approval, but embarrassed by his blatant scrutiny of her physical features. She wished she had been privy to those conversations in which Krish had described her to his father. Had the descriptions been entirely physical?

Erik embraced Kindra again, and this time she reciprocated the gesture stiffly. The King placed a kiss on each of her cheeks, and it surprised Kindra how soft the stubble of his white beard felt on her face. Krish kept his face smooth, but Tom's stubble had always been coarse and irritated her skin. Erik's facial hair was a little longer than

Tom had ever grown his. Was it possible that growing it longer would have saved Kindra from discomfort? Would she and Tom have enjoyed more time with their faces pressed close if he had grown a proper beard instead of keeping his face in a constant state of rugged scruff?

Kindra snapped back to the present when she felt the tug of Erik pulling away. He had needed to use some force to detach from Kindra, as she had been deep in her own thoughts. Kindra flushed with embarrassment. First, she had undergone the ruler's scrutiny of her physique, and now she had subjected him to one of her mental vacations. Though Kindra's friends were accustomed to her lack of presence from time to time, the King must think she was an imbecile.

To Kindra's surprise, Erik laughed. "I see my son did not exaggerate your propensity for deep thought at inopportune moments, either. Have no fear. It is comforting to know my son has chosen a female of thought and not one who is simple-minded."

Kindra relaxed slightly. She smiled at the King in thanks, but conflict swirled within her. She knew his words were meant to be a comfort to her, but it felt like he was being condescending. Kindra had not realized how badly she wanted to impress her future father-in-law until she stood here, failing miserably at amazing him.

Jess released a short, piercing whistle, and Erik's attention pulled from Kindra. Jess had seen her friend squirming and felt the need to bring Kindra some relief. Butch and Cassidy bounded from somewhere out in the garden and took their places at Jess's sides. To Jess's horror, Butch had one of the peacock-like birds in his mouth. Its long legs were moving as if it was trying to run side-ways in the air.

The king pretended not to notice as he came to stand before Jess and the dogs. Butch dropped the bird before Erik. The bird flopped around to gain its feet and then strode off, unharmed and full of indignation.

"Thank you for the gift, my friend," Erik said as he reached down to scratch Butch's head. "Which one of the ferocious canine duo might you be?"

"The bird snatcher is Butch, and this is Cassidy," Jess replied with her hand on Cassidy's head.

Erik leaned to his left to give Cassidy a scratch. "You must be Jess. I've heard much about you as well. You have a rare gift that has not manifested in a long time among our people."

"Yes. That is me. Gifted, and completely ashamed that my dog just tried to eat your bird."

"The prymmer is fine. No part of him was injured but his pride. He'll go strut around for the females and forget he was ever taken captive. I'm rather impressed with Butch's soft mouth. I hope the prymmer appreciates Butch fancying himself a retriever instead of a guard dog."

Jess smiled at the king, deciding to let him believe Butch was a gentle giant. Jess gave a mental warning to both dogs to refrain from maiming any of the garden wildlife. Verbally, she gave the 'down' command and both dogs put their bellies to the ground immediately. Confident the dogs remembered who was giving the orders, Jess held out her hand to greet the king. Ignoring her hand, Erik grabbed Jess by the shoulders and pulled her to him to place a kiss on each of her cheeks.

Erik moved on to clap Gunnar on the shoulder. "Cousin! It is always nice to welcome you to the palace. You shouldn't stay away so long."

"Thank you, cousin," said Gunnar. "I shall keep that in mind."

"Come," Erik addressed his visitors. "We shall have lunch brought out here to the garden."

Krish placed a hand on his father's shoulder as Erik turned to speak to his attendant.

"That won't be necessary, father. We enjoyed a delightful spread in Smalgroth before entering the portal. Since our time is short, we would like to go directly to the archives. We can join you for the evening meal in the dining room later."

Erik looked disappointed, but said, "Of course! You have important work to do. Don't let an old male keep you. I shall expect you at seven bells."

Krish nodded his thanks to his father, and Erik turned to walk back to the archway. His attendant walked beside him and the rest of the men took up positions in front and behind. Kindra now saw the entourage to be made up of an attendant and six guards.

Kindra leaned close to Krish and whispered, "How many men does he take with him when he actually leaves the palace grounds?"

"Oh!" said Krish, "he doesn't leave the grounds."

Kindra spoke the question in jest, but now she scrunched up her face in disbelief. There was no way anyone could remain home at all times. There was even a name for it, agoraphobia. People needed to get out. Then again, being confined to a palace was a little different from being stuck in some raised ranch in the suburbs. Kindra doubted the king wanted for anything while ensconced on the palace grounds.

Krish took Kindra's hand once again. He turned to her with concern on his face. It disturbed Kindra how similar his light green eyes were to his father's. Did the similarities between father and son go deeper than the obvious physical features? Did Krish view her as an equal, or was he more concerned with her looks and the perception the people of Lillerem had of her as a savior? Kindra had always felt that Krish valued her insight, but she was beginning to fear she might only have felt that way because it was what she had wanted to believe.

"Are you ok?" Krish asked.

"Yeah," replied Kindra. "Your father does have a way of making a person feel uncomfortable."

"Indeed, he does," said Krish. "There are many reasons I spend little time here at the palace, and you have now met one of them. My father is not a bad man, but he was raised to believe he is of a much higher station than he is. He is of the belief that there is no power greater than his, and when he speaks, he conveys those feelings unconsciously. It was not a pleasant way to grow up. I never felt as if I were enough."

"He is the king," said Kindra simply. "He commands more power than any other elf in the land. I suppose his feelings are justified."

"That is untrue," Gunnar broke into the conversation. "The king belongs to the people. The intention was never for him to be above them. Lars, Erik's father, was a terrible king. He witnessed the way the people lauded his grandfather, Andril, and even his father, Blaith, but he did nothing to command the same respect. Blaith maintained the respect of the people and came close to meeting the expectation that he would be as great as Andril. Blaith was an excellent king. He was fair, and the people liked him. Lars was of the belief that the people should simply worship their king without question. He never understood that Andril was the only king deserving of that treatment. Andril was the king that united Lillerem and was the last great king."

"Besides," continued Krish, "my father is king in name only. His adoption by Lars means he carries no royal blood. The people know this, but my father often forgets. You, Jess and Gunnar each have more royal blood in your veins than my father. Don't let his imperial demeanor bring you down."

Again, Kindra found words that were meant to comfort, unsettling. Krish was trying to convey that Erik was no better than she was and that she should keep her head up. The meaning behind his words went deeper, though. In reminding them that Erik held no royal blood, he had also reminded Kindra that Krish was not a royal by blood either. Only his marriage to her would legitimize his absolute claim to the throne of Lillerem. Kindra added that thought to the ruminations she was burying lately.

Hiding her inner conflict, Kindra nodded to Krish in affirmation and held out her arm in a gesture for him to lead the way to the archives. Krish smiled and turned in the direction his father had gone moments ago. He led the group through the archway and down a short walkway to a door set in a stone wall. The stained wood of the door looked dark against the sparkling stone wall. Krish reached for the iron handle and pulled the door open. Kindra was expecting an ominous creak, but there was no sound as the door opened on its hinges and allowed the group to enter the castle.

Jess was having trouble concentrating. Earlier, Jess was aware of her friend's discomfort, but she concluded it was a product of Kindra meeting her future father-in-law, and decided not to worry about it. That was the last moment Jess was in touch with the feelings of any of the others in the group. Currently, Jess was buzzing with anticipation. She had been away from the school where she taught math for too many weeks. Her mind was starving for intellectual thought and the resources to take in more knowledge. Jess thrived on facts and figures, and the prospect of having a royal library, in another realm, to comb through was making her skin tingle.

Jess barely noticed the statues, carved from the same rock as the garden path and the palace walls, as she followed Krish. She was no longer taking in the scent and sounds of the palace through the minds of Butch and Cassidy. Jess wondered if there would be a math section, like in the libraries of the human realm. Maybe there was a way she could convince the others that they should spend more time here in Lillerem City. Jess feared she might not be returning any time soon to explore the knowledge contained within these walls.

The group drew up to a large double door, and Krish knocked gently on the wood. Jess shifted her weight impatiently from one foot to the other. She looked down at the dogs, as if she had just remembered they were traveling with her. Krish caught her glance and sadly shook his head. Jess glanced around the area and saw nothing but cold stone floors.

"Let them roam freely," said Krish to Jess. "To his credit, my father is a dog person. Butch and Cassidy can enjoy the run of the palace, but Letha will not permit them entry to the archives."

"Letha?" asked Jess.

"Letha is the archivist. I'm not sure she actually leaves the royal library. She is ancient, even by Elven standards, and has traveled the world as a healer and historian. I have been told she decided she had seen enough pain, and about seventy years ago, she locked herself in the library and made it her mission to tend to books instead of people. Be kind to her. She has a wealth of knowledge, but also a few quirks. I find it best to let her do her thing."

Jess silently dismissed the dogs, sending them to explore the palace. Though apprehensive of the quirks Letha might possess, Jess wanted to speak to this female. The prospect of an intellectual conversation had her reaching for the door. Krish stopped her with a stern look.

"Remember those quirks?" he asked Jess. "One of them is that she treats the library as her private residence. Though it is open for all to use, and Letha would never deny anyone entry, she insists we knock and are officially welcomed into her home."

"It sure is taking a while to be welcomed," grumbled Kindra.

Krish smiled. "As I said, she is very old. Give her time. The library is expansive."

As Krish finished speaking, the sound of something being dragged could be heard through the door and a small, rectangular section of the wood slid open at eye-level. A pair of pale eyes stared through the opening. It seemed the eyes had once been blue, but the irises had faded with age until they were nearly white. It was safe to assume one reason Letha remained in the library was to avoid the sunlight.

"Krish! You look ravenous as always! So good to see you!"

Jess had not missed the way the old woman had swapped the word ravishing for the word ravenous, but that was not what held her curiosity. She was expecting Letha's voice to sound old. She would have been comfortable with a rasping voice, or one with a squeak to it. Instead, Jess found that there was no hint of age in Letha's voice as she greeted Krish with obvious excitement; and humor when you considered she had just hinted that Krish was starving instead of good looking. Letha's eyes disappeared and then the dragging sound came from the other side of the door again. The sound of several bolts being thrown came next, and then the door creaked open on its hinges.

A frail, stooped woman stood next to a wooden step stool. The room was so dark; there was nothing else to look at as the group stood in the doorway. Letha's white hair was pulled back into a braided bun at the base of her neck. There wasn't a single wisp of hair that was not slicked back to her head. The old female wore a robe of the same deep purple Erik had sported on his cape. Like Erik's cape, Letha's robe was gold-trimmed and elegant. The female looked up at Krish expectantly.

Krish motioned to Kindra to stand before Letha. "This is my betrothed, Kindra. Kindra, this is Letha, mistress of the palace library."

Kindra lowered her head in greeting and almost knocked her forehead on the top of Letha's head. The old woman was leaning in to get a better look at Kindra's face. Letha did not study Kindra's physical features the way Erik had. The ancient female was looking into Kindra's eyes as if she were analyzing Kindra's soul. It left Kindra feeling more uncomfortable than she had when she met the King in the garden.

At last, Letha released Kindra from her gaze and looked toward Krish for the next introduction. Kindra, feeling relieved, stepped forward into the dark room. As her eyes adjusted to the lack of light, she could see she stood at the center of a three-story hall lined with books. As Kindra pushed on, she saw giant rolling ladders and almost laughed out loud. She was getting that overwhelming feeling again of playing a part in a movie.

CHAPTER 13

Gunnar came up beside Kindra. "Krish is introducing Jess to Letha. It is comical. Jess may have been unimpressed when she met the king, but she is ecstatic over meeting an old archivist!"

Kindra turned back toward the entryway so she could witness Jess's reaction to Letha. Jess appeared to be shaking with excitement. She held both hands out and grasped Letha's extended arm. Jess offered something like a curtsy, combined with a bow, and then looked expectantly into the old female's eyes in anticipation.

"I am so happy to make your acquaintance, Letha. I've heard you have traveled all over and have many years of experience to share. It is such an honor to be in the presence of someone as wise as you."

Kindra rolled her eyes. It was plain to her, as usual; knowledge would trump everything for her friend. She stepped closer to rescue Jess from the embarrassing drivel spewing from her mouth, but stopped short when she heard Letha's reply.

"It is nice to meet you, Jess. Simply meeting you has me seeing you are quite culpable yourself. I'm sure you don't need the useless information stored in this old female's mind."

Kindra cocked her head. Had Letha said capable, or culpable? The joke with Krish at the door was cute, but Kindra did not find this one to be as funny. It had the effect of making a woman known for her wealth of knowledge sound ignorant. Letha motioned them all to follow her down the hall. After passing countless shelved books, Letha swept her arm to the right to show they should all enter a small room.

The room contained a wooden table with six chairs. On the table, three lanterns were lit to provide light. The lanterns reminded Jess of the old hurricane lantern her mother had kept as a decoration on a shelf in the kitchen. Jess's mother had never filled the lantern with oil, and Jess could not even remember if the hunk of decorative metal contained a wick. She wished she had made at least an attempt to use the antique when she saw how the three lanterns on the table provided the perfect light for reading.

"Now," began Letha. "Tell me exactly what you are researching. As I mentioned to Jess, I am sure you are culpable of finding your own information, but to save time, it may be more prudent for me to bring you tomes on the subjects you wish to research. Unlike libraries in the human realm, we do not use the Dewey Decibel System. The map for this library is in here."

Letha tapped her forehead as she spoke the last sentence. Kindra saw the concerned look on her friend's face and threw her own look in Krish's direction. This time, Kindra had distinctly heard the woman use the word decibel instead of decimal, advertising that she did not even know the correct name for the most famous library cataloging system ever created. Kindra, who had never been a top student, was feeling more intelligent than this ancient elf.

Kindra provided Letha with direction. "We need anything you have on Ulford's Elite Guard members. If you have family history or any stories about the group or the individuals, we'll take it. Also, we need to know anything we can about the hundespor and their arrival and time here in Alfheim."

"Give me a moment," Letha said as she turned from the room and disappeared.

"Ok Krish, what is the deal?" Kindra asked as soon as Letha was gone.

"I see you noticed one of Letha's other quirks. I promise you, she is not senseless. Letha is fluent in hundreds of languages. A working knowledge of any new language is all she ever feels the need to learn, after having mastered so many others. Once Letha felt she knew enough of the English language to communicate, she just stopped learning. Admittedly, it is unsettling the way she has simply decided certain words have certain meanings, but unless you are truly having difficulty understanding her, I recommend letting her believe her speech is flawless."

Jess looked relieved. That look showed Kindra she was not the only one who had questioned the intelligence of the ancient female. Undoubtedly, Jess was concerned that any information taken from the archivist might not be reliable. Kindra had concerns about that as well, but she was also worried about her future husband's ability to make rational decisions about whom he placed his faith in.

Gunnar said, "I feel like we are wasting time here. All four of us are sitting around a table in a dark library waiting for a crazy lady to bring us information. It would be a lot faster if we all looked through the archives. We need to get this done fast and get back to the human realm."

Gunnar never got a reply. Letha shuffled into the room with stacks of books in her arms. Several rolled manuscripts were dangerously close to spilling off the top of the pile. She bent awkwardly at the knees to place the stack on the table and quickly threw her hands to the sides of the pile to keep it from toppling. The rolled parchments fell to the table's surface. Gunnar carefully unfurled the document that came to rest before him. He spread a family tree out before him.

At the top of the parchment was Andril, King of Lillerem. The center portion of the tree was familiar. King Blaith's descendants right down to where Gunnar was gazing upon his own name. Leif's name appeared as well, but Jess and Kindra were not recorded in this tree. It was not a surprise to see the females' names absent, considering they were born in another realm. It was also unsurprising that King Lars was depicted as childless. He and his mate had adopted King Erik, and Erik was therefore not part of Andril's bloodline. The surprise was in the other two branches of the tree.

Every lesson on Elven lore Gunnar had heard told of Blaith as an only child. It was long believed that Blaith had never been the best choice to rule the kingdom after Andril, but that he had been the only choice. Looking at the tree before him, Gunnar supposed Blaith had been the only choice; just not for the reason the stories always offered. King Blaith had two sisters. This was the first time Gunnar had ever heard of them. It was common practice for Alfheim to only take a male ruler. This was the reason Gunnar's own mother was never considered for the throne, though she would have been a far better choice than Lars had ever been. It was still shocking to Gunnar that the female heirs had not only been overlooked when Blaith was chosen to rule, but they had been completely written out of history.

Gunnar traced the branches of Aldith, eldest child of King Andril. She had birthed four children of her own; all of them female. He followed the line through the generations. Toward the bottom of the parchment, his heart started racing. He spun the parchment around for the others to see and slammed his finger on top the names of two sisters at the bottom.

Kindra's head had snapped up from the book she had just opened when Gunnar gasped and spun the large parchment around. He had jabbed his finger at a place near the bottom right of the document. Everyone at the table leaned in to see what had caused Gunnar to be upset. Kindra drew in a sharp breath when she saw the names. She followed the branches up to the top of the tree and took note that these females were descendants of King Andril himself. Her heart sank as she realized she was being played for a fool. The names Gunnar had found, at the bottom of this long-lost line of King Andril, were Imra and her twin sister Syndral.

Kindra, too shocked to speak, allowed Jess to pull the parchment from her. She had been rash. She had believed Syndral to be an ally. Why would the female have shared so many secrets if she were loyal to Ulford? Worse than that, her twin was one of the Dredfall assassins Syndral had informed on. It didn't make any sense.

Jess, on the other hand, was not surprised at the revelation of Syndral being twin to one of Ulford's inner circle. Well, maybe the twin sister part was startling, but she was not shocked to discover Syndral had not been exactly who she claimed to be. As she perused the rest of the document, Jess noted that the other assassins descended from Blaith's younger sister, Hedda. She found Skalanis, Ruith, Morthil and Vander along the various branches of that side of the tree. Jess tapped her finger on a name at the bottom left of the parchment.

"What do you see?" asked Krish.

Jess turned the parchment toward Krish and said, "Other than the assassins we have identified, all other descendants of Aldith and Hedda are marked with death dates; all of them except Jacan. It is possible that he died and it was never recorded, or that he is simply not part of Ulford's goon squad, but I don't think either is the case. I'm afraid we have a previously unknown assassin."

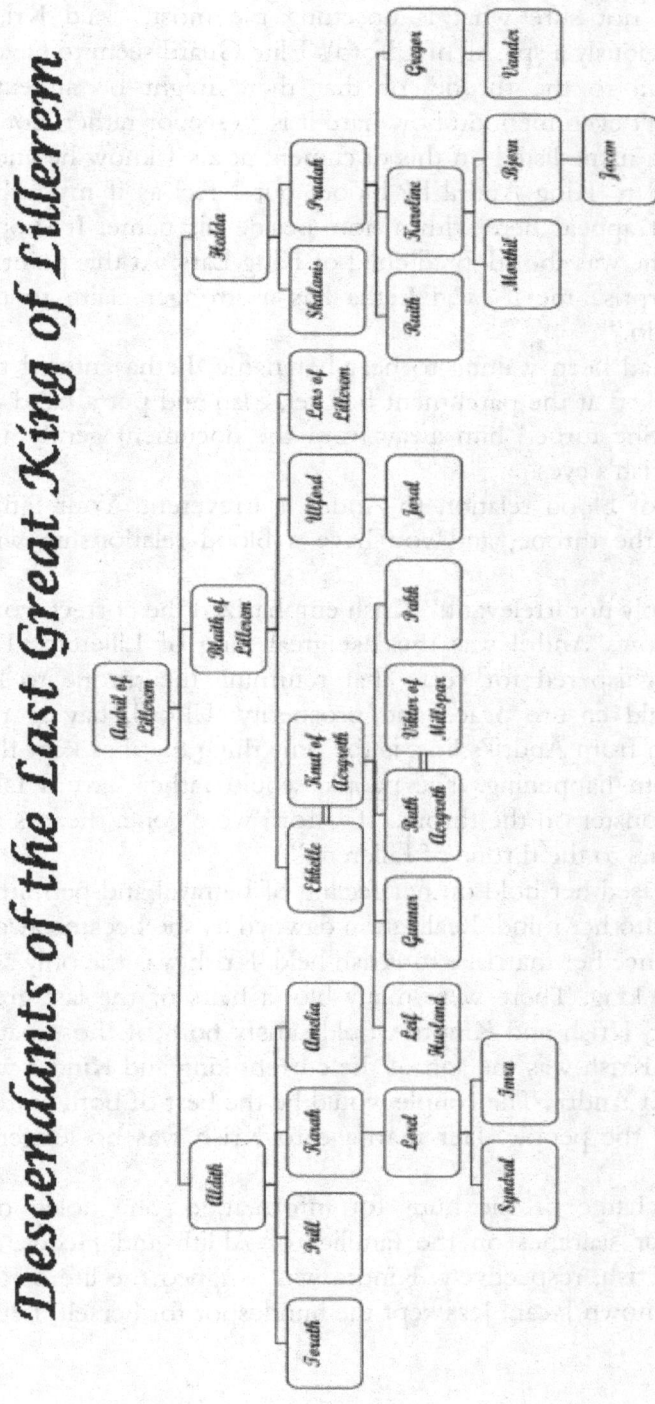

Descendants of the Last Great King of Lillerem

"I'm really not sure what is upsetting me most," said Krish. "Syndral is obviously a spy, all of Ulford's Elite Guard seem to have a legitimate claim to the throne, or that there might be an extra assassin. I won't even mention how hard it is to see; or rather, not to see my father's name listed on this document at all. I know he and I are not related to King Andril by blood, but I feel as if my father should at least appear here with a note beside his name. It should delineate that he was the adopted child of King Lars. At this point, it would not surprise me if even Letha has a stronger claim to the throne than I do."

As if she had been waiting to hear her name, Letha entered the room. She looked at the parchment before Krish and put a hand on his shoulder. She turned him away from the document gently and looked into Krish's eyes.

"The lack of blood relation to Andril is irreverent. Your father currently has the throne, and you have a blood relationship with him."

"It is certainly not irrelevant!" Krish emphasized the correct word. "Everyone knows Andril was the last great king of Lillerem. The people have whispered for years that returning the throne to his bloodline would ensure peace and prosperity. Ulford, having the strongest claim from Andril's line, is the only thing that has kept that very thing from happening. The people would rather have a false king than a monster on the throne. If Ulford were gone, there is no shortage of heirs to the throne of Lillerem."

Kindra released her hold on her feeling of betrayal and permitted fear to creep into her mind. Realization dawned as she became aware of the importance her marriage to Krish held. Krish was the only son of the current king. There were many blood heirs of the last great king. Together, Krish and Kindra would satisfy both of those paths to the throne. Krish was the son of the current king and Kindra was a descendant of Andril. The couple would be the best of both worlds in the eyes of the people. Her marriage to Krish was no longer a choice.

Jess took charge of the hunt for information. She doled out assignments for searches on the families of Aldith and Hedda, to Gunnar and Krish, respectively. Kindra was assigned the life of the previously unknown Jacan. Jess kept the hundespor for herself. Letha was sent back to the bookshelves to see if there were any records specific to Blaith's sisters. The group began to work in silence.

Jess was in the middle of a chapter from a book called 'Creatures of the Elvenwood', a book that read more like a collection of fairy tales than a work of nonfiction, when Letha returned to the room. Having found little useful information, the group looked up from their work hopefully. Letha placed a thin, softcover manuscript on the table. The title, 'Females of Alfheim,' was hand-written in beautiful script on the cover. Kindra carefully pulled back the cover to reveal a title page written in the same hand. A name she recognized was scrawled under the title.

"Gunnar, you're not going to believe this," started Kindra. "It says the author of this book is Ekkelle, princess of Lillerem. Your mother must have written this while she was living here at the palace and then added it to the library."

Gunnar took the hand-bound book from Kindra. He stared down at the cover without speaking. Kindra was certain she saw tears in the male's eyes. He ran his fingers over the paper lightly. Gunnar stood and walked slowly away from the table, never taking his eyes from the book. The big male, put his back to the wall and bent his knees to slide slowly to the floor. He sat there, resting the book on his bent knees, slowly flipping through the pages.

Jess was working very hard to contain her impatience. Her heart understood that this was a special moment for Gunnar, but logic was screaming for her to go and pluck the book from Gunnar's hands. The book's author captivated Gunnar, and even Kindra, but Jess fixated on the book's title. That title suggested the exact information they wanted was within the pages. The females of Alfheim were primarily inconsequential. They had not been written out of history; they had simply never existed. Ekkelle, the rebellious teenage elf, may have been the only person to record the history of the female royals in Alfheim. Jess hoped Princess Ekkelle had put the same effort into the contents of her writing that she had used for the carefully drawn script on the cover. Jess had almost no interest in Kindra's love of genealogy, but she found herself hoping that Kindra's dedication to the hobby had come from her grandma Ekkelle.

Come on, you big goon. It's a book. Your mom wrote it. I get it. Now give it up so we can get our information in time to have our meal with the King. Jess was trying not to hop from foot to foot like one of her students waiting for the bell to ring at the end of period nine. She watched as Gunnar put the book down beside him, at last. Jess counted to ten slowly, and then swept in to snatch the book from the stone floor, bringing it back to the table.

"Are you kidding me?" Jess's voice was far too loud for the library setting. "What language is this? It makes no sense at all. I recognize all the letters, but they're joined in ways I can't even pronounce, let alone understand."

Krish chuckled. "From the description you are giving, I'm going to guess it's written in the old language. Many of the languages used in your realm were born from it. You might have some luck if you think of it as a cross between Norwegian and Irish with some dashes of German."

"Irish? Seriously?" moaned Jess. "Almost no one knows that language anymore, and you're telling me this one is older? How are we ever going to get it translated?"

Krish was slowly shaking his head. "In Alfheim, we do not simply throw things away because they are old. Almost everyone can speak some of the old language. Those of us raised as part of the Court speak it well, in fact."

"That's lovely," said Jess sarcastically. "I'll be sure to remember that when I need someone to speak to Ekkelle after we raise her from the dead."

"Lucky for you," said Krish, "I am a prince. It was a requirement of my education to learn to read and write in several languages. Those languages include English, Norwegian, German, Irish, French..."

Krish let his voice trail off. Jess stared at him, waiting. She displayed no amusement. Krish was drawing this out just to get a rise from her. Krish read the impatience on her face, at last, and dropped the hand on which he had been counting off the languages in which he was proficient.

"I can translate the book for you," said Krish.

Kindra clapped Krish on the shoulder and spoke, "It's ok, Krish. You're not the first one to cease his shenanigans when Jess uses her teacher-face. Your pride will only hurt for a short time. Now, you better pull your chair close to Jess and read that entire thing to her as fast as you can."

Krish sat down next to Jess and shuffled his chair a little closer to her. He opened to the first page and began reading the text. It didn't translate word for word, so Krish read some of the writing, then translated it out loud, in English. He had only done this twice when Gunnar stood.

"We should get going. That book is my mother's and was never part of the Royal Archives, anyway. We'll simply take it with us. Now, let's go thank the king for his hospitality."

Jess pulled the book in closer. She didn't want Gunnar snatching it and striding out the door. She frantically searched for a reason not to leave. *But Gunnar, your mother wanted this book here in the archive. I don't know Gunnar; maybe we shouldn't be stealing books.* Gunnar was through the doorway before Jess could decide on the best argument. She had not even had time to discuss topics in science and mathematics with Letha. She still didn't know if there was a math section in this library. There could be a forgotten mathematical revelation on a shelf just outside of the room. Jess pushed Ekkelle's book into Krish's hands.

"Learn to read while walking. You can summarize what you read as we travel. I'm going to locate my dogs," said Jess as she pushed past Gunnar.

Jess pushed through the giant door and into the stone hallway. Seconds later, Kindra came through the door after her.

"What was that about?" Kindra asked.

"What was what about? I didn't say anything."

Kindra raised an eyebrow and said, "You didn't need to say anything. I know you held back. I could see the look on your face. What is your issue with taking the book and heading back home?"

"Well," Jess said, "for starters, I thought we'd spend at least one night in the palace. This might be my only chance. I was really looking forward to seeing what a palace wardrobe would choose for me to wear to dinner."

Kindra allowed herself a smile. The best part about Alfheim was never needing to pick out clothing. She often griped about the inability to drag one of Alfheim's magic wardrobes back into the human realm. Still, Kindra was not about to let Jess redirect the conversation.

"Jess, you actually looked panicked at the thought of leaving. This is not about missing out on the indulgences of palace life."

Jess took in a breath. "There is so much information in that archive. I didn't even have time to find any information on the hundespor, let alone investigate mathematical discoveries or pick Letha's brain. I feel like I am missing out on an opportunity."

"You knew this archive existed. You never even asked to visit while you were here previously. When you were recently stuck in this realm, you were dying to get home. You spent all of your time trying to increase your magic so you could return. Why aren't you excited about getting back now?"

Jess sighed. "I wasn't dying to get home; I was dying to get back to you. I was dying to get back to Butch and Cassidy. This time, I have you all here with me."

Kindra squinted her eyes at Jess as she said, "I notice there is one important person you failed to mention while listing the people you wanted to return to."

Jess said nothing. She stared back at Kindra and willed her to intuitively recognize her conflict. Jess did not want to have this conversation. She desperately wanted to feel the sisterhood that came with a shared understanding, but she wanted to skip the part where she had to explain her feelings. Krish exited the archive and caught the attention of Jess and Kindra. The conversation was put on hold. Jess was not sure if she was relieved or disappointed. Though not excited about doing it, she needed to talk to Kindra about Sean.

CHAPTER 14

Krish did not seem to notice the women were engrossed in an intense conversation. He started speaking before he was within five feet of Kindra and Jess. His voice echoed off of the stone walls and floor.

"I know Gunnar is suddenly desperate to get back to the human realm, but I don't think we can depart immediately. My father expects us at seven bells. We skirted lunch in the garden, but I do not see us avoiding the formal meal."

Kindra cocked her head toward Jess. "I'm sure someone is happy to hear that. Jess was crushed by the thought she might miss the experience of a magical wardrobe choosing her dinner attire on this trip to Alfheim."

Krish seemed slightly perplexed by Kindra's decision to meet his trepidations with levity. Jess understood her friend's motivation. Kindra was breaking the tension created by the conversation Krish had interrupted. It was a signal to Jess that Kindra was going to let that topic drop for now. Kindra might not completely understand Jess's current predicament, but she was attuned to Jess's reservations about discussing it.

Krish ignored Kindra's dismissal of his own concern and continued. "I will have the servants show you to your quarters and you can bathe and prepare for dinner."

Kindra was about to protest that there was no need. There was no way Gunnar was going to allow the party to spend the night, so sleeping chambers were unnecessary. She opened her mouth to alert Krish to this fact, but he turned to her knowingly.

"Relax darling. I am no fool. I am well aware that there is no option to spend the night. You, on the other hand, seem to have missed the impropriety that would be caused by changing into dinner attire in the middle of the palace grounds," said Krish as he chuckled.

There it was again. Since beginning to analyze her own relationship with Sean, she had been more attuned to relationships between other couples. *Was Krish really making a joke about running around the palace naked, or was he demeaning Kindra by pointing out that she had not been smart enough to realize the reason rooms were needed?* Jess let the unpleasant feeling in her gut pass and smiled brightly.

"Oh, thank goodness," Jess practically gushed. "I can't wait to get out of these wretched clothes!" She added a giggle at the end for good measure.

Krish completely missed the message Jess was trying to send, but Kindra caught it. Jess had seen Kindra's eyes widen. A servant appeared and motioned for the women to follow. Kindra lowered her voice so there would be no way Krish could hear her, even with the way the stone walls amplified voices.

"Tell me you don't like being treated like a silly girl without telling me you don't like being treated like a silly girl," Kindra said.

Jess pulled her head back and stared at her friend. "It wasn't the assumption that we would be so interested in getting dolled-up that I didn't like from him. It was his assumption that you were too stupid to realize you would need to change behind closed doors."

"I'm not stupid!" Kindra whisper-yelled at her friend.

"I am well aware of that fact," replied Jess with concern in her eyes. "I'm just worried Krish might not feel that way."

Kindra rolled her eyes at Jess but did not reply. Jess suspected Kindra was as in need of a talk with Jess, as Jess was in need of a talk with Kindra. Both women had a lot to sort out regarding their chosen partners. *Are we finally at that age where we get to have a mid-life crisis? That can't be. Maybe Kindra is the type to have that sort of predicament, and it wouldn't even need to be at the middle point of her life, but I always know what I want.*

Jess was internally horrified as she followed Kindra and the servant through the twisting halls. She was, once again, missing the marvels of the palace. If someone engaged her in conversation at a later date about the fruit trees growing in large pots under the many skylights, Jess would only have a vague recollection of the sight. She was not noticing how the sunlight streamed through the glass in the ceiling, brightening the halls and warming them. There just was no way Jess could admit that she might be at a point in her life in which she was unsure of herself.

The servant opened the door to a room and tipped his head to indicate Jess should enter. Kindra moved to follow Jess, but the servant cleared his throat.

"This way, Princess. The King has provided you with your own quarters."

Jess nodded to Kindra. "I can't wait to drool over the outfit your furniture picks for you. See you shortly."

Kindra followed the servant down the hall. Jess watched as the servant opened a door on the opposite side of the hall and about twenty feet away. Kindra's eyes grew wide, and she rushed out of view. Jess closed her eyes and reached out to Butch and Cassidy. Through the dogs' eyes, she could see Erik on a plush settee somewhere in the castle.

Butch and Cassidy were lounging on the rug at the male's feet. King Erik was munching on something from a small bowl. He flipped a piece of it to Butch, and Jess could taste the flavor instantaneously. Dried meat smothered in molasses. Jess didn't mind the dogs getting the bits of meat, but she was not sure how she felt about them ingesting too much molasses. Jess called silently to the dogs and was satisfied when they stood from the carpet and walked out of the room. She had not missed the look, glimpsed through Cassidy's eyes, on Erik's face when the dogs suddenly abandoned him without cause. A small smile touched Jess's lips.

Entering her own room, Jess was overwhelmed by red and gold. She supposed it was...elegant. It did not mean the décor was pretty, though. *Didn't the decorator understand that it was impossible to match the multitudes of reds in the color palette?* The dark red carpet in the center of the room looked faded when contrasted with the similarly colored bed covering. The floor length drapes took on a pinkish hue against the carpet. She supposed the silly carpet was intended to tie the room together, but it was not working. To give the place a bit more elegance, all the red materials in the room were adorned in glimmering gold embroidery or edging. Jess was grateful she would not need to spend the night in here. The color choices were born from nightmares and would certainly cause Jess to have them.

Once Jess's senses adjusted to the redness of the room, she identified the piece of furniture she was longing to see. Proudly standing in the corner, was a giant wardrobe. There was a chance Krish had been correct in his assumption that a change of clothes would be enough to make a woman happy. Jess delayed running to the ornate wooden closet, stripping off her boots and clothing instead. Placing her feet on the carpet, she thought she might be able to forgive its hideous coloring. It felt as if there were clouds under her feet. Jess wondered if she could manage to make her way around the room with her eyes closed just so she could enjoy the sensation of the rug without having to see it. Jess happily squished her toes into the fibers the entire way to the bathing chamber.

Water steamed in the soaking tub, and a basket of soaps and scents was waiting on a little stand. Jess climbed into the tub and breathed in the lavender scent wafting from the water. *Not that there is a competition, but the baths in Alfheim are right up there with the wardrobes.* Jess scrubbed the day's traveling dirt from her skin. The experience felt much more luxurious than the hasty shower she had taken when she stopped to see Sean. Her muscles relaxed almost immediately.

A loud scratch came from the door as Butch pawed his way in authoritatively. He sat at attention by the foot of the tub. Cassidy strolled in a moment later and curled up on the small towel on the floor beside the tub. The two Shepherds might look nearly identical, but there was no mistaking the difference in their personalities.

Cassidy rolled over onto his back and Jess draped her hand over the side of the tub to scratch his belly. Cassidy was entirely aware of how to enjoy the dog-life. A low growl came from Butch, and he stood. Jess rolled her eyes, initially thinking that Butch was scolding Cassidy for relaxing on the job. She opened her mind to Butch and was surprised to find the dog was actually on high alert. He smelled something he didn't like. Butch emanated enough concern that Cassidy rolled over, got to his feet and joined Butch at the door leading into the hall.

Jess sat up in the tub. She listened intently, using her own Fae hearing, as well as Butch and Cassidy's ears. Nothing. Jess smelled the air for danger through her dogs' senses. There was something different. Jess didn't know what it was, but it just seemed like something was off. Suddenly, the door pushed open, nearly throwing Butch and Cassidy across the small room.

A young servant girl stood wide-eyed in the doorway. "I am so sorry, miss! The door to your chamber was open. I thought you had dressed and left for the meal."

Jess saw the fresh towels in the girl's hands. It occurred to Jess that she had climbed into the tub before Butch and Cassidy had come to her chamber. Jess had left the door open for them and only closed the door to the bath chamber enough to keep out prying eyes. This young female was silent enough to surprise Jess and the dogs, even when they had already been listening intently. Then again, Butch was on alert due to his sense of smell, so the servant had not really been unnoticed.

"Give me just a moment," Jess said to the young female. "I should be getting dressed for dinner anyhow."

The servant went back into the hall, shutting the door behind her. Jess climbed from the tub and toweled off. Butch and Cassidy grumbled as the water from Jess's hair sprinkled them. Jess sent them a mental apology and wrapped her hair in the towel to protect the dogs from the evil water droplets. She walked into the sleeping area and called the dogs to join her. Jess shut the door to the bathing area, and Butch and Cassidy jumped up onto the bed. Cassidy snuggled into the pillows and Butch assumed the 'down' position at the foot of the bed.

Jess turned to the wardrobe and allowed herself to enjoy the shiver of excitement as it ran over her skin. She swung the doors open and reached in to grab her gown for the evening. *You've got to be kidding me. There is no way this thing is working correctly.* Jess held a red satin gown in her hands. After her senses had been overwhelmed by so much red in the room, she was hoping to find any color other than red. The dress was very pretty, but Jess hung it back up. She pulled out a dress of deep purple instead. *This is more like it!* Jess draped the gown on the bed and reached into a drawer to pull out a pair of slippers in the same purple. The color was not as dark as the purple on the King's cloak and Letha's robe. It didn't appear black under any light. The color reminded Jess of a ripening plum.

After braiding back her blonde hair and pulling a few stray strands out of the rope to frame her face, Jess reached back into the wardrobe and removed a thin silk ribbon in the same color as the dress and slippers. She tied off her braid with the ribbon and pulled the gown over her head. Jess reached back to fasten the buttons running up the back of the gown, but could only fasten the bottom button. Jess tried sitting on the bed and pushing her one arm up with the other to reach for the next button. She twisted right and left and tried holding her breath. At last, Jess sighed and admitted defeat. There was no way she was going to be able to fasten this dress on her own. Sliding the slippers onto her feet and holding the dress to her chest to remain decent, Jess stood and left her chamber to get help.

Holding the dress up with one hand, Jess knocked on Kindra's door with the other. There was no answer. Jess scanned the wall of the hall for a door to Kindra's bathing chamber. Unlike Millspare, this palace did not appear to have servants' entrances into all the rooms. The servant that had startled Jess a moment ago had entered from the main hall, so Jess figured there must be a similar entrance into Kindra's bathing area. She saw it. The door was disguised in the same wallpaper and wainscoting as the wall of the hallway. A black handle was the only evidence that this area was more than a wall and would not be noticed unless someone was searching for it or already knew it was there.

Jess banged on the door and listened for Kindra's voice. Again, there was no answer. Jess grabbed the handle for the door and depressed the latch. She pushed open the door, expecting to find Kindra submerged in the tub with her ears covered by water, making it too difficult for her friend to hear Jess knocking. The room was empty. The floor was wet, so Kindra had recently vacated the tub. Jess had only started for the door to Kindra's bed chamber when Butch burst into the room and flew by Jess. He entered Kindra's room, growling with Cassidy on his heels. Still holding her gown up over her chest, Jess followed the dogs with panic blossoming inside her.

Jess had little more than a few seconds to register the bright pink of the room's décor before she heard a dog yelp from the far side of the bed. She ran to it, struggling to climb up with her gown half fastened. She couldn't pull the skirts from her legs and hold up the bodice at the same time. Jess wriggled to the far side of the mattress and took in the fight ensuing on the floor. Kindra, wet hair stuck to her face, was on her back. A male was straddling her. He held her wrists to the floor above her head and was using his ankles to hold

Kindra's legs. Cassidy, jaws clamped on the assailant's calf, was growling and tugging at the figure, desperate to remove him from Kindra's body.

Jess reached up and grabbed the lamp orb from the sconce above the bed. She launched the ball of green light at the head of the attacker and it connected. Limping and dripping blood from his calf and shoulder, the male ran for the door as best he could. Kindra pushed her damp hair from her face and rolled onto her stomach. She crawled toward the bed and Jess reached out a hand to help her up.

Jess became aware of a soft whimpering and froze. She reached out with her senses and a wall of pain rolled over her. Butch was badly injured. Cassidy emanated concern as he stood in the corner, staring at the floor close enough to the bed that Jess could not see the area from her elevated position. Kindra reached back and pulled a towel from around her legs. She was likely wearing it as a robe when she was attacked and it had slipped off of her body. Jess slid off the foot of the bed and slowly peered around the side to get a look at Butch. The white towel Kindra had just grabbed was already turning bright red. Butch lay on his side, half under the bed, with a dagger protruding from behind his shoulder.

Jess drew in a sharp breath. Oh, God no! Not Butch. I can't lose him. Jess took a step toward the dog. He let out a ragged breath. Kindra, naked and on all fours. met Jess's eyes.

"I've got pressure on it. Call for a healer."

Jess didn't wait. Holding her gown to her chest with one hand and hiking up the skirts the best she could with her other, Jess ran into the hall through the same door the attacker had used. She screamed for a healer as she ran, and it didn't take long before several servants took up the cry as well. Jess almost collided with a male emerging from one of the rooms. In her haste to move out of his way, Jess's grip on her bodice slipped, and the front of the dress fell to her waist. The male did not show any indication that he was aware of Jess's exposed breasts.

"I am a healer. How can I help?"

Jess briefly acknowledged the male's station as a healer as the explanation for his lack of reaction to her bare breasts as she led him back down the hall to Kindra's room. The male's serene demeanor remained intact as he entered the room and witnessed Kindra's naked form crouched over Butch's motionless body. Jess crashed to the floor next to Cassidy and let the tears fall. She buried her head in the dog's fur and pulled him into her lap. She wanted to go home. *Why did I bring Butch and Cassidy to this place?* Butch didn't deserve to die, and it was Jess's fault.

The tears were being licked from Jess's face as she made the decision to strip off her silly purple gown and leave this realm. She squeezed Cassidy tightly and inhaled his smell. Jess had no idea how the two of them were going to go on without Butch. The licking on her face stopped and someone was trying to loosen Jess's grip on Cassidy. In her grief, she was probably strangling the poor dog. Jess loosened her hold enough for a second dog to wiggle his way into her lap. Butch, having successfully removed Cassidy from Jess's lap, resumed licking Jess's tears.

Jess sat back in confusion. The healer was sitting on the edge of the bed. Jess frantically ran her hands over Butch's side. She couldn't find the wound. Blood was congealing in a pool on the floor. A large dagger was nearly submerged in the sticky mess. Kindra was sitting on the floor beside the puddle. She had pulled the sheet from the bed and wrapped herself in it. She was watching Jess with amusement.

"I really hope you'll be half as distraught if I am ever stabbed in the act of defending you," Kindra said, as she shook her head.

Jess ignored her friend and turned to the healer. "Thank you. Thank you so very much. I don't know what I'd ever do without him."

The healer gave a slight bow of his head. Jess worked her way out from under her dogs and stood. She helped Kindra off the floor and Kindra sat down on the edge of the bed, still wrapped in the sheet.

Jess addressed the healer. "My name is Jess Bennett, and this is Kindra Powers. These are my dogs, Butch and Cassidy. I was so sure Butch was gone. There was so much blood. How did you help him? It is as if he was never injured."

The healer scratched Butch behind his ear. "I suppose it just wasn't this one's time. This is the Royal Palace of Lillerem. King Erik makes it a point to keep powerful healers in residence. It makes it difficult to die here as long as one acts swiftly."

Jess joined the healer and Kindra on the edge of the bed. The three of them sat in silence and allowed the adrenaline to drain. Cassidy was dutifully licking Butch's face and the area where the dreadful knife wound had been. Jess could feel Cassidy's relief. That made her happier than her own relief over Butch's miraculous recovery.

At last, the healer addressed Kindra. "If you'll finish preparations, I'll escort you all to dinner."

"Do you have a name?" Kindra asked the healer.

"You may call me Trego. Quickly now, I am not a fan of arriving late."

CHAPTER 15

Kindra ran to the bathing chamber as soon as the healer left the room. Jess gave each of the dogs an extra scratch on the neck, stood from the bed, and smoothed the skirts of her gown. She sat at the small table beside the window and looked into the mirror. Her blonde curls were still pulled back in their braid, but more locks framed her face than earlier. Jess decided she liked the look of all the ringlets that had pulled free. She looked down to where her hand was still clutching at the purple material that made up the bodice of the gown and realized she was covered in dog hair. Jess groaned and plucked the hairbrush from the table. Instead of using the brush on her hair, she used it to collect the chunks of fur clinging to her dress.

Kindra re-entered the room and pulled open her wardrobe. She flung a nearly black gown onto the bed. Dropping her towel, Kindra belted Forsvarer around her waist and stepped into the dress instead of pulling it over her head. She carefully pulled the bodice of the dress over the sword and offered Jess her back so Jess could fasten the buttons up the back. Jess wrinkled her nose as Kindra pulled on her socks and boots. When Jess caught Kindra's eye, her friend only smiled.

"You may enjoy dressing for high society, but experience has taught me that it is better to be prepared than pretty," said Kindra.

Jess stood and turned her back to Kindra so the bodice of her own dress could be fastened at last. "That's the thing," said Jess. "You just created a completely beautiful, yet utterly practical dress. I feel as if I've failed in my role as the friend with common sense.

There was a time where I was the brains and you were the pretty face. I'm starting to think you are both of those people now."

"It sounds as if you are calling me stupid and referring to yourself as ugly," Kindra said as she bent over to brush her copper hair toward the top of her head. She straightened and secured it with a leather cord and two combs.

Jess separated a chunk of hair from Kindra's ponytail and quickly braided it. She wrapped the braid around the base of Kindra's ponytail and tucked the end under the cord. She pulled her friend's shoulders so Kindra was facing her.

"You are not now, nor have you ever been, stupid. I have always been envious of your slender figure and beautiful face. My face is the shape of a full moon and all these freckles are impossible to cover. I thought my role in your life was to keep you in line; to protect you from your own impulsive ideas. It seems as if you have gone and matured behind my back and now I'm worried I no longer have a job in this relationship."

Kindra stared into Jess's blue eyes. "I won't tell you how beautiful you are. I've said it enough times to know that saying it once more will not change your opinion of your looks. I will emphasize that there is no way I could navigate life without you. You are my conscience, you are my sounding board, and you are my entire support system. Please don't underestimate your value in our friendship."

Jess looked at the floor. "I know you feel that way, but I'm trying to be realistic. What will happen to my place in your life once you marry Krish? I know we stayed as close as ever when you married Tom, and even once I married Sean, but this is different. You will literally live a realm away!"

Kindra looked as if she was going to reply, but Jess continued, "Do not even dream of saying that you will visit all the time. You are marrying the Crown Prince of Lillerem. You will have responsibilities, beyond what you feel now, to an entire kingdom."

It was Kindra's turn to look at the floor. Jess saw conflict on Kindra's face. She wasn't sure if she should prompt her friend to speak. Jess was not looking for a fight, and she certainly was not looking to push her friend away. She held her breath, wondering if she had gone too far already.

At last, Kindra spoke. "I don't think I love him. I know I have to marry him. I have no choice. At first, I thought my feelings were a product of rebellion against the expectation that this marriage was a foregone conclusion. All I have been doing is thinking about the ramification of marrying or not marrying Krish. I have been afraid to ask, but I know something is on your mind too. I didn't want anything else to think about. I feel like a terrible friend."

Jess sat down on the bed. She drew in a deep breath. Jess raised her eyes to meet Kindra's. She could see the heaviness there. Her friend, an eternal beacon of life and happiness, looked more worn down than Jess had ever seen her. It occurred to Jess that she might have exactly what her friend needed. The essence of Kindra's personality was rooted in the need to help others. Jess was in need of help.

"Kindra, it isn't my fear of losing our friendship that has been weighing on me. Selfishly, I am concerned about how the changes in your life relate to me, but I only think about it to avoid the actual issue. I don't want to return to the human realm because I am avoiding Sean. What I said earlier about wanting to get back to you and the dogs was true. You were on the mark when you pointed out that I did not include Sean in that equation. I didn't miss him. I didn't miss our life. Sean just felt like one more responsibility I had waiting for me."

Kindra sat on the bed beside Jess. "What happened? Did he cheat on you while you were gone? Is he drinking too much? Has he been violent?"

Jess held up a hand to stop Kindra before she worked herself up. "That's the thing; nothing happened. Sean is exactly the same as he always was. He has not changed. He still lets me do his laundry and clean up after him. He still sits on the couch watching sports while I take out the trash and do the food shopping. I don't know what I expected when I returned home, but I walked in that door and all I saw was all the work he had created for me."

"You just need to talk to him. I'm sure he would be willing to help out around the house."

"I'm not so sure about that. When we got married, I was happy to take care of him. I was supposed to get pregnant and leave teaching. I was going to make a full-time job of taking care of the house and our children. When we didn't have children, and my focus switched to my career, his expectations didn't change. I honestly don't think it would be fair of me to ask him to change. Helping to take care of the house wasn't supposed to be part of the package for Sean. He wanted a wife and mother, not an individual. I was happy to be exactly what he wanted. It was my dream too until it became apparent it was not going to happen."

"I stopped by to see Sean a few times while you were stuck here in Alfheim," said Kindra. "I saw the house. It was as if he was just waiting for you to come home to take care of all of it. I'm not sure he washed a single dish while you were gone."

Jess smiled. "I appreciate you taking my side, but I don't really need you to give me more reasons to avoid returning home."

"I did tell him you weren't going to be happy. I suggested he clean the place up before you returned."

A tiny laugh escaped from Jess. "Well, I could tell he cleared off the coffee table. What you said must have made an impression."

Kindra smiled at her friend. "See! It's not hopeless. He's willing to make an effort."

Jess let out an enormous sigh. "Honestly, it feels better to laugh about it a little. Everything happening has hit me pretty hard, and it's all wrapped up in a giant mess of emotion. I know I'm losing you to this realm, and I keep thinking about what I am left with. I have a classroom full of unappreciative students, parents of those students who think I exist to give their children anxiety, and a husband who thinks it's ok to be stuck to the bathroom floor by his own urine. I'd rather stay here than deal with all of that anymore."

"I am hearing that you are unhappy with the way you are treated at work," Kindra said softly to Jess. " I hear that you are unhappy with the state in which Sean leaves - "

Kindra stopped when she looked at Jess's face. The-teacher-glare-of-death was piercing Kindra's eyes and making them burn.

"I'll ask you once to stop treating me as if I am a client on your couch. You are not required to parrot back my words to demonstrate how invested you are in my problem," Jess said.

Kindra raised an eyebrow. "Would a better reaction be for me to offer to beat Sean to a pulp until he understands that he needs to stop taking you for granted? I can also suggest you quit your job and live carefree as a vagrant. I can use those words instead, but it doesn't change my feeling that you are just overwhelmed and in need of a break."

"Well," said Jess. "Those words did have a better effect on my emotions. I wonder if you might consider taking a similar approach with the students? I can't imagine anyone who is angry and frustrated enjoys hearing their words repeated back to them. Solutions, even ridiculous ones, have a more calming result."

"Seriously though," Kindra began, "I know how distraught Sean has been since he accepted where you really were and that you never intended to abandon him without a word. Maybe your absence was what he needed to snap him out of his lethargic life where he waits for you to serve him tirelessly?"

"I'm not sure what will happen when I return home, but I feel better now that we have defined and acknowledged the problem." Jess smiled at Kindra in thanks.

"See, talk therapy prevails again," replied Kindra. "I just need to remember not to take such a passive approach with you when I apply the technique."

Jess gave her friend a playful shove. "Ever the psychologist! Now, what are you going to do about your relationship with Krish?"

Jess watched her friend's eyes become unfocussed. Though she was well practiced, Jess always found it difficult to wait out Kindra's vacant moments. She knew her friend was replaying moments between herself and Krish. Once, when the women were younger, Jess was convinced Kindra was suffering a seizure when Kindra went vacant, like she had just now. When Kindra snapped back to reality, Jess had demanded a detailed explanation of what Kindra was just experiencing. The conclusion Jess reached was that Kindra experienced her thoughts in a way that was similar to watching television. Kindra replayed scenes from her own life vividly, and it took several minutes.

As Kindra came back to the present and met Jess's eyes with her own, Jess could see her friend had not come up with a solution. There was determination on Kindra's face, but no direction. Jess put her arms around Kindra and gave her a tight squeeze.

"Listen Kindra, we don't need to fix it now. We'll get there. For now, we look absolutely stunning and should take advantage of the spread of food that is undoubtedly waiting for us."

"Oh wow! I forgot about Trego!" Kindra jumped up from the bed. "Do you think he's still waiting in the hall?"

Jess glanced at Butch and Cassidy and they immediately stood, ready to follow the women to their next destination. Jess dragged herself to a standing position, checked her hair in the mirror, and headed for the bedroom door. The door swung open before she ever touched the knob. Trego's face was passive, but Jess could feel the impatience roiling within the healer. *Maybe it wasn't impatience? Did I just hear the elf's stomach rumble?*

Kindra and Trego entered the dining hall first. Trego escorted Kindra to a seat between Krish and Gunnar. He then walked around to the other side of the table and took his own seat. There were several empty chairs at the end of the table farthest from the king, but Jess understood she was expected to take the seat between the king and Trego, nearly at the head of the table. This put Jess in a seat of equal importance to the seat Krish occupied at the king's left. Jess was unsure how she earned this honor until she sat and watched Butch and Cassidy take positions under the table, facing the king, making no attempt to hide their anticipation of table scraps.

Stroking Butch's head, the King addressed Jess. "I'm glad to see I did not cause these two any offense. We were relaxing in the sitting room earlier when the two of them took off suddenly."

"They still seem to be drawn to you," Jess said as she watched the king slip Cassidy a sliver of meat under the table. "I should tell you, though, we nearly lost Butch. Had it not been for Trego's intervention, you would currently have one less mouth to feed."

The king looked uncomfortable for a moment as he recognized he had just been admonished, however subtly, for feeding the dogs at the table. He brought both of his hands back into sight and wiped them with his napkin. His face changed as he realized what Jess said before the gentle reprimand. The king looked at Trego expectantly.

"It seems, Your Highness, that there was an attempt on Kindra's life. The canine defended the female and took a dagger in the fray. The assailant was gone, and Butch was near death when I arrived in Kindra's chambers."

The king reached below the table again and found Butch's head. He scratched the dog behind the ear. Seeing no food in the king's hand, Butch and Cassidy dropped to the floor to sleep off the depravity. Jess was comforted to see the concern for Butch on Erik's features, but noticed the king had not even glanced at Kindra to see if she was injured. Instead, Erik called to one of the guards at the door. The guard quickly approached the king and dipped his head.

"Where is your commander?" Erik demanded of the guard.

The guard's eyes went to an empty chair at the table and the muscular male withered under King Erik's scrutiny. The guard's gaze went to those of the other guards stationed around the room. None of them offered any relief. They continued to stare straight ahead.

"I am not sure where he went. He has not been seen today."

"Was his absence not a cause for concern?" pressed the king.

"I expected to see Captain Jacan here at the table. It is not until I saw the empty chair, and am now hearing of this attack, that I had cause for concern. I suppose he may have been a victim of the assailant as well, though no other guards have been reported missing. I shall send a team to scout for other casualties."

"Don't bother," Krish's voice cut in. "You say your captain's name is Jacan? I suspect he was no more a victim of an attack than I am a fairy princess."

Krish's eyes smoldered as he shared the discovery of Jacan's existence and connection to Hedda, daughter of King Blaith. Jess, already knowing about the discovery in the archives, concentrated on Krish's demeanor as he spoke instead of his words. She could see his anguish. There was so much anger and concern balled within him. Jess found herself wondering if it was Krish's love for Kindra and discovering she had been seconds from losing her life, causing his light green eyes to fill with angry amber specks. It was also possible that his demeanor was simply a result of him being bested. Someone had reached Kindra while under the protection of the palace. Krish would certainly feel as if he was partially to blame for that. When Krish's rigid grip on his utensils became the focus of Jess's attention, she decided on a combination of both reasons. This amount of rage stemmed from multiple causes.

Jess shifted her attention to Erik. She was unsure what reaction she was expecting from him, but she was expecting some response. Instead, Erik sat passively. There was no evidence of concern, anger, or fear displayed on his features. When Krish finished speaking, the king turned to the guard that had remained at his side, listening.

"Organize a search," Erik commanded. "I want Captain Jacan found if he is still on palace grounds. Otherwise, I want proof of his departure."

Erik turned to his son. "This book of Ekkelle's has been in the palace archives since her childhood. I am disturbed by my own ignorance and intend to speak to Letha. Knowledge of these lost branches of King Andril's family tree would have prevented Jacan's ability to work in service to the crown, and therefore prevented the attempt on my future daughter-in-law's life."

There it was. Jess let out a sigh of relief. King Erik had acknowledged Kindra as his son's fiancée and was, indeed, concerned for her safety. *At least, I think he is showing concern for Kindra. It's possible his only issue with the attack is that it occurred in a place he is charged with protecting. He might only be upset because he is aware that information was kept from him.* Jess decided not to question the king's motivation. It made her feel better to continue assuming Erik cared about Kindra's safety.

"Now," the king addressed his son again, "where is this handmade book you discovered in my archives?"

It was Gunnar who answered. "With all due respect, Your Highness, the archives belong to the palace, not to the people living within it. I have possession of my mother's journal, if you wish to see it."

Erik narrowed his eyes at Gunnar. Jess could tell the king was uncertain of Gunnar's intentions. At last, the staring contest concluded, and King Erik proffered a smile.

"I accept your offer, Gunnar. I shall send my personal servant to your quarters to retrieve the book after our meal."

Feeling the tense situation was at an end, Erik motioned to Kindra to pass the salt. Gunnar's hand slowly came off the table and dipped into the satchel he wore around his waist. From the bag, he pulled his mother's manuscript. He held it out to the king.

"Please be careful. My mother scrawled this when she was barely an adult. For me, the mere existence of this book is a treasure," Gunnar said with sincerity.

Jess could see the King understood the promise laced in Gunnar's words. Erik read through the first two pages and then flipped through the document several pages at a time.

Seeming to find little of interest, he handed the book back to Gunnar. "I never knew your mother. From what I see here, she felt the importance of documenting the lives of the female elves of royalty and took it seriously. I am not sure she had, or would even have today, many supporters. I do see that this book is special to you, though, and I can understand why an heirloom like this might make you feel close to your mother. I shall permit you to take it with you when you leave."

Gunnar had barely opened his mouth to reply when Kindra kicked him. Jess was grateful she had done so, because if it were up to Jess to deliver the kick, she may have accidentally bruised the wrong shins from this side of the table. Erik was well aware that Gunnar had intended to leave with that book; with or without permission. By publicly granting authorization for the book to leave the palace grounds, Erik maintained control in front of his men and his courtiers. Instead of arguing, Gunnar dipped his head to the King in thanks.

CHAPTER 16

Bane was waiting for them when the group entered Smalgroth from the palace portal. He did not look happy. It occurred to Jess that Bane never looked happy, but at this moment, he looked even more 'not happy' than he usually did. Krish must have seen it too because he left the rest of the group behind and quickly went to Bane. The two males spoke in hushed voices as Gunnar and the women walked toward Kanin's home.

Krish's voice rang out from behind them, "Our rations are packed for travel. We are out of time."

Jess and Kindra exchanged a look, but Gunnar simply continued up the porch steps. He grabbed several small satchels from Kanin at the door and was walking back toward Jess and Kindra in a heartbeat. He dropped the satchels at the women's feet and continued past them. Kindra shook her head sharply to let Jess know she was unaware where Gunnar was going and then bent to pick up two of the satchels. Jess retrieved the other two bags and followed Kindra toward the stables.

Branka stomped a hello to Kindra when she approached the mare's stall. Kindra rubbed Branka's fuzzy face to return the greeting. When Jess stepped up to the stall with Butch and Cassidy at her sides, Branka lowered her head and snorted. Butch took a step back, but Cassidy stretched out his tongue and planted a canine kiss on the horse's nose.

The stable hands had Gunnar and Krish's horses saddled and ready. Jess narrowed her eyes at Gunnar's arrogant mount as she attached one of the provision bags to his saddle. She considered opening her mind up to Krish's stallion to see if he possessed a similar personality, but she decided she'd rather not know. Jess knew Branka had a loving heart, and that was all that mattered for keeping Butch and Cassidy happy. She fastened her second satchel to Krish's horse as Kindra unburdened herself of her two provision bags by entrusting them to Branka and Bob.

Kindra and Jess mounted up and exited the stable. Jess looked down at Butch on her left and Cassidy on her right. The dogs trotted beside Branka easily, as if they were all part of the same pack. She marveled at how accepting the dogs were of the mare. It was a true testament to Branka's demeanor, considering Butch still wouldn't go within fifteen feet of the other horses and Cassidy made no move to befriend them. Gunnar hurried down the road toward the stable with something tucked under his arm. Jess raised her eyebrows at Kindra, but her friend only shrugged.

Krish's voice could be heard coming from the stable. "By the Gods, Gunnar! We're in a rush here!"

Krish and Bane rode out from the stable and pulled up in front of Jess and Kindra. Krish turned in the saddle and looked beyond the women to see if his cousin was following.

"It seems Gunnar felt a visit to his female friend was more important than getting back to the human realm to warn Leif and Joral about that hundespor you saw," said Krish. "We'll get moving, I'm sure he'll catch up."

Female friend? Did Gunnar have a girlfriend? Jess didn't need to think about it for long. She should have known that comment was not getting by Kindra without questions.

"I see you gave Gunnar's horse to Bane. Is that some kind of punishment for Gunnar going to see his girlfriend?" Kindra asked sweetly.

"It's not a punishment. Bane was ready to go. It was senseless to wait for another horse to be readied."

"So, you might say Uncle Gunnar's girlfriend," Kindra emphasized the word girlfriend, "is actually to blame for the delay?"

"I see what you're doing there, Kindra. I have no details about the relationship between Gunnar and his female friend. I only know he went to see her, despite our need to keep moving."

Bane kicked his horse into motion and led the group out of town and through the surrounding fields. Instead of going straight up the hill to the forest, Bane took the horses on a path that meandered. Jess opened her mind to the equines and felt appreciation. Jess was wondering if all elves were as considerate of animals as the princes were. Bane was surly and abrupt when interacting with people, but his first thought had been for the horses' comfort as they ascended the steep incline. Jess liked the enormous male a little more at that moment.

There was a minor issue as the group reached the edge of the forest. Butch refused to go on. Jess felt fear and irritation from the dog. Through Butch's mind, Jess saw images of the Little Folk reaching out from the bushes to smack Butch's nose. In Butch's memory, those smacks were much harder than Jess remembered them in her own thoughts.

"Ok, you big baby," Jess said to the German Shepherd dog. "Just walk in front of Branka. Stay in the center of the trail. The Little Folk are more afraid of you than you are of them. They will not risk being seen to step out of the bushes."

Butch gave Jess a look that even those who could not read his thoughts would understand. He did not believe, for a second, that the Little Folk were afraid of him. He did center himself on the path and enter the forest, though. Following Butch, atop Branka, Jess saw the little eyes in the bushes. Butch continued on with his hackles raised. After about ten minutes, the eyes in the bushes thinned, and then disappeared. Butch's hackles lowered, and he was more at ease. Jess sent thoughts to Butch to let him know she was proud of him. He had ignored the Little Folk long enough for them to get bored and leave him in peace.

Gunnar caught up to the group about a mile before they arrived back in Aergroth. There was no sign of the bundle he had been carrying when he entered the stables back in Smalgroth. He must have put it in his saddlebag.

"Sooooooooooo, Uncle Gunnar," Kindra began in a teasing voice.

Jess smiled. Kindra had likely been thinking about Gunnar's female friend for the entire ride. Since the group had kept a swift pace, there had not been a lot of conversation, and Jess was certain

145

Kindra would have lost herself in a soap opera version of her uncle's life.

"Krish told Jess and I, you have a lady friend back in Smalgroth."

Gunnar didn't flinch. "Frida is the town leatherworker. There is history between us, we are only friends."

"History, huh?" Kindra taunted.

"A long time ago, when I first returned to Alfheim, Frida was kind to me and showed me the land. We spent a lot of time together and grew very close. A little less than thirty-five years ago, Frida's mother became ill. I was wrapped up in the war against Ulford and trying to convince Leif to return to the realm. We saw each other less, and we grew apart. We are now friends."

Kindra wasn't buying it. Jess could see it on her friend's face, and she understood why. There was not a female in any realm that would simply let someone she loved fade away from her life. Even if Frida had needed to spend much of her time caring for her mother, Jess knew the elf had likely never stopped thinking about Gunnar. It was simply incomprehensible to think that she could have just forgotten all the years they shared. Sneaking a glance at Gunnar, Jess was doubtful he was happy with his current relationship status, either. The powerful male looked deflated. It was as if revisiting his years with Frida, even briefly, had sucked the air from him. Jess was glad Gunnar had stolen a few moments with his female friend, even if it made him run a little behind. They were all together now, and approaching the stable at Millspare.

The group thundered into the stables, causing the other horses there to whinny with anxiety. Krish and Gunnar did not even wait for their horses to stop moving when they gracefully dismounted and handed the reins to the waiting stable boys. The two of them pulled their packs from the horses and started walking back out of the stable, the same way they all had entered. Jess sent Kindra a questioning look. *Are we going to follow them?*

Kindra shook her head. "I don't care how much of a rush we are in. We're stopping in to see Einar and Mildred before we return to the human realm."

Bane grunted his agreement as he dismounted and hit the ground heavily. Bane had no magic. The little grace bestowed upon the half-troll elf came from his Elven blood alone. Bane, unable to travel through the portal to the human realm, was just as insulted as Einar and Mildred would be with Gunnar and Krish's hasty departure.

"Do you think we should go after them?" Jess asked Bane.

Bane did not respond. He pulled his pack from his beautiful horse and walked through the stalls toward the passage into Millspare. Kindra climbed down from her horse with considerably more grace than Bane had. She scratched Cassidy on the head and started working the knots on her own satchel.

"Send the dogs," Kindra suggested to Jess. "If the boys return, great. If they choose to continue on, then at least they'll see the dogs return to us and understand that we intend to visit for a little while."

Jess considered her friend's suggestion. Connecting her mind to her dog's consciousness, Jess sent out silent directions. She ensured the dogs were aware that the primary directive was to retrieve Gunnar and Krish, but also to return if the mission failed. Emitting a quick bark, Butch tore out of the stable as if he were chasing a squirrel. Cassidy lingered long enough for a quick scratch behind the ears from Jess and then trotted after his brother.

"Butch thinks he's a police dog," Kindra laughed as she helped Jess from Branka's back.

Marveling over the differences in the dogs' personalities, yet again, Jess thought about Sean's description of the dogs. One of Sean's coworkers had invited Sean and Jess for dinner. The coworker's wife had asked what kind of dogs she and Sean owned. Sean had told the woman they had a Belgian Malinois, named Butch, and an Old English SheepDog, named Cassidy. Jess had been incredulous that Sean would lie about the breed of the dogs. She had looked at Sean disgustedly as she corrected him for the benefit of his coworker and the wife. Sean had been hurt and said he was only joking, but Jess, a stickler for the facts, did not see anything funny about providing incorrect information.

Having just watched her two German Shepherd dogs take directive with completely different attitudes, Jess couldn't help feeling as if Sean may have been more factual than she thought at the time. Butch took his tasks seriously and was almost always alert and ready for the next encounter. Cassidy was laid-back. As long as the sheep were safe, he saw no reason to get worked up over anything. Jess felt a twinge of guilt for how she viewed her husband. Sean may not be as meticulous about the care of the dogs as she was, but he certainly recognized them as individuals. Maybe even more than Jess did. She had always viewed Butch and Cassidy as a unit. They were 'the dogs'; plural, rarely singular.

"Hey," Kindra tapped Jess on the shoulder. "I was unaware that my daydreams were contagious. I would have tried harder to suppress them when around those I care about."

Shaking her head to clear her thoughts, Jess smiled at her friend. "Maybe you're just not as weird as we all think."

Kindra gave Jess a little shove and walked past her friend to follow Bane. Jess hurried after her friend. Since being stuck here at Millspare, Jess's senses had strengthened along with her body. She didn't need to ask if there was food on the table in Einar's kitchen. The scent of roasted quail wafted down the hall and pulled Jess forward. *Do I smell sweetbread? I definitely smell sweetbread.*

Jess pushed through the doorway and into the kitchen area. She wound her way around the open fire and took a seat at the table next to Kindra. Einar was just bringing out plates of quail, but there were a few sweetbread morsels left on a platter in the center of the table. Jess dunked a piece into a dipping sauce and popped it directly into her mouth. The sound of a throat clearing behind her almost caused her to choke on her food.

From behind Einar, Mildred's voice scolded Jess. "Manners, child! You've barely been gone a week and you've returned to your savage ways!"

"Forgive me, Mildred," Jess grimaced as she spoke. "I feel it is Einar's cooking that is to blame. It is only when I'm confronted with his delicacies that I find my manners lacking."

Jess scraped the remaining sweetbread onto her plate and drizzled sauce on top. Looking up and seeing Mildred's wide-eyed look, Jess realized she had spoken with her mouth full when she gave her apologetic excuse for her poor manners. She sighed, placed her fork next to her plate, chewed, and then swallowed. She raised her napkin from her lap, wiped her face, and then placed the napkin back in her lap.

"Forgive me Mildred," Jess said with an empty mouth. "There is no excuse for my behavior."

Mildred's eyes crinkled with her smile. "There's the young lady I know. Where are your fluffy bodyguards?"

At the mention of the dogs, the door creaked open. Butch and Cassidy came in and immediately assumed positions under the table. Gunnar quietly entered on their heels. Krish did not follow. Gunnar went to Mildred and gave her a hug. He clapped Einar on the shoulder and then took a seat at the table beside Bane. Jess felt the tension building in the room. Nothing seemed out of place as the group enjoyed the delicious quail and Einar peppered them with questions about Gulentine and King Erik, but Jess knew her friend too well. As if Einar was not currently speaking, and with fire blazing in her eyes, Kindra directed her own question at Gunnar.

"Would you care to explain to me why my fiancé is not currently in attendance?"

Gunnar put his fork down. He took his time chewing his food. He probably should have masticated his food a little longer because the answer he provided was less than satisfactory.

"As Crown Prince, Krish has a duty to protect the realm. He has continued with his duties while we enjoy respite."

Jess was concerned Kindra's eyes might fall right out of her head and onto the table. Her eyelids were no longer visible. Her eyes were pinned open as wide as they could go. Gunnar saw the look too, and he was wise enough to understand that his answer had been insufficient.

"I believe Krish wanted us all to enjoy a good meal and some good company. He took it upon himself to forgo the pleasantries so we could indulge," Gunnar tried again.

Kindra drew breath to speak, but Mildred beat her to it. "Stuff some more quail in your mouth, Gunnar. I wasn't going to bring it up because I didn't want to sound selfish, but now that I know it isn't just me who is offended by Krish's actions, I'll have you stop making excuses for him. Don't paint him out to be a martyr, allowing you to enjoy a brief stay at Millspare. That boy has a duty alright, and it's not to the realm! His duty is to this family and the female who is his future. I taught him better than that. I know you are all in a rush, but he should have at least stopped in and shown his face."

Kindra's face softened a little. Mildred was like a mother to all the princes. Like any mother or grandmother, Mildred had expectations for those she cared for. There were Bingo halls full of older women in the human realm complaining that their children and grandchildren rarely visited and had no time for them. Mildred, it seemed, was no different. Kindra forgot the criticism she had been about to spew in Gunnar's direction. Instead, she turned to Mildred.

"I agree with you. Certainly, we are pressed for time, but it would be inexcusable not to visit with the two of you. It also gives us a chance to recharge with some of Einar's delicious food. I assure you, Krish will hear about how we feel about his choice to skip this visit."

Mildred's eyes softened and fell on Kindra. She said nothing, but Kindra could feel warmth from the older female. Though Kindra's own emotions had been blazing moments ago, she felt calmed now. There was a mutual understanding between her and Mildred. Mildred trusted that Krish's transgressions would be appropriately addressed, and that she had been heard in a way that mattered. Kindra nodded to Mildred to show she understood the feelings responsible for the fire inside Mildred.

Gunnar stood. "I'm not sure what the contents of this silent conversation are, but it's time to end it. We really need to get moving. Thank you for the food and company. We shall return with more time on our side in the future."

Gunnar went to Mildred and put his arms around the old elf. He dipped his head to Einar and turned for the servants' door at the back of the room. Jess stood and followed Gunnar after throwing smiles to their Elven hosts and Butch marched away at Jess's heels. Cassidy walked by Einar and got a scratch behind the ears and then gave Mildred a tiny lick on the hand as he loped by her to fall in line with Jess.

"Please give Aunt Ruth and Viktor our best. I'm sure they are busy, but will be unhappy to hear we skipped a visit with them," Kindra said. "Thank you for the meal. We will return soon."

Kindra was pretty sure Lady Ruth and Lord Viktor would feel no disappointment at having missed the group passing through Millspare. It wasn't that the rulers didn't enjoy seeing Kindra, Jess or the princes; it was simply that they were busy. Greeting guests, even guests that had recently saved Aergroth and Castle Millspare, was nearly impossible to schedule into the day. Turning away from Mildred and Einar, Kindra stepped away from this realm and headed off for the portal.

CHAPTER 17

Things were wrong in the human realm. Even before crossing out of the portal and into Leif's basement, Jess felt discomfort from her dogs. They were more on edge as they re-entered the basement than they had been during the uncomfortable transition into the human realm at the center of the tunnel. Listening through the dogs' ears, Jess heard shouting before both of her feet were on human soil. Gunnar, already at the top of the stairs, opened the door to the first floor of Leif's cabin and the shouted words became clear. Well, half of the words were clear.

Loud, and exceptionally slurred, speech came from Leif. "You weren't here. It's gone. I should've known."

Krish's answer was clear as glass. "You had one job. You chose to remain here with Joral and the descendant army. I should've known you would not be capable of one paltry task."

"I never asked for that task. I never asked for all these people at my cabin. I never asked for any of this!"

If Leif's almost unintelligible speech had not been enough of an indicator, Jess was positive Leif was plastered when she reached the top of the stairs. She joined Gunnar as she watched Krish attempt to raise Leif from the floor. The material at the front of Leif's pants was dark and the scent of urine permeated the air. Not only was Leif drunk, he had been so for some time. Gunnar went to Krish's aid. The two princes dragged Leif to his feet. Finding Leif could not stand on his own, Gunnar and Krish dragged Leif past Jess and down the hall. Butch bared his teeth as the trio struggled to squeeze down the hallway. The dog placed himself between the males and Jess.

Jess sent a mental command to Butch to fall back and relax. She stepped to the bathroom doorway in time to see Krish and Gunnar dump Leif into the tub, still fully clothed. Krish turned on the water and closed the drain. As the water filled the tub, Krish continued to berate Leif. Leif attempted to climb from the tub when he finally realized it was filling with cold water. With no control of his limbs, Leif only managed to hit his head on the soap dish. The sound Leif's head made when it connected rolled Jess's stomach and she expected him to slip, unconscious, into the water.

"Fuck!" screamed Leif. "Get the fuck off of me!"

Jess was surprised Leif was still alive after cracking his head, but she was even more startled to see Krish and Gunnar back away. Krish took a seat on the closed toilet lid, and Gunnar leaned back against the sink. No one said anything as Leif lay in the cold bathwater, with his eyes closed, head back, but still breathing. After several silent moments, Krish cleared his throat.

"Let's leave this wretch to marinate in his own filth for a time. I need to tell you both what I found upon my arrival. Where is Kindra?"

Jess fielded the question with ease. "No doubt, Kindra is avoiding her darling father while he is in this state. She probably made it to the top of the steps and then headed right out the front door. We can catch her up later.

"Depending on the direction she chose, Kindra may have more details than you and Gunnar have at this point," Krish replied as he led the way to the kitchen.

Seated at the table, Gunnar and Jess listened to Krish. Jess rubbed Cassidy behind the ears as she contemplated the relationship between Krish and Leif. Krish had seen Leif passed out on the living room floor as soon as he entered the cabin. Instead of checking on Leif, Krish left the cabin and went to the encampment to find Joral. She almost missed Krish's description of the encampment as she considered the kind of person it takes to ignore a body on the floor and just walk off in the other direction.

"...and the gore was indescribable," Krish was saying. "This was after Joral had picked up all the body parts he could find and burned them. Not a soul survived. Each elf who came here to help with training, and every descendant with too little magic to travel to Millspare, is gone. I sat with Joral on a log by the fire for some time as he described the carnage he, Leif and Syndral, had found when they entered the clearing."

Jess held up a hand to stop Krish from speaking. "Syndral was here? She witnessed the attack as well?"

"No one actually witnessed the attack," Krish explained. "Joral, Leif and Syndral were arguing in front of the house when it happened. It wasn't until they picked up on the unnatural silence that they even considered something might be wrong."

Gunnar grimaced. "Knowing what we now do about Syndral's lineage, it would not surprise me if she was an intended distraction."

Krish agreed. "I thought the same as soon as Joral described Syndral's sudden appearance with additional information about Skilanis. Joral and Leif had been suspicious of her intent, even then."

Jess narrowed her eyes. "It must've been some pretty important information to distract two elves that were already suspicious."

"That is another disturbing part of all of this," said Krish. "Joral said Syndral shared information about having seen a hundespor at the workplace of a known Pakk descendant. Joral and Syndral were very wrapped up in explaining the origins of hundespor and the significance of one being in the human realm. It would be enough to hold the attention of both Leif and Joral. Joral then went on to tell me it appears the attack on the encampment was a hundespor attack. That sneaky female used the threat of the event that was occurring at that moment as a distraction from that occurrence! Basically, she told Leif and Joral the truth to keep them from being able to thwart the attack. It was only after Syndral left, and Leif and Joral were burning the bodies, that they realized how foolish they were and how easily Syndral duped them."

"I hate to defend my brother in any way," Gunnar placed Ekkelle's book on the table. "But neither he nor Joral has seen this. Though they were always suspicious of Syndral, we see it much more clearly than they would have. We are all aware that she and the rest of Ulford's Elite Draw are descendants of King Andril. The more competition for the throne they eliminate, the better. The parchment we found in the archives, in concert with my mother's writing, delineates just how many people have a claim to that throne. That is, after taking into account the innumerable Andril descendants that have been eliminated by the assassins already."

Krish did not lift his eyes from the floor as he spoke. "They call me the Crown Prince. It's a joke. Of all those claims to the throne of Lillerem, my claim is but a pittance. I may be the only being raised as a prince of Lillerem, within the walls of Castle Gulentine, but I have no blood connection to King Andril. I am not a descendant of the last great king. Even after Kindra and I marry, her blood claim is weaker than many of the assassins'."

Jess cocked her head. "Kindra..." Jess whispered. "No cars left. She's probably seen the camp by now."

"I'm sure she has," said Krish. "Joral is there. I'm sure she is shocked, but Joral is probably explaining how the attack occurred."

"Regardless, I think we should go find her," said Jess.

Jess got up and walked out the back door. Butch followed immediately, but Cassidy did a lap around Gunnar's legs as an invitation for him to come along. Cassidy trotted out the door. One side of Gunnar's mouth turned up. He shook his head, got to his feet, and followed behind the canine. It was Krish's turn to shake his head. He was pretty sure he had just witnessed a smile from Gunnar. No person ever got that reaction from the stoic male.

Krish placed his hands on the table for leverage and was about to rise from his seat when Leif entered the kitchen. His hair was damp, and he was wearing clean clothes. Joral waited for him to speak, but Leif was in no rush to say whatever it was that was on his mind. He nodded once to Joral and walked out the door. Again, Krish was shaking his head. He did not understand either of his cousins. Gunnar was impossible to read, seemingly impassive in almost any situation, and Leif was a maelstrom of emotion. Krish rose to his feet and followed the enigmas out into the rear yard.

When Krish arrived at the location of the former encampment, Kindra was not there. Joral still sat by the fire. He did not appear to have moved since Krish had sat with him earlier. Jess and Gunnar walked the area with Butch and Cassidy as if they were scrutinizing a crime scene. Krish stepped up next to Leif, who had not left the woods, and entered the clearing. The two males watched in silence for a brief time before Leif spoke.

"I know this is entirely my fault. I was a fool to think I could be an agent of change. I have always known my presence causes more harm than good, yet I returned to Alfheim and got myself involved. You all would have been better off without me. I was useless. There was nothing I could do."

Krish wondered if Leif's statement was supposed to be an apology or if it was intended to elicit pity. Was Leif offering himself to the others as an excuse to explain why they were experiencing failure on such a grand scale? Krish decided against all of those options. He was fairly certain Leif thought everything that occurred here, as well in Lillerem, was a result of Leif's involvement.

"I don't think I've ever met a more selfish and self-centered person in my life," Krish said to Leif. "You seem to think that all of this is a direct result of you having done something other than get drunk and mind your own business. While it is true that involving yourself earlier, or not involving yourself at all would have changed the plot, this story would have played out with or without your participation. The world does not revolve around you. You are not the singular reason for anything happening or not happening. I suppose I should be happy you haven't reached the point of saying that you were unable to stop any of this because Joral was in the way. Maybe you would prefer to blame Gunnar and me for having been in Alfheim? I suppose you worked past blaming others quickly and moved straight to blaming yourself. Did you even wait until the bodies were buried before opening the bottle?"

A small laugh escaped Leif's lips. "I started the first bottle while we dug the graves."

"You are impossible and have completely missed the point. Joral sits there, broken and alone. You didn't even like any of the people in the camp. You were happy to have an excuse to go drown yourself in booze instead of moving to action. You could have helped pull Joral from his own sorrow. You could have gone after Syndral. You could have come to Alfheim to find us. You could have done so many things, and you chose to pass out in your living room in a puddle of your own piss. You say you were useless, and I've heard others call you such, but it is far worse than that. Useless is not something you are; it is something you are choosing to be."

Krish stepped into the camp and went to sit beside Joral at the fire. He placed a hand on the elf's shoulder. Joral had been through more than any of them. The scar on his face was a daily reminder of Ulford's evil. Joral had never spoken about what he had done to earn the scar, but he had shared with Krish that he had been barely old enough to walk. It was very difficult to scar an elf. One needed to suffer a grievous injury to experience marks that did not fade, even over decades. While the rest of them knew Ulford only as a tyrannical king, Joral had spent his early years knowing the embodiment of evil as his father.

Sometime after bestowing his only legitimate son with the scar he would wear forever, Ulford had killed his own wife. There was a lot of speculation about how the murder had transpired, but Krish only knew for certain that Joral was sent to live with the slave children once his mother was dead. Unlike the adult slaves, Ulford did not keep the children shackled. He believed the children were of no threat and should they escape, they would certainly die in the forests surrounding Dredfall. The slave children were fed and clothed and even had opportunities to play together when chores were complete. Most enjoyed their lives, especially when compared to trying to live alone in a forest. Bane and Joral had not been normal slave children. They had decided to take the chance of attaining freedom. The two of them had experienced a harrowing adventure and saved each other's lives several times before arriving at Millspare in the back of a cart. When they stowed away with the cargo, they had not known the ride they took would be their salvation.

Krish sat beside Joral trying to imagine what it must be like for the male to have finally felt as if he had built something good; something that might help those who had selflessly raised him and work to destroy the evil king that was his father, and now be sitting among the evidence of its destruction. Krish could not fathom having been close to every soldier, and every descendant that was lost here. Joral had known many of their families. There had been children here. Krish did not even try to use words to console Joral. There were no words to expel any of the grief the male beside him was feeling. Krish just sat beside him quietly, with his head bowed.

Jess and Gunnar were walking the grounds slowly. It felt wrong to miss even a single, horrible sight. Jess felt as if missing any part of this atrocity would be disrespectful to those who had endured it and then perished because of it. Jess had not seen the hundespor when Kindra had glimpsed it as they left Leif's cabin. She was trying hard to reconcile the remnants of gore she was seeing here in the camp with the Irish Wolfhound breed she knew of. Jess understood a hundespor was not a dog, but it was the most similar thing she could picture in her mind.

"Gunnar, have you seen a hundespor?"

"Yes," he replied.

Jess stopped walking and waited for Gunnar to go on. Gunnar bent to pick up a sword from the ground. The blade was clean. Whoever had held the weapon had never had the chance to use it. Gunnar placed the sword on a nearby table. Jess understood that Gunnar did not intend to elaborate on his answer when he continued walking.

"I'd appreciate it if you'd tell me a little more about when you saw it," Jess prodded.

Gunnar turned to face her. He looked at Butch, standing on Jess's right, and then looked over at Cassidy, standing on Jess's left. He lowered his eyes to the ground, turned, and began to walk again. Jess couldn't believe he was just going to ignore her request. Hundespor were not dogs. *Why did Gunnar just look Butch and Cassidy over before deciding not to answer?* Gunner stopped at the table where he had left the sword with the clean blade. He turned back toward Jess and leaned on the table. There was resignation in his eyes when he finally spoke.

"Hundespor are not dogs, but so much about them seems similar. They have a humanoid form, though I don't know that I have ever seen it. I know it is hard to comprehend, but we only know that form exists because it must be so. How else would they be able to move among us and be seen so infrequently?"

As a math teacher, and math major in college, Jess could easily understand this logic. Imaginary numbers were not tangible. They did not exist somewhere on the number line, but we know of them and need them to exist when dealing with quadratics in some fields of physics. Jess nodded her head to show that she fully accepted the existence of the hundespor's humanoid form.

"As far as we know, hundespor attacks occur when in the form similar to a canine. Like wolves, or wild dogs, they prefer to hunt in packs. Many times, hunting parties will go off into the forest and never return. Sometimes parts of the hunters' bodies are recovered, and other times it is as if the people vanished; no trace left behind at all. Since hundespor are the only predators capable of shredding an entire party of hunters without leaving anyone alive to report on the cause of the carnage, all such occurrences are attributed to hundespor."

Jess interrupted Gunnar's explanation. "You don't seem as if you believe every attack is the work of the hundespor."

"I'm not sure. The first time Castle Millspare was attacked, after Kindra came to Alfheim, we fled into the forest. We were attacked in the middle of the night by humanoid creatures that smelled of rot and disappeared into mist when cut with a blade. None of us had ever seen them before and we suspected they might be from a different realm, similar to the hundespor. The woods outside Dredfall are notorious for unknown creatures. It is as if that area breeds their ilk. We accepted the mist monsters, deciding they had simply strayed from the forest of Dredfall, possibly following Ulford's soldiers. There could be a multitude of beings from other realms walking the earth. As rare as the hundespor are, they might be some of the better known monsters."

Jess's mind started making connections and she shared them as they formed. "Syndral was here under the pretense of telling Leif and Joral about the hundespor. She told them the sight of one reminded her that Skalanis had the power to bring the hundespor into Alfheim from another realm. What if those are not the only dark creatures he has pulled through? What if he is moving his new pets into the human realm?"

Jess looked into Gunnar's eyes and could see he had picked up on where her mind was traveling. His perpetually serious features seemed to become even more staid. It made him more beautiful. The lines on his face did not crease with concentration. His face was serene, and Jess knew he was lost in his thoughts. Gunnar shook his head and met Jess's eyes as he spoke.

"I fear the human realm may have yet to experience some of Dredfall's secrets. The number of discovered descendants has been dwindling, and those who were camped here are now gone. That can only mean that any remaining nightmares are coming after us. We're going to need to make some important decisions as soon as possible."

Jess felt her skin prickle. The awareness that her descent from King Andril made her a threat to Ulford was ever present, but Jess had convinced herself that she was low on that list. With the number of blood-heirs dwindling, it dawned on Jess that she was moving closer to becoming a primary target for Dredfall.

Though there was no immediate threat in the area, she mentally called Butch and Cassidy in closer. Jess drew comfort from the dogs' proximity as they closed ranks. She took one last look around the camp. She saw Krish, and the hunched form of Joral still sitting by the fire, and then turned and started back toward the cabin. Without food and rest, Jess was ill prepared for making logical decisions.

Gunnar watched Jess walk off toward the cabin. There must be a way to find the hundespor. He approached the fire pit and sat down next to Joral.

"I know you're hurting, cousin. It won't change what happened here, but going after those things might provide a distraction from the pain you currently feel. You're an excellent tracker and the hundespor pack may still be in the area."

Joral only nodded. Krish, liking Gunnar's idea, took up the call to action.

"You're our best tracker, Joral. I'll head out there with you. Right now. Let's get after those beasts."

Joral pushed himself from the rock he was using as a bench. His eyes roamed over the destruction throughout the camp. His gaze settled on an area at the edge of the clearing where the foliage was thoroughly trampled. Without a word, Joral started walking.

"I'll be here," Gunnar said to Krish. Watch your back. Don't engage them unless you are sure you can take them out."

Krish nodded and stalked off after Joral. He met Joral's pace as they entered the woods. There was no need for Joral's skill with tracking. The hundespor left a wide swath of trampled undergrowth to follow.

Joral pulled the pistol Leif had procured for him from the holster on his belt. Krish sighed. He hadn't been comfortable with the sleek black weapon Leif had provided for him. He had never used one and felt much more comfortable carrying his sword, even though he couldn't walk around freely with it outside of Leif's property. Krish drew the sword and held it before him as he followed Joral.

A tree branch creaked above the males. A hairy form fell from above and onto Joral. The beast's rear claws tore through the back of Joral's shirt, causing blood to bloom on the material along the ragged edges.

Moving quickly, Krish ran his blade into the creature, just behind its left shoulder. Krish's blow was a perfect strike to the heart. The beast appeared not to notice the puncture wound to its body.

Joral spun to face the hundespor. He brought the gun up and took aim at its head. Joral could not fire. Krish was still standing behind the creature and there was a risk a bullet would pass through the beast and hit Krish.

Now on all four legs, the hundespor swiped at Joral's legs and made contact. Joral's legs were pulled from beneath his body and he fell onto his side. The impact forced the pistol from his hand. Joral could only watch as the creature lunged for his face to finish him off.

Before the beast could strike, Krish yanked his blade from where it protruded from the hundespor's side. Krish stepped in with his left foot and arced his sword down from above his right shoulder at an angle. The blade sliced cleanly through the neck of the hundespor. Its head fell onto Joral's chest.

"Sword one, gun zero," said Krish as he reached out to help Joral off the ground.

"The trail continues on. The rest of them are still out there," said Joral, still winded. "I had been thinking of them like wolves, but wolves don't leave a scout behind after an attack."

"Let's keep going," said Krish. "By the way, aim for the head only. I don't think these beasts have a heart."

CHAPTER 18

The next morning, Jess woke and rolled over to find Cassidy's sad brown eyes gazing back at her. It didn't matter what the dog was actually feeling, his eyes always looked sorrowful. Cassidy stuck out his tongue and gave Jess a wet kiss. Jess sat up and checked her surroundings. She was in Leif's room, having slept at the cabin. Butch, lying on the floor beside the bed, lifted his head and waited to see if it was time to wake up. Jess swung her feet to the floor and Cassidy jumped off the bed. Butch hopped up, and Jess let the two dogs out of the room.

In the kitchen, Jess grabbed a mug of coffee from the pot sitting on the burner. She sat at the table, holding the mug. *What am I doing? This is ridiculous. There's nothing for me to do here.* Jess's leg bounced impatiently under the table. Jess was never comfortable with inaction. She jumped out of her seat and dumped the rest of her coffee in the sink. She walked out the front door, Butch and Cassidy following, and climbed into her SUV after giving the dogs access to the back seat. The engine roared to life when Jess turned the key, and she drove down the bumpy driveway to the road. Jess turned the vehicle left and did something she had not planned to do today. She went home.

The driveway was empty when Jess pulled up to the house. It was only 5am, so Sean must be working an overnight shift. If that were the case, then he would be home soon. Jess let the dogs out of the car and went inside. She filled the dogs' bowls and then stepped carefully into the bathroom. Jess was pleasantly surprised to find she did not stick to the floor. She stripped off her clothes and took a fast shower. Toweling her hair with one hand and scooping her filthy clothes off the bathroom floor with the other, Jess went to the bedroom she shared with Sean. She tossed her old clothes in the hamper and plucked a plain dress out of the closet. There was an overwhelming sense of ineptitude as she pulled the dress over her head and wondered what the wardrobe back at Millspare would think of her choice. Jess grabbed a pair of black pumps and wiggled them onto her feet.

Standing before the full-length mirror, Jess inhaled deeply. She ran her fingers through her damp, blonde curls and grabbed a hair clip off the dresser to pull some of it back from her face. This was as good as it was going to get. Jess made sure the doggie door to the backyard was unlocked and gave each dog a scratch on the head. The dogs' emotions flowed to Jess. They understood they were staying behind and they were not happy about it. Jess sent them calming thoughts and told them to be good while she was gone. Butch and Cassidy watched Jess walk through the front door as she started the second activity she had not planned to do today. She was going to school.

Jess strode through the front door of the brick building about a half hour before any sane teacher would show up to school. She stopped in the main office and checked her mailbox, found it was empty, and smiled. Whoever had been taking care of her class had collected her mail. It was likely stacked in a neat pile on the corner of her desk. The training Jess now executed daily made the stairs to the third floor less of a challenge than Jess remembered. She had an extra spring in her step as she made her way to the end of the hall and unlocked her classroom.

The student desks were in disarray. They were not in rows, groups, or any other discernible pattern. It looked as if the students had simply dragged them wherever they desired during period nine on Friday and left them that way. Jess made quick work of putting the unruly desks into six groups of four and then fired up her desktop computer. Clicking the icon for her school email, Jess held her breath. When the application opened, 438 new e-mail messages were waiting. Jess hung her head in defeat. Keeping up with school emails was a challenge even when a teacher wasn't absent. Jess had missed several weeks of class. Checking the box used to select all messages, Jess closed her eyes and pressed down on the left mouse button. She opened her eyes and clicked once more when a dialog box asked her if she was sure. Just like that, Jess accomplished something else she had not planned to do today or any day in her life. She deleted every email in her inbox. *If it's that important, there will be another email, or someone will actually come and speak to me face-to-face.*

Jess clicked the button to compose a new message and sent an email to all staff to announce that she had returned and asked everyone to cut her some slack while she acclimated to school life again. She knew she would get no such reprieve, but it couldn't hurt to remind everyone that she had been gone for a while and would likely not be at the top of her game. Jess dug through the neat piles on her desk to get some idea what the substitute had been doing with her students. There was an answer key for a worksheet on applications of Pythagorean Theorem and one for finding the surface area of pyramids. The smile that broke out on Jess's face made her eyes crinkle to the point where she almost couldn't see. It was the last three weeks of the school year and her substitute had kept both levels of math students exactly on schedule. Math teachers, such as Jess, were sticklers for adhering to the class scope and sequence to ensure the entire curriculum was covered each year.

Swinging her focus back to her computer, Jess went into her files and pulled up her lesson for surface area of composite figures. She made a few changes and added today's date to the title page before letting out an uncomfortable laugh. In twenty minutes, twenty-three middle school students would enter the classroom for homeroom. If Jess missed fifteen minutes of class, her students would pepper her with questions about where she had been and why she was not in the room on time. In this instance, Jess had missed weeks of school. Legally, Jess could ignore any questions the students asked, but this was not her first year. The kids might look as if they were watching the lesson and hanging on each of Mrs. Bennett's words, but they would be learning nothing. Every one of those students would spend the entire class wondering where their math teacher had been and probably sneaking instant messages to other classmates on the subject each time Jess turned her back. She sat back in her chair and sighed. It looked as if Mrs. Bennett would be skipping the math lessons today and holding a question-and-answer session instead.

Jess took the two answer keys off her desk and went to the copy room. She scanned the documents to her email and spun to leave the closet-sized room. She collided with Mr. Brownlee, the head of the science department and the president of the teachers' union. He stared at her for a moment, trying to reconcile her presence in the hallway with his incorrect assumption that Jess would not be returning this year. Jess could see the questions blossoming in the eyes behind his thick glasses. Jess smiled at the science teacher and waited. She knew he would never ask where she had been.

"Wow! Welcome back, Jess. You are back, right? Not just visiting?"

"I am back," Jess kept smiling as she spoke. "It made good sense to get back as soon as I could and finish out the school year."

"Well, I'm glad I ran into you this morning. The kids will be buzzing with the news of your return. I still have some time to adjust my plans to account for the diminished attention spans your return will cause in class today."

The average person would think Mr. Brownlee's comment was negative, but Jess knew better. She had just been reminded that the students liked her enough to set aside their tendencies to be self-absorbed and make her return the focus for today. Mrs. Bennett's return would be the social media hashtag for the day. Jess was also wise enough to understand that Mr. Brownlee had just laid out a choice for Jess. He had reminded her that she had a choice between writing her own narrative, offering an explanation for her disappearance to the science teacher now, or letting the kids pass the information around until Mr. Brownlee inevitably heard the story from them. The corner of Jess's mouth turned up. Today was full of firsts. Normally, Jess would head off the gossip, but since returning from Alfheim, she had been a different version of herself.

"Yeah, sorry about that. It wasn't until this morning that I was sure I'd be coming back this week. I knew I was gone too long when I started writing lesson plans and thinking I would actually get a chance to talk about math today."

Mr. Brownlee waited a moment to see if Jess would go on. When she offered no insight regarding where she had been, Mr. Brownlee wished her luck again and entered the copy room to run off his worksheets for the day. Jess smiled the entire way back to her room, and the whole time she uploaded the answer keys to her class website. An idea was forming in her mind, and if it played out as she expected, it would be a source of amusement for Jess and her students. She created a single slide for the day's lesson, telling students to first check the answers to the homework on the class website, and then use the slips of paper found on their desks to write down any questions they had for Mrs. Bennett. Jess stacked some printer paper and used the paper cutter to create rectangles about the size of an index card. She left three of the papers on each student's desk.

At eight o'clock, the students started to trickle into the classroom. Some kids spun on their heels and dashed back into the hallway to tell friends that Mrs. Bennett was back. In true middle school fashion, most of Jess's students approached her immediately and asked her, point blank, where she had been, why she had come back, and if they would need their chromebooks today, all in one breath. To the chagrin of those students, Jess did what any seasoned teacher would do; she said nothing and simply pointed at the directions on the board at the front of the room.

After taking attendance and reminding multiple students that the questions must be written on paper if they were to be answered, Jess walked around the room and collected the paper slips. She dragged a stool to the front of the room and sat down. Even when middle-school students were quiet, they were not silent. There was always a pen tapping on a desk or a metal water bottle falling to the floor. Jess's classroom was a tomb as her students waited for the first question. She looked down at the first slip of paper and read the question out loud.

"Where were you?"

Jess looked up from the paper and moved her gaze around her noiseless classroom. As she would when teaching, she made eye contact with many of the students as she did so. Jess smiled, and then answered with the truth.

"I had to go to a different realm to share important information with my friend. Unfortunately, I was stuck there once I arrived."

Students furiously scribbled on the small sheets of paper remaining on their desks. Jess could only imagine how many new questions she had inspired in her students with the answer to the first query. She decided to save her students a few scraps of paper.

"Before you ask, yes, I am completely serious. On to the next question. Someone in here wants to know if I am back for good. Yes, I am back for good. The next question is asking if we are doing math today. Not today, but certainly tomorrow, and for the next two weeks."

Jess answered each unique question in the pile, throwing the doubles into the recycling bin as she went. She then walked around the room and collected the new sheets of paper with questions her students had come up with while Jess answered the first round of inquiries. She, once again, took her place at the front of the room. *I wonder if I could use this method to generate the same kind of inquisitiveness during a math lesson. Unlikely.* Jess began answering questions again.

"The name of the realm is Alfheim. There were magical creatures there. I did not see any dragons. No, I have not taken up drinking, and I'm sorry to hear it had that effect on your grandfather."

The question-and-answer session continued until the bell rang. Unlike the end of a math lesson, the students did not view the bell as an opportunity to sprint out into the hall. Many of the kids stayed behind, attempting to weasel the answers to new questions from Jess. She shook her head apologetically, saying she was sorry that the period had ended, and suggested the students speak with friends. Maybe they would be able to get different questions answered in later periods throughout the day.

After four similar class periods, where the questions gradually became more specific, and the answers grew seemingly more spectacular, Jess grabbed her bag to leave the building and pick up lunch. This time she collided with Zelda Pinkerton. Mrs. Pinkerton was the English and Language Arts teacher. The woman had been at the school for over thirty years, and Jess was pretty sure she should have retired. The students had a difficult time relating to her and saw her as more of a grandmother figure than their teacher. Zelda, still the right side of sixty, was spry but very out of touch with current trends in technology and fashion. It was likely Mrs. Pinkerton still had a lot to offer with regard to her subject area, but the students had difficulty taking her seriously.

"Hey Jess, I wanted to pop by and welcome you back. The students are in a tizzy over the fantastical stories you've been spinning about your adventures in Elf Home!"

"Alfheim," Jess corrected.

"Considering we were unable to make much progress with our class discussion about our current book, I had the students fill me in on the details they have collected so far about your journey. I don't think I've ever seen eighth-graders so excited to discuss plot and scene in my life. You should consider turning your adventure story into a novel. I must say, this is certainly not something I expected from you, though."

Jess narrowed her eyes at the older woman. "What do you mean by not expecting this from me?"

"Well, you're the math teacher! It's your job to fill their heads with facts and formulas. I am surprised, in a good way, to see so much interest and intrigue spilling from your classroom."

"I was unaware you were so concerned about the lack of interest in mathematics," Jess said as she tried not to roll her eyes. "It has been a pleasant change and I'm enjoying myself."

"Just don't enjoy yourself too much, Jessica! Some of our students actually believe the story you are telling. We don't want them getting too carried away with this. There are still two more weeks of classes before the final exams and we don't want pandemonium on our hands."

"I'll keep that in mind."

Jess turned and walked away from Zelda. Her conversation with the older woman was causing the same feeling the kids must get from conversations with Jess. It was as if she had just been politely reprimanded by her mother. Jess used her phone to place an order at the local deli as she left the school building. She climbed into her RAV4 and pulled out of the parking lot, still thinking about her grandmother. Her mother's mother had been the only grandmother to live long enough for Jess to remember. She and Kindra spent many days after school playing at Jess's grandmother's house. There had been a birdbath in the front yard, surrounded by a garden of lilies that she and Kindra had used as their home when they played house as little girls. *Speaking of Kindra, she must have cooled off by now. Why haven't I heard from her?*

Jess pulled into the parking lot of the deli and ran in to grab her sandwich. She came back to the car and dialed Kindra's number. It rang several times before Kindra's cheery voice message indicated that she would not be answering the phone. Jess disconnected the call. She unwrapped her sandwich and took a bite. After considering that she had not, yet, experienced a catastrophe caused by the string of first time acts committed today, Jess perpetrated another first. She sent Kindra a text message describing some details about telling the students the truth about why she was absent from school. After hitting send, Jess finished her sandwich. Ten minutes later, Kindra had still not replied. Jess had not realized how upset her friend must have been after seeing Leif in his drunken bastard form. She had not expected Kindra to be able to resist replying in the search for more information about the students' reactions.

When Jess returned to school, the students stared at her as she walked down the hall. Truthfully, many of her colleagues were staring, too. While the students' gawks were quizzical and full of awe, her colleagues were doing something similar to glaring, at Jess. *I'm going to guess they are none too pleased with the derailing of their plans for the day.* Jess continued down the hall to her classroom. Study hall started five minutes later, and it proved to be the most challenging period of the day. The students kept slipping pieces of paper with questions for her onto her desk. Since study hall is a silent period, Jess was writing the answers to the questions on the backs of the papers and returning them. This resulted in Jess writing the same comments over and over because the students were unaware of which questions were already asked. It was a lot like grading tests, actually. Multiple students usually made the same mistake and in some cases, Jess had to fight the urge to write "ask Johnny" as the comment when she took off a point, since she had just written a long explanation about the same error on Johnny's test.

Eventually, the day ended. The bell rang at the end of ninth period and the students filed out. One student stayed seated. The girl remaining at her desk was named Riva, and Jess found her irritating at times. Though thirteen years old, Riva often had small stuffed animals on her desk and was prone to crying when she did not understand something in class. These were behaviors Jess associated with younger students and Jess had to bite her tongue to keep from sharing this with Riva… often. Outwardly, Jess had been patient with the little girl all year, but this was June and Jess was less than twenty-four hours out from witnessing the remains of a slaughter back at Leif's cabin. Putting on a happy face, Jess took the seat across from Riva and gently informed the girl that the day was over and no more questions about her whereabouts would be answered.

The small girl's eyes started to fill with tears, and Jess almost stood up and ran out of the room. That was exactly the kind of reaction that Jess did not need from this tiny little eighth-grader. As if sensing the effect she was having on Jess, Riva took a shaky breath and calmed herself. She reached into her school bag and left her hand sitting inside. The girl was definitely petting one of those stuffed animals just out of sight.

"Um, so, Mrs. Bennett, I um... I think I am an elf," the girl said in a soft voice.

Jess was not surprised by Riva's words. What did surprise her was that more students had not come to the same conclusion. Maybe more had, but had not shared their thoughts. Riva was just immature enough to not understand that there were things one did not share aloud, and especially not with the math teacher. Jess struggled to rein in her desire to tell Riva she was not an elf and to go home to her family.

"What makes you think you are an elf?"

Riva got up from her seat and went to the door of the classroom. She closed the door and locked it. The little girl just stood there, tears building in her eyes again. Jess was starting to get a little concerned. She was contemplating calling Riva's parents when she realized she had broken out in a sweat. The room seemed to be getting warmer. The air was thicker. The sudden humidity was oppressive. Jess got up and went to the heat register. Putting her hand over the vent, she felt no warm air coming from it. She turned back to Riva to ask if she felt like the room was warm and found water soaking her shirt. It was raining in her classroom! Jess dove to cover her computer.

"Turn it off, Riva! Riva! Turn it off!"

The rain stopped. The room cooled. Jess grabbed the front of her dress and squeezed the material. Water trickled to the floor. With all Jess had seen and learned to accept, this had her reeling. Riva and Jess locked gazes. Jess went to the girl and pulled her in for a hug. Jess added this to the list of things she had never planned to do today and acknowledged the hug was more to calm her own nerves than Riva's. The girl seemed calm at the moment.

"Does anyone else know you can do this, Riva?" asked Jess.

The girl shook her head in the negative. Jess walked Riva back to her seat. Riva sat and Jess went to her computer. She looked Riva up in the school's information system and found her address. She grabbed her purse from her desk drawer and turned back to the girl.

"We'll make a stop at your locker, and then I'm going to drive you home. I think I should have a talk with your parents."

CHAPTER 19

"Riva, throw your bag in the back and jump into the front seat."
Jess opened her own door and climbed into the driver's seat. She watched Riva in the rear-view mirror. The girl was a statue behind Jess's car. Jess gave the horn a little tap, and something furry flinched in the passenger side mirror. Jess checked the rearview again and saw Riva was pointing at the passenger side of her car and backing up toward the school building she and Jess had just exited.

Jess was not entirely sure what was happening, but something was not normal. She turned the ignition and she saw that thing startle in her passenger mirror again. Jess threw the car in reverse and backed out of the spot, cutting the wheel so the passenger side door was parallel to Riva. Riva pulled the door handle and jumped into the car, placing her backpack on her lap.

Jess was not watching the girl. When she had pulled the car out of the spot, she had revealed the hundespor that had been waiting between the SUV and another car. It stood in the spot now, ten feet from where Jess sat behind the wheel. Saliva dripped from its maw, its ears twitched, and it saw low on its back legs as if it were about to...

The hundespor lept for the SUV, landing on the hood right in front of Riva. It stared the little girl down, running its tongue over the front of its nose and muzzle in one swipe.

Jess pressed the accelerator and the car sped down down the parking lot aisle. At the end of the row, Jess slammed on the brakes. The beast slid from the hood of the car. Jess didn't even watch it roll to the pavement. She already had the car in reverse. At the other end of the row, she swung the car toward the exit for the lot and into the street without even checking for oncoming traffic.

"Look out!" Riva screamed.

The hundespor was running from the lot. It was trying to intercept Jess's car as she passed the lot. Jess pressed harder on the accelerator and sped by the mangy-looking thing before it made it to the road. Stealing glances in the mirror, Jess saw the hundespor pursued them, but the RAV4 was putting distance between her and the beast.

Relaxing only a little, Jess looked over at Riva. The girl's eyes were wide as she sat staring at the passenger mirror, watching the hundespor shrink in the distance. Jess did not bother stopping at the next corner, but watched for any oncoming traffic as she turned right. With their pursuer out of sight, Jess turned left at the next intersection. She was no longer driving at top speed, but she was still moving the car above the posted speed limit at she drove her car up the ramp to merge onto the highway.

"I've seen those things before," Riva said softly. "I'm pretty sure they have been following me. They never attacked though."

"Well," said Jess. "I guess they no longer have a reason to hold back."

<hr/>

When Jess pulled up to Leif's cabin with Riva in the back seat, Gunnar was waiting in the driveway. Jess had called ahead to say she had gotten permission from Riva's parents to bring her to Alfheim. Leif had argued that she should leave the little girl with the parents. He was sure they would call the authorities as soon as Jess drove off. Not only would Jess lose her job, she would likely be brought up on charges of kidnapping. For years, Leif had ferried children with Elven blood to Alfheim, but he insisted they be at least eighteen. The child needed to be of an age where the parents could not interfere. He had colorfully explained all of this to Jess over the phone. Insisting Riva's circumstance was different, Jess promised further details when she and Riva got to the cabin.

Riva sat frozen in the passenger seat, stroking the head of a stuffed dog. Jess wondered if it would have been wise to pick up her own dogs before speeding off to the cabin from Riva's home.

Watching the girl stroke Cassidy's head would be much less unsettling than watching a young teen rub the head of a stuffed animal. This had been a stressful day for Riva. First, she and Jess were attacked by a hundespor while leaving the school, then Riva had needed to leave the only parents she had ever known. Jess decided she'd let the little girl pet her stuffed animal if it comforted her.

Gunnar beckoned the arrivals inside, but Jess shook her head. She climbed from the car and waited near the hood for Riva to gain the courage to take an adventurous step from the vehicle. She eyed the claw marks on her hood as she walked by it.

Intent on speeding up the process, Gunnar took several purposeful steps toward the vehicle. Jess held up her hand. The last thing she wanted was for Gunnar to storm over to the car and wrench the shy girl from her seat. She needed Riva to trust Gunnar. Gunnar slowed his pace and stopped his approach entirely when he reached Jess.

"What happened to your hood?" Gunnar asked.

"We ran into a little trouble with a hundespor. We lost it, but it proves we are being targeted. Riva said she felt like they had been stalking her. It doesn't appear they are concerned with staying hidden any longer."

He and Jess waited in silence for several more minutes, pretending not to be full of impatience. Riva unbuckled her belt and let it slide off to her right. She tucked the stuffed dog into her backpack and pulled on the door handle. She sat that way, with the car door only opened a crack for a few moments. Jess held her breath and placed a hand on Gunnar's forearm to prevent him from moving.

In one motion, Riva pushed open the door and propelled herself from the car. She slammed the door behind her and stood with her back pressed against it, staring off into the woods. Gunnar's gaze bounced from the back of the girl's head to Jess's face and back to Riva's frozen form. Jess willed Gunnar to be patient. Though it seemed it might take most of the evening to coax the girl away from the car, Jess knew Riva would hop back in and lock the doors if Gunnar approached her before she was ready. Jess and Gunnar watched as Riva slowly spun to face them. It was as if the girl's body was attached to the car with a powerful magnet and it took a momentous amount of effort for her to turn. Her body remained in contact with the car door the entire time.

"Joral and Krish are tracking the beasts. Leif caught up to them last night just after one attacked Joral and Krish in the woods. It was as if the pack left one behind to spy on us."

"That is rather unsettling," replied Jess. "It had to be watching us when we were walking around the remains of the camp."

After staring at Jess and Gunnar through the passenger and driver windows from the other side of the car for several seconds, Riva started inching her way toward the hood. Riva dragged her body along the car as if it were a lifeline she could not release. Jess wanted to scream at the girl not to scratch the paint, but what did that matter at this point. The hood looked like a huge cat had used it for a scratching post. At the front of the car, Riva stopped to open her bag and pulled out the stuffed dog. She hugged it to herself and pushed away from the side of the car.

Kindra would have a field day with the psychoanalysis of this girl!

With the dog squashed to her body, Riva moved to stand before Jess and Gunnar. Jess wished Gunnar was one of her dogs, as she silently sent useless messages to Gunnar, begging him not to move or speak. Gunnar deserved more credit. He was still. Jess thought he might even be trying not to scowl.

"Riva, I'd like you to meet my friend Gunnar. Don't let his appearance scare you. He won't hurt you, and he loves dogs as much as you do." Jess gestured to the stuffed animal as she spoke.

Riva plucked one of her small hands from the plush dog and gave Gunnar a little wave. Jess had to hold in a laugh as she watched Gunnar awkwardly lift his hand from the hilt of his sword and give the same wave back with his much larger hand. Jess couldn't help making the parallel between Riva's stuffed dog and Gunnar's sword. Kindra was rubbing off on Jess; she knew a security blanket when she saw one.

"Riva, would you be able to show Gunnar what you showed me in the classroom?"

The tiny thirteen-year-old nodded once. Her dark curls fell in front of her face, obscuring her bottomless brown eyes; soulful, like a dog's. It took a moment before Jess felt it, but her skin grew bumps and her hair stood up. Instead of growing hotter, this time Jess felt as if the surrounding air temperature had dropped drastically. It was June and Jess's dress had no sleeves. Her toes were growing numb; exposed by her open-toed sandals. A snowflake fell slowly and landed on Jess's nose. The heat from her body melted it as Jess marveled at the mysterious June flake. All intrigue fled from Jess as more flakes fell and Jess found herself standing in a sundress and sandals in the midst of a blizzard.

"Thank you, Riva. That will do it!" Jess half commanded and half begged.

A slow smile appeared on Riva's face. Jess turned to follow the girl's gaze and let out a chuckle. Gunnar had an icicle hanging from the tip of his nose. It was melting quickly as the air returned to June temperature and Gunnar was watching it with crossed eyes. The warrior looked absolutely ridiculous. Jess could not have wished for a better icebreaker. Riva's entire body relaxed when Gunnar, realizing he had an audience, swiped the remainder of the ice from his face and returned to looking resilient and expressionless.

Gunnar spoke to Jess without taking his eyes from Riva. "I think you've found something more than a descendant, Jess. In this realm, I am not able to scent it, but I suspect Riva is an elf."

"I know," said Jess. "Riva thought so too. I went to her parents' home to try to figure out her lineage. I thought she must be a descendant of Pakk or Leif to have such strength in magic."

"Let me guess," said Gunnar. "Riva's parents adopted her?"

Jess nodded. "Not only did they adopt her, but they have met Riva's biological mother. It seems the mother suffered from mental illness and she believed she was from a place called Lindel, located in a different realm. Riva's parents were barely twenty when they took Riva in as an infant. The couple is now in their sixties, and this is only one of many places the family of three has lived over the last forty years. At this point, Riva should be married and have a family of her own, but..."

Jess gestured to Riva. The girl stood quietly, listening to Jess tell her story. Gunnar's face softened. He squatted down in front of the girl, the sword at his side clanging when it hit the gravel of the driveway. Gunnar looked up into Riva's turned-down face and spoke to her through his eyes. Jess could see understanding radiating through the warrior's features. He understood exactly what this young female was experiencing. Riva was not a human carrying Elven blood. She was an Elven child, hidden in the human realm, exactly like Gunnar and Leif had been, so long ago.

Gunnar turned his head to look at Jess. "I assume it would be safe to venture inside at this point? Has the potential for weather disruptions passed?"

"Indeed," said Jess. "I thought Riva might enjoy hearing some stories about you and Leif growing up in Norway."

"I can understand why you would feel that way, and I agree." Gunnar turned back to Riva. "I expect you and I have more in common than you could ever imagine."

Inside, Jess set Riva up on the couch with a glass of water and some chocolate chip cookies. The cookies had likely been hidden in the pantry by Kindra, but Jess didn't think her friend would mind sharing under the circumstances. Jess paused on her way back to the kitchen to grab a napkin for Riva. *Where the hell is Kindra, anyway?* It was now twenty-four hours since she had last spoken to the woman. Jess returned to the living room and placed several napkins on the coffee table next to the cookies. Though she didn't think Leif would care about water rings staining the wood, she placed a napkin under Riva's glass and slipped back into the kitchen to call Kindra.

Again, there was no answer, but this time Kindra's phone had sent Jess directly to voicemail. Kindra had turned the phone off, was in a dead-zone, or the phone battery had died. It was unlikely the phone was dead. Kindra was rarely disconnected from the Internet. Jess poked her head back into the living room where Riva and Gunnar were silently sharing cookies.

"Have you heard from Kindra, Gunnar?"

The male shook his head. "I figured she was pissed off..." Gunnar looked over at Riva. "I figured she was annoyed with Leif and went home. Send her a text and tell her she should come back here. She's going to want to meet Riva."

"I texted her earlier and got no reply. I think I'll swing by her house on my way home. Maybe she grabbed one of the cars out of the driveway last night without us noticing."

Jess stepped outside onto Leif's wooden porch. Every time she stood here, she had visions of Leif tottering around in a stupor. Jess feared she would never rid herself of the vivid first impression Leif had left with her. Jess scanned the area outside Leif's cabin that had served as a parking lot for all the descendants recently lost in the attack on the encampment. The little blue Subaru Jess had borrowed, and then asked Kindra to drive back to the cabin, was sitting where

Kindra had parked it. Jess had never done an inventory of all the cars that had collected in Leif's driveway, so she had no way of knowing if Kindra had borrowed one. Instead, Jess was left guessing about Kindra's mode of transportation. She went to her own vehicle and left for Kindra's house.

Jess steered her car into Kindra's driveway a half-hour later. Kindra's Honda

Civic was parked to Jess's left, but that would be meaningless if Kindra had borrowed a car from Leif's cabin. Doubting she would find her friend at home, Jess went to the front door, knocked and turned the handle to enter. It was locked. Jess used her own key to enter the house. A locked front door meant Kindra wasn't here. She flipped on a few lights and did a quick circuit of the home. Nothing seemed out of place. There was a stack of dirty dishes in the sink and laundry coating the bedroom floor, but this was not unusual. The dishes had likely been there for days, or maybe weeks, but they were Kindra's dishes. This meant the length of time the dishes spent in the sink did not correlate to the length of time Kindra may have been absent from the house. *Well, this was a completely useless trip.* Jess locked the door behind her and went back to her car.

Jess pulled her phone from her bag and dialed. She held the phone as far from her body as possible while she listened to the loud belch and the rest of Leif's repulsive voice recording. Once the message had safely concluded, Jess moved the phone closer to her mouth's proximity. She recorded a message stating that she had not heard from Kindra and was concerned. She explained that she was currently in Kindra's driveway and Kindra's car was here, but Kindra was not. Jess disconnected the call without giving a sign-off of any kind. With no other ideas, Jess decided it was best to go home. It was getting late and there was school tomorrow.

Butterflies took over Jess's stomach when she pulled into her driveway. Sean's truck was parked in its spot and blue television light flickered through the front window. There was no avoiding this reintroduction. Jess would walk through the front door and be confronted by her husband. It had once been painful for Jess to be separated from Sean for even a short time. She missed him each time one of them was working and the other was home. At the start of their marriage, she and Sean had even run errands together, so they wouldn't need to be apart. As recently as a few months ago, Jess found herself watching the clock at school and counting the minutes until she could go home and tell Sean about her day. Since traveling to Alfheim, and her subsequent return, she had felt little more than loathing for Sean. *Isn't absence supposed to make the heart grow fonder or something like that? Where have I heard that? Was it mom quoting someone?* Regardless of who had said it, Jess was not feeling the fondness. She felt dread and her mind conjured images of her shoes sticking to the bathroom floor.

The curtains in the front window wiggled. Jess felt both warmth and protectiveness, pressing on her thoughts. She sent back warm feelings to the two canines on the far side of the curtains. Jess strode to the front door and fought the urge to fling it open and let the dogs run out to greet her, and then jump in the car and flee. She pulled on her "big girl" pants, opened the door, and then walked inside. She immediately dropped into a squat and permitted wet licks to cover her face as she stroked the fuzzy necks of Butch and Cassidy.

After the dogs' initial reaction to her homecoming faded, Jess permitted herself to look around the room. It was spotless. Sean sat on the couch with an arm thrown across the back and the other hand holding the television remote. He rose when Jess stood and Jess dropped her bag and gave Sean a hug. He held her for several minutes before Jess gave him a kiss on the cheek and pulled back.

"The place looks amazing! I can't describe to you how happy this makes me!"

"I can see that," replied Sean. "I wish it were the sight of me making you this happy, but I'll take it any way I can get it."

Jess felt a swell of love for Sean then. She supposed it never really went away. Her love for Sean had just been buried under mounds of responsibilities. With all Jess felt she needed to accomplish, there had been no room to feel anything. She had been in survival mode, simply pushing forward and ticking tasks off her list as she climbed the mountain that had become her life. Jess didn't hide her surprise as she went from room to room basking in the cleanliness. She stopped in the bathroom and made a point of taking off her shoes and sliding around a little on the clean tile. Going back to the living room, Sean was still standing. He had watched her with a smile on his face, enjoying Jess's happiness.

"Before you ask," Sean started. "The dogs have been fed and both of them have gone out. I saw you were home this morning to dress for work, so I figured I'd see you at some point this evening. I left a salad for you in the fridge if you're hungry."

Jess gave Sean another quick squeeze and then disappeared into the kitchen. She pulled the salad out of the fridge and doused it in ranch dressing. There were no forks in the drawer, so she opened the dishwasher. The dishes were clean, but the dishwasher had been loaded wrong. It took her a moment to find all she was looking for, but she pulled a drinking glass and a fork from the appliance. Jess bit her tongue as she filled her glass with water so she would not comment on how the dishwasher had been loaded incorrectly. There would likely be more discoveries of things done the wrong way, and it would be up to Jess to accept this and be grateful it was done at all.

When Jess seated herself on the couch next to Sean, she silently commanded Butch and Cassidy to seek attention from Sean instead of attempting to curl up with her. This allowed Jess to eat in peace, and it would boost Sean's ego a little. He was forever commenting about the dogs loving Jess more than they loved him. Butch acquiesced begrudgingly, but Cassidy was content to grab some pets and scratches wherever he could get them. Jess sent mental apologies to Butch and made a mental note to add a little broth to the top of his breakfast tomorrow as a thank you. Eternally vigilant, Butch was still reading Jess, and he licked his lips at the thought of the treat.

Scratching the dogs' ears, Sean asked, "So, Elven stuff, huh?"

"A man of so many words, as usual. Yes. Elven stuff. Would you like to see the latest?"

Sean nodded. Butch climbed off the couch and stood facing Sean from the other side of the coffee table. Cassidy propelled himself off of the sofa and hurdled into the kitchen. A moment later, he sprinted back into the room and launched over Butch's back, hit the floor, and tore up the hallway toward the bedroom. Cassidy walked back into the living room, raised to his hind legs, took a few steps, then dropped his front paws on Butch's back, turning his head to Jess and Sean as if he were waiting for applause. Butch stared back at Jess unhappily. He sent a vision of steak being sliced up on the counter, and Jess sent back a silent affirmation.

Sean slowly turned his head toward Jess. "There have been times where I have wondered if you were trying to get the dogs to hate me, but this is ridiculous. They'll do whatever you want? I guess I'll be more careful not to upset you or I'll never be safe in my own home again."

Jess planted a kiss on Sean's mouth and raised an eyebrow after pulling back. She made a show of scrutinizing her husband as if she were looking for reasons to send the dogs after him. She lowered her eyebrow and gave a quick nod to her dogs. The dogs curled up on their beds across the room. Once the dogs were settled, Sean settled as well. Jess filled Sean in on some of the things that had occurred since she returned from Alfheim. She carefully omitted the parts that might hint at how close Jess had come to deciding she should leave Sean. The problem was far from solved, but right now it felt as if Sean understood things needed to change and there was no need to beat him over the head with it.

CHAPTER 20

After school the following day, Jess was walking to her car when a text came in from Leif. She read the message and anger immediately boiled to the surface. Leif was well aware of Jess's policy on not conveying important information via text message. Plopping down into the driver's seat of the RAV4, it occurred to Jess that her policy was probably the motivation for Leif texting in the first place. There was a reason Leif's contact information was "Asshole" on Jess's phone, as well as Kindra's. Jess dialed Leif and did not give him the satisfaction of letting him know she had been rattled by the text.

Calmly, Jess said. "I got your text. Care to explain?"

"Did it even occur to you who you had sitting in your period nine math class this entire year?"

"What? Riva? Why would it have occurred to me to think anything about her up until yesterday?"

"Exactly, Jess. Have you given any consideration, since yesterday, as to who young Riva actually is?"

"Of course I did! Gunnar and I agreed. All evidence points to her being a full-blooded elf, hidden here in the human realm by her parents."

"Think a little harder, princess of logical reasoning. I'll give you a moment."

Jess dove through everything she knew about Riva in her mind. She recalled the names of her adoptive parents, and the little girl's address. She pulled up information filed in her brain about the birth mother and adoptive parents having met. The birth mother was mentally ill. She insisted she was from Alfheim. Wait. No! The adoptive parents had never said the mother was from Alfheim. The older couple told Jess the birth mother was from Lindel. Jess had known Lindel to be a city in Alfheim and had held fast to the information she felt was pertinent at the time. Jess had only been concerned with the notion that Riva's mother was from the realm of Alfheim, she had not bothered to connect the name of the town with the only other person they already knew to be from Lindel. Riva was Syndral's daughter.

Leif's voice broke into Jess's thoughts. "I will assume your silence is an indicator that you have drawn the conclusion that I made immediately when I heard where Riva's mother came from. I can't believe you were just driving around with that girl in your car, and you brought her to my cabin, where Syndral and the hundespor could return at any time?"

"Oh my God. They'll be looking for her. Meet me at Gretchen's house. Bring Gunnar and Riva."

"We're already half-way there. We didn't know exactly where we could meet up with you, but we need to decide on a plan of action. We decided it would be best if we started heading in your direction."

Jess hung up and called Sean. He answered on the first ring.

"There's my baby girl! The dogs and I are here waiting for you. How was your day with the little heathens?"

"Sean, I love that you are asking about my day and I love even more that you have adopted Gretchen's pet name for the students, but there is something happening. Can you please feed the dogs?"

"I can certainly do that. Is there anything else I can do for you?"

Jess was pretty sure a little sarcasm was leaching its way into Sean's speech. She supposed she couldn't blame him. He was working really hard to be the perfect husband and now Jess was about to tell him something else was more important than he was…again. Jess had lost track of the number of times she had done something unlike herself over the past few days, but she added another to the list.

"Sean, you are my husband and I want to share my entire life with you. After you feed the dogs, it would mean the world to me if you would meet me at Gretchen's house. I could use your input on the latest problem that has come up."

"Of course! I'll be there as soon as Butch and Cassidy are taken care of."

Jess heard the happiness in Sean's voice and she knew she had done the right thing. She wasn't sure if Sean would truly have anything to offer when it came to things of the Elven nature, but all he really needed was to be included instead of overshadowed by the new things in Jess's life. She turned the ignition and guided the car out of the school parking lot. The wheels in her mind started spinning immediately.

By the time Jess pulled into Gretchen's driveway, she had come up with three general plans that might be practical. The first plan required confronting Syndral and demanding that she offer every bit of information she could in exchange for her daughter's safe return. The second plan would be to bring Riva to Millspare and have Mildred and Einar look after her. A third plan seemed to be the most radical. Sit in wait at Gretchen's house and use Riva as bait. They could wait to be found by Syndral, the hundespor, or one of Dredfall's assassins.

Sean pulled into the driveway as Jess unlocked the front door of Gretchen's house. Jess left the door standing open for Sean as she went around the house turning off lights and turning others on. Jess and Kindra did this each time one of them dropped by Gretchen's since the woman had left for Norway. At first it was Jess who dropped in, picked up any mail and performed the light routine. Once Jess was lost in Alfheim, and Kindra was aware that Gretchen would never return to her home, Kindra had taken up the task of caring for the house.

Sean came through the door, closing it behind him, and removed his shoes. Even Jess had not thought to take her shoes off as she entered the house. She savored the gesture of cleanliness for a moment as Sean wrapped her in a hug. He rubbed small circles in the small of Jess's back and it was soothing. The man might not have much to offer with regard to Elven crises, but he had always been extraordinarily good at making Jess feel like everything would turn out in the long run. She pulled back and gave him a kiss on his lips.

"Thanks for coming," said Jess.

Sean did not have time to reply to Jess before the sound of a car pulling up turned his attention to the front window. "There is a car here. Multiple occupants. Two adult males and a female child."

Jess smiled. Sean was in cop mode. Maybe she had been wrong. This might actually be a situation where Sean was very useful. After a nod from Jess, Sean opened the door. Butch and Cassidy were standing sentry on the porch. Sean waved the new arrivals inside.

Gunnar entered first, followed by an uncomfortable-looking Riva. Leif twisted in the door as he dodged a snap from Butch. Butch followed Leif to the couch, emitting a low growl until Leif was still. Cassidy came through the door last and rubbed up against Riva's side. Jess wasn't sure if the dog had felt the command through her or if he was using his own intuition to discern that the girl needed some comfort. Jess went into her old room, now a sunroom, complete with a loveseat and television. She called Riva over and handed her the television remote. Cassidy gave a little tug on Riva's shirt and she went and sat down. Cassidy hopped up next to her and made himself comfortable.

Returning to the living room, Jess took a seat with the men. She mentally coached Butch to back up a few inches so Leif felt more inclined to breathe. The male was an ass, but he was Kindra's father. She would likely be unhappy if Jess allowed Butch to eat him. She considered going to the kitchen to see if there was anything she could offer them all to drink, but reconsidered. This was not a social call. They were gathering to come up with a plan of action as quickly as possible. With luck, the plan would be in motion before any refreshments were required. Jess was about to share the framework for the three plans she was considering on her drive over when Sean beat her to it.

"First of all, hello. I know Leif, and based on the description Jess has given me, you must be Gunnar. Thank you for training my wife so she was able to come back to me. Yesterday, Jess told me one of her students was a young elf. I'm guessing that elf is currently watching television. Before we come up with a plan of action, I think it's important we all share any information others might not have."

Leif spoke up. "The only new information that you haven't reviewed already is that we are nearly certain that Riva is the daughter of Syndral. Syndral is..."

"...a former soldier of Dredfall. She claimed to be willing to support you in your battle against Ulford and the Dredfall assassins, but you've since been betrayed by her," Sean finished. "You don't need to explain. My wife has filled me in on all of the details except for those discovered today."

Jess had never seen her husband like this. He exuded confidence and was taking complete control of the situation. The most interesting part was that Leif and Gunnar had submitted to Sean's lead. Her husband had never seemed more attractive and Jess found herself shifting in her seat as she thought about it. Hopefully there would be time later this evening for Jess to further remind herself how attractive her husband could be.

Sean continued. "Assuming this Syndral person is likely to come looking for her daughter, the girl needs to be protected. I think it's obvious that she has no idea who she is. Her parents did the best they could to raise her, but they are aging and moving around constantly has likely become a burden. Jess's description of elves and the powers they can hold have opened this little girl's eyes to what she might be and she is undoubtedly scared. She was just removed from the only parents she has ever known and entrusted to strangers."

Jess cleared her throat.

"Well," Sean said, "A bunch of strangers and her math teacher and I'm not sure that makes things any better."

This time Jess shot Sean a glare and leaned over, giving him a good shove.

Sean continued. "The way I see it, you have two options. You can hide her somewhere here in the human realm, or you can take her to Millspare. Syndral will likely expect you to take her daughter to Millspare, but Riva will have protection there and Syndral will not be able to walk in and just take the girl back."

Gunnar quietly interrupted. "Let's not assume Syndral even knows the girl is in the area. It could be a coincidence. Syndral gave Riva up when Riva was a baby, and that was about forty years ago. The family has moved around a lot since then."

Leif replied, "If Syndral is anything like me, she knows exactly where Riva is. Since Syndral is Elven, and she is female, she would not have the opportunity to have anywhere near as many offspring as I do and I know where every child of mine is."

"Well, you do now," said Jess. "You lost track of Kindra for about the same number of years Riva has been alive."

"That was different!" Leif shot back. "Her mother forced me to stay away! I sincerely doubt Syndral's adoptive parents set the same rules. They legally adopted Riva so they would have no reason to think they would need to keep Syndral away. I'm willing to bet Syndral has been watching Riva from a distance since she gave the girl up."

Sean took control of the conversation again. "All bets aside, we don't know anything for sure. Riva having Jess as a math teacher may have been what clued in Syndral and the assassins to what you were all doing here with the descendants. It is also possible Syndral never knew Riva and Jess had daily contact for the majority of this year. Honestly, there is no way we will have enough information to be completely comfortable with our choice. We do need to make that decision though. What's it going to be? Pick a realm."

"I vote Alfheim," offered Jess.

"I do too," said Leif. "We've got enough shit going on here. We don't need a little girl to babysit on top of everything else."

"If she goes to Alfheim, I'm going with her," said Gunnar. "Millspare has fewer defenses than it usually does. Bane is currently the only prince in Alfheim, and he doesn't even reside at the castle full time. Now that the camp is...now that there is no camp, Joral will likely return to Millspare as well."

"It sounds as if it's decided," said Leif. "I'm not going back. I only returned to Alfheim to ensure Kindra's safety. Now that she is back in this realm, there is no need for me to be there."

The room grew silent. All eyes were on Leif. Jess's mouth hung open. Leif was sober, so it did not take him long to realize his mistake. He pushed out his lower jaw and nodded his head once in resignation.

"Ok. So I am not exactly sure if Kindra is currently safe because no one seems to know where she is. I'm pretty sure you get my point though and it's one more reason I need to stay. I'd like to know my own daughter is ok before I take care of someone else's."

Jess had to hold in a laugh. She was trying to imagine Leif taking care of anyone. She stood up to go check on Riva to cover the smile on her face. She stuck her head into the back room and Cassidy raised his head from the little girl's lap. She looked tired, but the anxiety seemed to have left her for now. Jess left her to her television show and went back to the living room.

Jess addressed the room. "Ok. Gunnar and Joral will take Riva to Millspare. Leif and I will stay here and try to figure out where Kindra is. Yesterday, I would have assured all of you she was fine and just needed some time to herself. At this point, she has been incommunicado for far too long. I am now concerned. Syndral has not shown herself in almost the same amount of time as Kindra has been missing. There must be a connection there."

Sean swung his head to Jess. "Why didn't you say Kindra was missing?"

"To be honest, I really wasn't thinking of her as missing until recently. We came back from Alfheim Sunday evening and Leif was so ossified that he had passed out in a puddle of his own urine right in the middle of the living room. Kindra was upset. I figured she needed a break and some time to herself. At this point though, it has been more time than she should have needed."

Sean put his hand on top of Jess's. "Listen, we'll find her. She probably stormed outside and ran right into Syndral. If Syndral has her, then at least we have some leverage."

"I don't think I like you referring to a little girl as leverage," said Jess.

Gunnar interceded. "I'm sure it won't come to that. Sean does have a point though. If Syndral is aware we have Riva, she will make sure no harm comes to Kindra."

Jess sat in silence while the males in the room started to work out the finer points of the plan to move Riva to Millspare. She was ruminating on Kindra's disappearance. It's not that she didn't care about Riva's safety. She did like the girl, despite her obsession with stuffed animals and propensity for crying. Jess was suddenly very concerned about Kindra's safety. Worse than her friend possibly being in danger, Jess was concerned that she might be to blame for anything that befell Kindra. Jess had not been needed to help out with Leif at the cabin. Krish and Gunnar had taken control of that situation. Jess had been busy watching "the Leif Show" when she should have chased after her friend to support her as soon as Jess discovered she wasn't right behind her. Jess had made the choice to let Kindra deal with the impact of Leif's dive into the bottle alone. Jess stood from her seat next to Sean.

"I have school in the morning. Let me know what you need me to do, once you work everything out."

The males barely acknowledged that Jess had spoken. They were completely engrossed in planning Riva's protection duty as she was transported to Millspare. Jess didn't mind. She really needed a break from all of this. Butch was at Jess's side immediately. Cassidy joined them by the time Jess reached the front door. Jess strode down the walk, Butch on her left and Cassidy on her right. She opened the door to the SUV, and the dogs hopped in. Jess could not wait to get home and go to sleep. Battling assassins was tiring, but returning to the classroom had Jess feeling completely exhausted.

CHAPTER 21

Following school the next day, Jess fought the urge to drop by Gretchen's and see how Gunnar and Riva were getting along. Sean had arrived home after midnight the previous night and interrupted Jess's sleep to tell her Riva would be skipping school and staying at Gretchen's with Gunnar. Jess suppressed her genuine curiosity in favor of something much more important. She really needed to talk to Krish.

Jess wound down the desolate country roads to the drive that led to Leif's cabin. She bumped her Toyota up the path and parked before the front porch. She jumped from the car and climbed the steps two at a time. After throwing open the front door, Jess found Joral sitting listlessly on the couch in the living room. The television was not on, there was no book in his hands, and he was just sitting there. This time, Jess permitted herself to be distracted from her primary focus. She sat down in the rocking chair and faced the forlorn male.

"Will you be returning to Millspare with Gunnar?" Jess asked.

"I will. There is no longer a need for me here," replied Joral flatly.

Jess waited for the elf to look at her before she spoke. "You know what happened to them is not your fault, right?"

Joral met her gaze. "I am no fool. I know I would likely be among the casualties if I were in the camp when it was attacked. It doesn't prevent me from mulling over the possibility that I could have been less distracted by Syndral. I could have been more aware of the changes in the surrounding air. I was less than a mile from it all when it happened. I heard nothing, and I smelled nothing."

"I'm sure you'll find a different reason to blame yourself after hearing this, but we did find information about the hundespor in the palace archive. It wasn't much, but what little we found provides details about why there are few witnesses to hundespor attacks. They are extremely secretive, and though they hunt and travel in packs, they have a way of cloaking their movements. It's almost as if they can enclose the entire group in a bubble to remain undetected."

"Syndral spoke of something similar to that."

Jess saw anger flash in Joral's eyes as the female's name left his lips. Jess was not the type of person to hug or even touch another person to comfort them, but she wondered if that was what she should be doing now. She lifted her hand and used it to pat Joral's thigh. As soon as she did it, she realized how ridiculous the action was. Maybe it would have been soothing if it had come from someone else, but Jess didn't know how to connect the action to feelings of comfort.

"I know you lost a lot here, Joral. You put a great deal of work into training those men and it must be devastating for it to have ended like this. Selfishly, I am glad you are no longer tied to this cabin though. I know you don't really know her, but I feel this little girl needs your protection. I trust you will do everything you can to keep her safe."

Joral was emotionless when he replied, "I will protect her with my life, as I would anyone. The girl really does not know who she is?"

"No," said Jess. "I truly believe she thought she was relatively normal. Rivka's parents moved her around so often she might not even be aware how slowly she aged!"

Joral stared at the far wall. He looked less miserable than he had earlier, but he was far from content. Jess, not knowing what else she could offer the male, stood. She walked through the kitchen and out through the back door. She followed the sound of an ax striking wood to the clearing where the camp had been. Krish looked up as Jess approached. He let the ax head drop to the ground and leaned on the handle. Jess strode up to the large male and gave the ax handle a kick. The ax swung out from under Krish's hands, causing him to stumble. Krish stared at Jess disbelievingly.

"Where's your fiancée?" Jess demanded. "I can only assume you know exactly where she is because you have not shown an iota of concern for her safety."

"Of course I'm concerned! You're speaking about my future wife; the future Queen of Lillerem!"

Jess noticed Krish had not said he was concerned for Kindra's safety because he loved her. His worry was that something had happened to the future queen. It might even be worse than Krish being concerned for his future ruler. Jess wondered if he was only concerned because his security as the future king was threatened. She didn't think Krish was that self-absorbed, but he was raised in a palace among power-hungry people. Some of that drive for power must have influenced Krish.

"I'm not sure why you are so angry with me," said Krish. "I'm not hiding her anywhere, and she hasn't even attempted to contact me. If you want to be upset with anyone, you should try directing that energy at Kindra. She's the one that seems to think she can just storm off every time she has an inner conflict. At first, I really felt for her. She was in a new world and had just discovered what an ass her father is. At this point, though, I don't have time for her games. I didn't chase after her at Millspare, and I have no intention of chasing her in the human realm. When she comes to terms with the reality of Leif's sparkling personality, she can come find me. She came to her senses in Aegroth, and I expect she will do the same here."

Jess's jaw was hanging open. She slowly shut it when she realized she was standing in the woods and any number of flying insects might find its way into her mouth. With her lips pressed together firmly, Jess bore into Krish's skull with her eyes. *Who does he think he is?* Jess answered her own question almost immediately. He is the Crown Prince of Lillerem and he has probably never needed to chase after anyone. Likely, everyone would be chasing after him. It didn't change the fact that Krish was unconcerned for Kindra's safety. It did point toward him not thinking there was any danger at all. If Krish felt Kindra was only pouting about her father being an unpredictable drunk, then Jess could understand why he would be undaunted. She still did not love the thought of her best friend marrying a man who couldn't sympathize with Kindra's feelings, though.

"I've known Kindra since we were only kids. I've seen her angry. At times, she has even been angry with me. She has never avoided speaking to me for days, in all those years I've known her. You might not be concerned, but I am. I think something happened to her. I came here to see if you would be interested in helping me find her, but it seems likely that you will think I am overreacting."

"Listen Jess, I suspect Kindra is fine. If we find something to specify otherwise, I'll be the first to mount up and go to her rescue."

Jess nodded her head and turned back toward the cabin. As she walked, she thought about all the indications there already were that Kindra might be in trouble. Her phone was off or dead. She told no one where she was going. It had been three days since anyone had heard from her. That might not be proof Kindra was in trouble, but it was more than enough to cause Jess to worry. There might be someone else who was worried as well.

Jess pulled up in front of Gretchen's house thirty minutes later. She jogged to the front door and let herself in. Gunnar jumped off the sofa, and a book fell to the floor. A sleepy-eyed Riva sat up, startled. Gunnar stooped to pick up the book and placed it on the table. Jess saw it was the book written by Ekkelle. Gunnar shifted on his feet uncomfortably.

"Were the two of you asleep on the couch?" Jess was laughing as she asked the question. "That might be one of the most adorable things ever!"

"Well, yes," Gunnar started. "Riva was bored, so I was telling her about the women in my mother's book. We needed to read through it anyway, and with everything that happened, the book was forgotten. It felt strange to just sit here reading in silence, so I started translating some of it for the girl."

"Those stories must be riveting! It's barely five o'clock and the two of you are out like lights," teased Jess.

Gunnar stiffened. "Actually, the stories about the women in the book are quite interesting. It has been a tough last few days though and-"

"You do not need to explain yourselves to me," said Jess. "You are certainly not the first people to fall asleep while reading. All joking aside, did you find anything useful in your mother's manuscript?"

"I'm not sure anything I read would be useful to us, but it is very interesting. It's shocking how little I know about the women in my family. Some of them accomplished incredible feats for and among the people of Lillerem. You would be surprised to learn many of the accomplishments attributed to King Blaith were actually a result of his sister's actions. It is as if they never existed and all credit for their deeds was ascribed to Blaith instead."

"I doubt I would be surprised," said Jess. It sounds a lot like Pythagoras to me. He organized an entire society of people who studied and discussed mathematics. All discoveries, by any member of the group, were attributed to him. To his credit, he did allow women to join his order, but we will never know if he actually discovered anything on his own. He has a famous theorem named after him, but it was discovered that the Egyptians used a similar method when working with right triangles, long before his time. Did I mention he decreed that beans were sacred? Anyway, regarding your mother's writings, I'm not surprised the accomplishments of females were credited to males at all."

Riva spoke for the first time. "Don't worry Uncle Gunnar. She always does this. One moment you think you are discussing a cute picture of a cat from the Internet and the next moment, Mrs. Bennett is telling you about some guy named Showdingler."

"Shrödinger," corrected Jess. "It was Shrödinger's cat."

"Yeah, that guy," said Riva. "Anyway, Mrs. Bennett likes to suck the fun out of everything and turn it into math. One time, I drew a caricature of her dogs for her based on a picture she keeps on her desk. She turned it into a lesson on proportions."

The corner of Gunnar's mouth turned up. "Mrs. Bennett does sound as if she can be very boring."

"Ok, you two, stop ganging up on me. I just swung by to see how you were holding up. I now see you are cut from a similar cloth and getting along swimmingly. Is there anything you need before I go home to my well-proportioned dogs whose faces show reflective symmetry? By the way, Riva, Butch can run about 60 miles in 3 hours. Can you imagine what his constant rate of speed would be?"

Riva covered her ears with her hands. "Ok! I give up! I can't take it anymore!"

Riva fell over onto the couch dramatically and covered her head with a pillow.

"Who knew math was such a powerful weapon?" mused Gunnar. "You killed her just by talking about it."

Jess was pretty sure she heard the girl giggle from under her pillow. She beckoned for Gunnar to follow her out of the girl's earshot. Jess turned to face Gunnar and let her eyes roam his face for signs of discomfort. There was some concern in his features, but he seemed more relaxed than she had ever seen him.

"Babysitting suits you," said Jess. "I noticed Riva called you Uncle Gunnar. As far as I knew, you banned Kindra from calling you that and you are her actual uncle."

Gunnar reddened slightly. "I wasn't sure what she should call me. She said it was impolite to call me by my first name and asked what my last name was. When I didn't have a succinct answer, she said she would just call me Mr. Smith. I decided I liked Uncle Gunnar better than a name that didn't belong to me at all. I thought it would raise far too many questions to suggest she call me Prince Gunnar, and I'm not a fan of that title anyhow."

Jess nodded. "Are you ready to go tomorrow?"

"Yes. Sean's shift ends at six tomorrow morning and he's going to come here to pick us up and bring us back to Leif's. We should be through the portal and in Alfheim before eight."

"Be careful, and good luck. I'd travel with you, but there are seven more days of classes left and I told the kids I'd be finishing out the year."

The pair stared at each other for a moment. Jess opened her arms and gave Gunnar a stiff hug. Jess did not think her level of comfort with touching people would ever change, but she was trying. It felt just as awkward as patting Joral's thigh and it did not help that Gunnar was not a hugger, either. They each took a step back and Jess decided she would not be attempting that form of goodbye with anyone other than Sean or Kindra anytime soon.

Exiting the house and returning to her car, Jess started thinking about her next tasks. She needed to go home and feed the dogs. After letting them out, she needed to sit down and put together a lesson on simplifying radicals for periods three and four and a chapter review for her other periods to review for the last test of the year. She pulled into her driveway, wondering if she should skip the lesson on radicals. It wasn't a requirement for this year's curriculum. Jess usually added the topic at the end of the unit on irrational numbers for her honors level classes. She just wasn't sure if this year's group could manage the work, especially after not having Mrs. Bennett in the classroom for several weeks.

Jess climbed from the vehicle and walked toward her front door. Something wasn't right. There was nothing unusual about Butch and Cassidy barking when Jess arrived home, but the sounds coming from the dogs were not the excited barking of a greeting. It was the kind of barking the dogs did to scare off evil people, such as postal workers and meter readers, where growls were interspersed with deep, throaty barks. Butch and Cassidy sounded as if they were about to come right through the front window and tear her throat out.

Quickening her pace and pulling her keys from her pocket as she went, Jess was about to mount the single step to the front door when she was tugged backward by the collar of her shirt. Jess landed on her back, her skirt hiked up to her waist. She stared up into a face she had not seen in almost a week. Syndral cocked an eyebrow at Jess.

"I was going to enter your house and wait for you on the couch, but I hadn't anticipated your guardians would be home." Syndral nodded her head toward the front window.

Jess closed her eyes and reached out to her dogs. Cassidy's thoughts were desperate. He was scratching and clawing at the window. Butch seethed with anger. He was backing up from the couch and preparing to launch himself through the glass. Jess took a deep breath. She calmly pictured the back door. She saw the doggie door in her mind. Butch froze. He turned and ran for the kitchen. Jess lost contact with Butch. Her connection to the dogs was not as strong in the human realm as it was in Alfheim. She could only hope Butch could figure it out on his own.

Syndral reached down and grabbed a handful of Jess's curls. She straddled Jess's legs and bent at the waist. Syndral pulled Jess's hair until her face was inches from hers. The rage in Syndral's eyes was explosive. Trying to reason with her would be fruitless. There was no way Syndral would hear a word Jess had to say, even if she could speak through the teeth she was clenching in pain. Syndral pulled her arm back and smashed her fist into Jess's cheek.

"Where is my daughter?" Syndral growled.

Jess did not get the chance to answer. Syndral jerked forward, her head crashing into Jess's shoulder. As Syndral fell, she threw out her hands to keep from smashing her face on the ground. In the process, she ripped a clump of hair from Jess's head. Jess closed her eyes against the sharp pain and rolled to her left. She looked up to see Butch crouched behind Syndral, waiting for her to move.

To Syndral's credit, she stayed on her stomach in the grass, frozen. Jess pushed herself up onto her knees and elbows. She looked over her shoulder at the front window and rolled her eyes at Cassidy. The German Shepherd Dog was standing on the back of the couch, looking out the window. He was quiet now and had his head tilted in confusion. Opening her mind to him, Jess chuckled as she realized Cassidy could not figure out how Butch had ended up outside. Jess climbed to her feet, pressing one hand to her face and one to the place where her hair had been torn from her head. She went to her front door and unlocked it. She turned the handle and pushed the door open.

After a moment, Cassidy came through the door and assumed a menacing position next to Butch. Jess plopped down on the front step. She was destined to have a bruise on her face and there was some blood on her fingers when she pulled her hand from her scalp. She took a moment to collect herself while the canine duo held Syndral still. Eventually, she pulled herself to her feet and walked over to Syndral.

"If I allow them to let you up, will you control yourself?"

Syndral gave the slightest of nods. Jess held her hand up to Butch and Cassidy and sent them a mental message to back off. Cassidy went to the down position. Butch remained standing, but took several steps back. Syndral rolled onto her back and sat up. She folded her legs up. Bent over, she hugged her knees and looked up at Jess. Mimicking Syndral's expression from a moment earlier, Jess cocked an eyebrow.

Jess spoke first. "Where is Kindra?"

"How the hell should I know? If my daughter isn't with you, then Kindra's probably got her. If I had known Riva was in your class all year..."

Looking over at the dogs, Syndral let her threat die. Jess was pleased to see Syndral was smart enough to know she was not in a position of power right now. Concern suddenly flooded Jess's thoughts. Syndral had only recently discovered that Riva was in Jess's class. Riva's parents must have shared that information.

"I see that look on your face," said Syndral. "Relax. The old couple is alive and kicking. When I stopped seeing Riva show up for school, I disguised myself as a truancy officer and dropped by their house. They informed me that she was safe and I could speak to her math teacher, Mrs. Bennett, for verification. A real truancy officer would have been pretty suspicious, but I understood the connection immediately."

Jess knew the best lies were mostly true. "I don't know where Riva is now. I spoke to her parents and convinced them it would be best for Riva to let her go. I think they were tired. As you said, they are not young, and they insinuated that there had been a lot of moving around in the time they had cared for the girl. I brought her straight to Leif's cabin."

"I was there, Jess. She's not at the cabin."

"As I said, I don't know where she is now. Did you speak to Leif?"

"Leif wasn't there either. It was only Joral, and he had little to say. You say Kindra's missing? Maybe she brought Riva to Alfheim."

Jess considered her next words very carefully. She did not trust Syndral, and she did not want to give Syndral access to Riva. Jess had been sure Syndral had been responsible for Kindra's disappearance, but she felt Syndral truly did not know anything about Kindra's whereabouts.

"Kindra doesn't even know about Riva. Kindra hasn't been seen since Sunday."

Syndral's head snapped back up, and now she was looking Jess in the eyes. "Sunday? Was she in the camp when the hundespor attacked? Leif insisted none of you were there!"

Jess was now positive that Syndral was not party to Kindra vanishing. Jess turned and walked back toward the house. She mentally called the dogs to follow her in. She did not close the door behind her. Jess grabbed two bottles of water from the refrigerator and an ice pack from the freezer. She sat down on the couch in the living room and waited for Syndral to join her.

CHAPTER 22

Syndral stepped into the house a moment later. She eyed Butch as she crossed the distance to the sofa. The female sat down and grabbed a bottle of water from the table. She took a long drink and then a deep breath. Syndral screwed the cap back on the water bottle and placed it before her. She did not take her eyes off Butch when she spoke.

"So, Riva and Kindra are both missing. What are the chances they are together?"

"They can't be together. Kindra was with me on Sunday after the attack. She got pissed off at Leif and stormed out of the house. It wasn't until the following day that I discovered Riva is an elf, and at that point, I had not even realized she was your daughter."

Syndral considered Jess's words. "What did Kindra say when she left?"

"I don't think she said anything. Why?"

Syndral thought for a second. "At first, I was wondering if she said something that might give us a clue where she went, but now I'm wondering something else. How did you know she was angry? Was it just the look on her face?"

The question staggered Jess. She replayed the events after returning from Alfheim. When she stepped through the passage and into the basement, Gunnar had already gone up the steps. Kindra was behind her. Jess had reached the top of the steps to find Krish dealing with Leif, so drunk he had been lying in the living room in a puddle of urine. Gunnar and Krish had dragged Leif to the bathroom and thrown him into the tub. Jess's eyes went wide as she realized Kindra had not been with her as she witnessed all of this. It was possible Kindra had never even followed Jess up the stairs. If that were the case, Kindra may have returned to Alheim through the passage. Though Jess found it hard to believe her friend would do that without telling anyone, it would explain why contacting Kindra by phone had proved impossible.

"You know what," said Jess. "I'm not so sure Kindra even came upstairs that day. She may have gone back to Alfheim before she ever really returned to this realm."

Syndral nodded her head as if she had already expected this was the case. "I suspect you could just wait her out. She's probably living it up at Millspare."

Jess nodded her head slowly. It was possible, but it just didn't feel right. Kindra might take off for a few hours and spend some time simmering, but it was not like her to disappear overnight. Jess remembered Kindra being ready to tear into Krish for slighting Mildred and Einar; she didn't think Kindra would turn around and do something like this. Even if she had, Mildred would have marched Kindra back to the human realm herself over the impropriety.

"It's possible, I suppose," said Jess.

"Ok," said Syndral. "We covered your question. Now, it's time for you to answer mine. Where is my daughter?"

Butch did not like the tone Syndral used when steering the conversation back to Riva. He hadn't removed his eyes from Syndral, but now he stood and bared his teeth. Cassidy remained prone, but his eyes were fixed on Syndral as well. Syndral straightened her spine and sat back against the cushions. She raised her hands in front of her body when she spoke.

"Listen, I'm not going to attack you again or anything. I just really need to know where she is. She could be in a lot of danger."

"Even if I knew where she was, why would Riva be safer if I shared that information with you?" asked Jess. "You were the one that gave her up to be cared for by a human couple when she was a baby. I can only assume you knew Riva would be safer if no one knew she existed."

"Well, that's the thing, isn't it? You and the princes know she exists, so it's no longer a secret. She is no longer hidden, and therefore, no longer safe."

Jess narrowed her eyes at Syndral. "Do you really think we would hurt a child? That's something your kind does. Lillerem has traditionally sequestered descendants of the crown here in the human realm to keep them unknown to Ulford. As one of his assassins, you are well aware that Ulford has figured that game out. He sent an entire squad to this realm, not just to kill Elven children, but any person with Elven blood."

Syndral just stared at Jess. Jess cocked her head to the side. It was clear Syndral was waiting for Jess to say or do something, but Jess had no idea what it was. She knew she was missing something, but it was out of her grasp.

Finally, Syndral spoke. "I thought you were supposed to be the smart one. You already identified the issue. You said it just now. Ulford is killing all hidden Elven children."

Realization dawned on Jess. She did have all the information already, but her mind hadn't made the correct connections. Syndral had a hidden Elven child that was a descendant of King Andril. The line differed from Gunnar and Leif's line, but the result would be the same. Gunnar and Leif descended from Blaith, Andril's son, but Blaith had sisters. His elder sister, Aldith, was Syndral's ancestor, and therefore an ancestor to Riva. Once Ulford eradicated all descendants of Blaith, Aldith's descendants would be the next in line for the throne. If Ulford was truly on a quest to eliminate every heir to the Kingdom of Lillerem, Syndral and Riva would be on the list.

"There is something I don't understand at all. Each of the assassins, including your sister, is in line for the throne in some way or another. Ulford has declared war on all descendants of King Andril. Why would he keep so many of them as his Royal Guard? Those would be the people he most trusted. It seems obvious to me that he would eventually need to remove them from the equation as well."

Syndral sat with her mouth partially open. She looked as if she was about to say something, but no words were being formed. Licking her lips, Syndral tried to reply, but stopped again, as if she were reconsidering what she was about to tell Jess. Jess saw tears in the corners of Syndral's eyes when the female finally spoke.

"I'm sorry," Syndral said. "I just... I didn't know you were aware of my sister. For months, I've worked hard to stop thinking of her as such, and it is just a shock to be reminded that she is still under

Ulford's spell. Imra is in love with Ulford. I think of her as a consort to him, though she is more than that. Imra is a seer. Well, maybe seer is an exaggeration? She can't see anything. She has feelings about which choices are right and wrong. When we were children, her feelings kept us out of some serious situations. It's the reason that I can't understand why she doesn't see the danger she is facing. The only plausible conclusion I can draw is that she is more focused on pleasing Ulford than protecting herself. I think it's possible that her feelings are steering her toward choices that ensure her a position of more favor with Ulford instead of guiding her in self-preservation."

Jess willed her mind to keep up. Her head ached from where Syndral had removed a chunk of her hair and her cheek was numb from the ice pack. The discomfort was making it difficult for Jess to think logically. At the palace archives, she had accepted that Syndral and Imra were sisters. That bit of information had caused Jess and the others to believe Syndral had infiltrated their group, intending to betray them. As Jess started putting information together, she revisited that conclusion, but wondered if it was incorrect.

Syndral continued, "Ulford must have informed the First Draw that they would be safe from persecution. I can't imagine another scenario where the assassins would not realize they would eventually be added to the list of people that posed a threat to Ulford uniting Lillerem under his hand. I didn't bother speaking to my sister. She is too wrapped up in pleasing Ulford to open her eyes. I had intended to speak to Morthil. Of all the assassins, I thought he would be the most likely to see reason. It was why I was following him and why I ended up at the library that night with Kindra. You already know what happened there and why I didn't get to speak to him. I did speak to Skalanis, though. I wasn't completely forthcoming when I talked with Leif and Joral."

"Shocker," said Jess, and then pressed her lips together.

Syndral ignored the comment. "I did see a hundespor at that mechanic shop. It did make me think about Skalanis and I did want to tell you all about it. I didn't go straight to speak with Joral and Leif, though. I actually ran into Skalanis on the property. I told him I was there on my own mission, and also sent by Ulford. I doubt he believed me, but it was enough to keep him from acting against me at that moment. I didn't ask him about the hundespor, but I did engage him in a conversation on a more philosophical level. I started acting like I was wondering out loud and asking him if he ever considered what Ulford's ultimate goal might be. I told him I sometimes wondered how long I had before I might no longer be useful to Ulford. It was a risk, and Skalanis never admitted that he had concerns as well, but he did say that we would all live beyond our usefulness at some point. Skalanis indicated that Morthil had once asked him if he ever wondered if Ulford was insane. He was curious to know if Ulford might get the entire First Draw killed in his quest to rule the realm. Skalanis had not replied to Morthil then, but he did admit to me that he was not worried. He felt secure in the idea that he could surround himself with his own blanket of protection. I assumed he meant his control of the hundespor, but I've since wondered if there are more than hundespor in his arsenal. Though hundespor are terrifying, he was far too confident to be backed only by a small pack of the creatures."

Jess made a decision. She needed to take a moment to contemplate how she would do it, but she decided Syndral should know that her daughter was traveling to Alfheim the following morning. She couldn't pinpoint where the feeling stemmed from, but Jess felt Syndral was not working for Ulford. It wasn't really that she was against him, but more that Syndral had realized that Riva's best interests and her own relied on Syndral removing herself from under Ulford's thumb. The female had tried hiding her daughter, but it was far too likely the hundespor would sniff her out, if they hadn't already. Ulford might never learn that Syndral had a daughter, but Riva might simply be eliminated because she possessed Elven blood in the human realm. Syndral might not be interested in destroying Ulford, but she was intent on doing everything she could to ensure her daughter's safety.

Jess said, "I know where Riva is. We have plans in place for her protection."

Syndral's eyes started smoldering once more. Either she was upset again that Jess and her friends had taken Riva in the first place, or upset that Jess had lied to her or both. Jess proceeded cautiously as she spoke.

"I told my students about Alfheim. I don't think many of them believed any of it, but it was fun to tell of my adventures as if it were a fairy tale. At the end of the day, Riva stayed after class and shared with me that she thought she was an elf. I didn't believe her at first. I figured she was just another middle-school student trying to find her place in the world and had latched onto the idea that she might feel out of place because she actually belonged to a different realm. It would not be the first time something similar went through one of my student's minds. She gave me a demonstration of her power right there in the classroom."

Syndral held up her hand. "What power? What power does Riva possess?"

Jess swallowed. "She made it rain in my classroom."

Syndral slumped in her seat. "I had no idea. Riva can control the weather? She is powerful enough to control the weather, here in this realm? The poor girl. She likely made connections between her emotion and weather phenomena years ago and there was no one for her to turn to for an explanation. She must have been so scared."

"Likely," said Jess. "Once she showed me what she could do, we went to speak to her parents. They admitted they no longer felt they could help her. I took Riva to Gunnar at Leif's cabin."

"As I said, I was there. No one is at the cabin," Syndral repeated impatiently.

"I know," said Jess. "When Leif realized who Riva was, I suggested they move her to Kindra's mother's house. That's where they've been. We also came to the conclusion that Riva would be discovered by the hundespor and decided she should go to Millspare. She will be protected there."

Syndral's eyes were wide. "Protected? Millspare! You intend to walk her right into Ulford's realm? I brought her here to keep her safe!"

Jess quickly replied, "We're not sure Riva has been detected in this realm yet. Even if the hundespor have scented her and she is on the menu for the near future, removing her to Alfheim will cause them to lose her scent. Once in Aegroth and living at Castle Millspare, she will only be another elf. By now, Ulford and the assassins will have determined that all of Blaith's descendants are accounted for. No one knows you have a child, and if they did, they would never expect her to be cared for by Ekkelle's family."

Syndral took a deep breath. "Even if Ulford goes after Lady Ruth, he will never suspect Riva is also a threat to him. Ruth has no children. Riva will live as Bane does. She will know her heritage, but will not share it readily. Those who need to know of her relationship with me will already be aware. Do you expect Lord Viktor and Lady Ruth to raise Riva as their own?"

Jess laughed. She laughed so hard, her head started to pound harder still. She winced and moved the ice pack from her face to the spot where her scalp had finally stopped bleeding. She cocked her head and gave Syndral a small smile.

"I can tell you have never met the Lord and Lady of Castle Millspare. I'm not sure either of them would know what to do with a child. The couple who would care for Riva is a bit older than Viktor and Ruth, and much more doting. I also expect Riva will have impeccable manners in no time."

Jess's phone rang. The caller ID displayed 'Asshole', so Jess sent it to voicemail. A text came through a moment later. The message implied that the joke was getting old, and that Jess was acting as if she were similar in age to her students; only the language was much more crass. The phone rang again. This time, Jess answered. Leif started speaking before Jess got a chance to greet him with a witty comment.

"Listen, we decided it would be best if we took the girl to Millspare tonight. Sitting around doing nothing is not getting us anywhere."

"That makes sense," Jess replied. "I'm going to meet you at your cabin. There is someone who will want to see Riva before she goes."

Jess hung up the phone and tossed the ice pack back in the freezer. She grabbed her bag and motioned for Syndral to follow. Syndral closed the front door behind her and followed Jess and the dogs to the car. Jess opened the back door and Butch settled himself behind Jess. Cassidy sat behind the seat Syndral was sliding into. Jess closed the door behind Cassidy and ran around to her side of the RAV4. She jumped in, started the engine, and then backed out of the driveway.

CHAPTER 23

Jess guided the Toyota up Leif's driveway. She parked in the spot in front of the porch and climbed from the car. For the second time this evening, Jess was grabbed by her shirt's collar and yanked backward. She flung one hand over her head to keep it from slamming on the ground and tried to get the other hand behind her. She only succeeded in landing awkwardly on her elbow. Butch and Cassidy were snarling and snapping at the side window, desperate to exit the vehicle.

A figure placed a foot on Jess's chest and pinned her to the ground as he said, "If your friend knows what's good for her, she'll stay in the car and keep those beasts company."

Jess tried to focus on the male's face. Like so many people in this realm, the figure was wearing a hoodie. The attire was no longer weather-dependent. People wore them regardless of temperature, and that made it easy to hide Elven ears and blend in with humans. Jess was almost positive her attacker was an elf, but she was still disappointed to see the ears blocked by the hood. Jess needn't have worried about discovering the assailant's identity. He simply told her who he was.

"My name is Jacan. We've met before, but we were never properly introduced. I was pretty sure you would have one less guardian after our last encounter. I have been using that as a consolation for failing to eliminate my intended target. Now I see I lost my place at the palace for absolutely nothing."

Jess's eyes burned with angry tears. This was the newly found descendant of Andril, the previously unknown assassin, identified by the parchment in the palace archives. Most importantly, though, this male had attempted to kill Kindra and had left Butch a breath away from his last. If it had not been for Trego, Butch would not be here now. Based on the sounds coming from the backseat, Butch was aware of who this male was as well.

"What were you doing at Gulentine, anyway?" asked Jess. "You couldn't have been waiting for Kindra. There was no way you could have known we would be visiting the palace."

Jacan gave Jess a kick in her side. The air left her lungs. She tried to roll on her side to protect the new area blossoming with pain, but Jacan returned his foot to her chest. Jess's back was quickly pressed into the gravel driveway.

"This isn't going to go down like it does in some mystery novel. There is no time in this story where everyone confesses their intentions and brings closure to the other party. The only thing that needs to happen here tonight is that you, Kindra, and the princes need to die."

Jacan pulled a small penknife from his pocket and flipped open the blade. He reached down and grabbed Jess by her blonde curls. Jess's scalp screamed from the spot where Syndral had already claimed a handful of hair. Jacan moved the blade toward the side of her neck. It was far too small a knife to cut her throat open. He was likely going to use the tip of the blade to puncture her jugular and leave her to bleed out.

"Hold up!" a voice rang out from the front porch. "I've got the one with the scar in here, but the other two aren't around. Scarface isn't talking, but that bitch might know where they are."

Jess saw the newcomer when Jacan relaxed his grip on her hair. Vander, commander of the First Draw and leader of the Dredfall assassins, stood at the top of the steps. If he was on the steps, then Joral was either unconscious or restrained. Vander came down to the bottom of the steps and hauled Jess up by the back of her shirt. She tried to walk, but was primarily dragged up the steps to the cabin entrance.

Vander said to Jacan, "Stay here and make sure nothing gets out of that car. We'll deal with the other one once we find out where the other princes are. It will be tricky getting by those hounds."

Jess tried not to react to his words. These males had no idea it was Syndral in the passenger seat of her car. Jess really hoped Syndral was wise enough to send a text message to Leif or Joral. She had not liked letting Syndral partner with them initially, but she was currently very thankful they had exchanged phone and that the female was with her when she arrived here tonight. Butch and Cassidy were incredible weapons, but it would take someone with thumbs to use a cell phone.

Vander dumped Jess on the couch. Joral was at Jess's feet, bloody and unmoving. Jess stayed very still as she stared at her friend. Relief flooded her when she saw his chest rise and fall. In the movies, captives always tried reasoning with the bad guys. It was supposed to help the evildoer see the captive as a person, and it made sense to Jess. It had not worked when she tried the tactic with Jacan, but she tried again with Vander.

"There is no need to hurt anyone else. I'm sure we can work it out so you can get—"

Vander cut Jess off. "Enough. This has nothing to do with what I want. I have orders. Now, where are the others?"

"How the hell should I know? I went to work, and then brought a friend with me to check on Joral. He just hasn't been himself since you killed all his friends."

"If neither you nor Joral here has the information I need, then there is no need for you to remain breathing. I'm sure Kindra will wonder where you are soon enough. Eventually, she and the princes will return here. If you can't tell me where they are now, then you die and I simply wait."

Vander drew a large blade from a leather sheath at his right side. He tossed his head back before advancing on Jess. Stringy black hair fell back in his face immediately. The male's hair was so greasy, it looked wet. Jess saw no emotion in his dark eyes. There was no anger or regret. This was only a job, and Vander had no qualms about removing Jess from the realms. *Wait. He had expected Kindra to be worried about me and show up looking for me. How is it that neither Syndral, nor the assassins knew Kindra was missing?*

Jess spoke as Vander moved his knife to her throat. "The princes might show up eventually, but you missed your chance with Kindra. It's possible she is already in Dredfall. It would be pretty embarrassing if the First Draw failed to protect its king because it was in the human realm hunting the very female who ended Ulford's life."

Jess thought she had found the right thing to say. Vander paused and looked as if he might pull back and ask for details. Instead, his eyes hardened in resolution and Jess closed her eyes. She waited for the blade to slice her neck. There was a thud and Jess pulled her eyes back open. Vander lay face down before her with a dagger protruding from the base of his skull. A trickle of blood and spinal fluid ran down either side of the male's neck and dripped to the floor.

Jess looked up in time to see Gunnar cross the room. *I'll never get over how quiet elves are.* Gunnar retrieved his dagger and wiped it on the edge of the throw rug sticking out from under the coffee table. Krish entered the room, and both princes went straight to Joral. Jess scrambled off the couch as the princes lifted their unconscious brother and laid him where Jess had just been sitting.

"What about Jacan? He was out on the porch."

"Got him," Krish said. "Leif took him out and Gunnar and I entered the cabin through the bedroom window. Currently, Leif is amusing himself with Syndral."

Jess left Gunnar and Krish to tend to Joral and ran for the front door. She hoped she was in time. There was a good possibility Leif had already killed Syndral. Jess slowed as soon as she exited the cabin. From the porch, she could see Leif trying to find a way to enter the car. Whichever door Leif tried to open, Butch hopped to the seat nearest the door and growled and snapped at Leif. To anyone else, it would look as if Butch were protecting Syndral who remained in the passenger seat, but Jess could feel Butch in her mind. All the dog cared about was getting out of the SUV and tearing Leif's limbs from his body.

Jess went to the RAV4 and opened the door to the backseat. Instead of charging Leif, Butch looked from Jess to Leif for a moment. Love and relief won out and Butch jumped from the car and jumped on Jess. He was joined by Cassidy. When Jess reached down to rub the dogs' heads, Leif made his move for the car. Instantly, Butch and Cassidy turned their attention to him.

"I'm going to bring Syndral inside. Do you have a certain someone here with you? You might want to bring her inside, too," Jess said.

Leif scowled at Butch as he turned and walked down the driveway. The trio of princes must have approached the house on foot and left Riva in the car. Jess gave Butch and Cassidy the greeting she had attempted moments earlier, before they had redirected their attention to Leif. She then opened the passenger side door to find Syndral sitting in the seat, eyebrow cocked, with her cellphone in her lap.

"That fucking beast has barely let me move since you got out of the car. I saw Jacan coming toward you even before you closed the car door. I pulled up my hood and texted Leif to tell him the assassins were here and they needed to hurry, but approach with caution. He replied right away, saying they were nearly at the cabin already. I couldn't have Jacan knowing it was me in the car, so I sat still. I'm sorry I didn't help you. When Vander stepped out on the porch, I knew I'd made the wrong choice, but by then Butch wouldn't let me move a muscle. He and Cassidy were so worked up that anytime I moved, they snapped at me. They couldn't get out of the car and they didn't understand that I needed to move to let them out. They were in such a frenzy. I thought they might shred me just because they couldn't get to Jacan or Vander."

Jess realized Syndral was close to hysterics. It was a shock to see the female in this state. Jess understood. There was little that could break a calm female with strength. Helplessness. That had to be the cause. Syndral had been forced to sit in the car and watch an attack on Jess. She couldn't have known what was happening in the cabin. Syndral had nothing but time to think about how her daughter was about to be dragged directly into this situation and be presented to Dredfall.

Jess, uncomfortable with comforting people in distress, had no idea where to begin with this particular frantic female. She started by extending her hand to Syndral to help her from the car. Syndral didn't take Jess's offer, but the gesture seemed to spur Syndral to move. The warrior female regained her composure as soon as she stood on the gravel driveway.

"Thank you. I'm good. Let's just go inside," Syndral said.

Jess shook her head at change in Syndral's demeanor and followed her, throwing a thought back to Butch and Cassidy, telling them to follow after her. Butch seemed reluctant to release his stare from where Leif had disappeared down the driveway, but he turned his attention toward the cabin and both dogs mounted the steps to enter.

Jess took a seat next to Joral on the couch. He was sitting up and his eyes held a determination that Jess had not seen from the elf since before the attack on the training camp. She was sorry Joral had been beaten so badly, but it was a relief to see him less despondent than he had been lately. Dried blood smeared the area above his lip, but it didn't seem that he had any serious injuries. Jess thought of what her own face must look like after rough treatment from Syndral, Jacan, and Vander. It was likely she looked worse than Joral.

Syndral quietly took a seat in the rocking chair, but Krish and Gunnar remained standing. They looked as if they were still channeling too much adrenaline to relax. The front door opened and Syndral was back out of her seat seconds after she had taken it. Riva came through the doorway. The little girl froze and took in the entire scene. Her eyes lingered on Jess and Joral's injuries as she scanned the room. After taking it all in, her gaze stopped on the person who had been stalking her.

Syndral took two steps toward Riva and then stopped. She seemed to want to hug the child, but then realized the young female probably saw her as a predator. Instead of continuing her approach, Syndral dropped down to her knees about five feet before she reached Riva. The little girl's hand dipped into the backpack she held, and Jess knew she would be stroking some bothersome stuffed animal. There was a moment where mother and daughter just stared at each other. Syndral tried to collect her thoughts while Riva waited in confused anticipation.

"Hello Riva," Syndral began. "It has been a long time since we lived together. You were so small at the time, that you will have no memory of me. I am Syndral, and I am your mother."

Riva did not move a muscle. She waited for Syndral to continue. Jess wasn't sure what Syndral had expected Riva to do next, but it was obvious the female had not considered what she would say after her initial confession. Leif, who had entered the cabin behind Riva, guided the girl to the rocking chair and sat her down. He took a place behind the chair and Syndral rose to move before Riva. She lowered herself to her knees again and continued her story.

Seeming to forget the room was full of other people, Syndral told Riva about her birth in Alfheim, and her trip to the human realm shortly afterwards. She explained how she had introduced herself to Riva's adoptive parents and they had agreed to raise her. Riva kept her hand in her backpack and never took her eyes off Syndral. When Syndral finished telling Riva how she had checked in on her often and followed her to each place her family had moved her, Riva finally opened her mouth to speak.

"I can smell who you are. You smell like a part of me. I knew you were my mother as soon as I walked into the cabin. When I saw you before…on the street, I don't think we were close enough for me to smell it," Riva said.

Jess was transported back to the day where Kindra had met Leif at the bottom of the driveway to the cabin they all currently occupied. Riva's words echoed Kindra's at the time and the similarity gave Jess goosebumps. Syndral had relaxed slightly hearing Riva's words, and was now speaking again.

"I am sure you have many questions, and I want nothing more than to sit down with you and talk. Truthfully, I never want you to leave my sight again, but right now, you need to go with these people. They are going to protect you. Right now, no one can know you are my daughter. It is the only way to keep you safe. They will take you to a magical place. It is the realm where you were born. I will come to you as soon as I can."

Riva said nothing. The young elf had likely not even processed the magnitude of Syndral being her mother. It was even less probable that she understood she was about to leave the human realm with people she had only recently met. There was no time to let the girl process any of the new information, though. Jess sent Cassidy to Riva's side, and the girl stroked his fur absently.

"Ok," Gunnar said from the other side of the room. "Let's get going."

The entire group followed Gunnar down the stairs to the basement. Jess sank down and sat on the stairs. She watched Gunnar and Joral take positions on either side of Riva. Joral stood on Riva's left. Like Butch, who always stood at Jess's left, Joral was fiercely protective. He was quick to anger and willing to lay down his own life in defense of another. Cassidy looked as fierce as Butch, but he was a lover at heart. He always stood at Jess's right side, equally ready to defend her life or offer emotional support at a moment's notice. Gunnar, at Riva's right side, was very similar to Cassidy. He was gruff and often silent. He looked terrifyingly fierce, but he felt his emotions strongly and was the first to recognize when people were distressed. Jess smiled. That little girl had no idea how strong the weapons at her sides were.

Riva looked back over her shoulder and found Syndral's eyes. She turned and went to her mother. She reached up and hugged her. Syndral was frozen for a second before she let her arms wrap around Riva's body. After a moment, Riva pulled back and gave Syndral a nod. There were so many unspoken words in that gesture, and Jess could see how they melted Syndral's heart. Riva returned to her place between Joral and Gunnar and took the warriors' hands. Leif moved forward and placed a hand on the wall.

Riva's mouth fell open as a chunk of the stone slid back slowly, revealing the passage. There was a loud clang as something hit the dirt and stone floor of the cellar. Something had fallen out of the passage as the wall slid away. Jess got to her feet to see what the object was. There, on the floor, naked without its scabbard, was Forsvarer.

EPILOGUE

Kindra attempted to coax her eyes open. She failed. When she tried to raise her hands to her face, she found them bound behind her back. She fought the panic bubbling up from her stomach. Breathing deeply, Kindra investigated her surroundings with her ears and nose. The air smelled damp, and there was an undertone of rot. She had experienced the sliced mushroom smell once before, in the forests outside Millspare. It was not a comforting memory. She pushed the thought aside and focused on what she heard.

The sounds filtering through her ears told her she was in Alfheim. It wasn't what she heard, but how she experienced it. The unremarkable sounds of dripping water and the sounds of dragging chains accompanied by an occasional snuffle or growl were crystal clear. She had to be in some kind of kennel. Beyond the sounds of caged animals was the sound of voices. Kindra instinctively knew the voices were much farther from her than the sound indicated. She could discern enough of the language shared to determine there was a market nearby.

Relatively sure that she was locked in a cage alone, Kindra tried to recall how she had come to be here. She had been following Jess as they neared the tunnel to the basement at Leif's cabin. Krish's angry voice hinted they would be walking into an argument. Kindra watched as Jess exited the passage and started up the steps. Butch and Cassidy bounded past her to reach the top of the stairs first. At that point, Kindra had felt a chill run up her spine and she had automatically drawn Forsvarer from its new scabbard across her back. Kindra had never made it into Leif's basement. She had stepped forward, and a hand had closed over her mouth and nose. Within seconds, her vision had faded to black.

That was all there was to remember. Kindra was now in a cage somewhere in Alfheim. She didn't know who had taken her or why. She also didn't know how long she had been here. Kindra searched her feelings and found she was a little hungry, but not starving. She could not have been here for more than a few hours to a day. Her mouth was dry after her involuntary sleep.

"Hey!" Kindra called out. "Is there anyone out there?"

It did not take long for Kindra to hear a metallic lock being opened, followed by the screech of a metal door or gate opening and then closing. She heard no footsteps approach, but was aware someone had joined her.

Hands pulled Kindra into a sitting position and moved to the back of her head. Seconds later, a blindfold fell from her face and into her lap. She could now open her eyes. She was, indeed, in a cage. The floor was dirt, and the walls were made of large rectangular stones. The space covered about twelve square feet.

Kindra turned her attention to the small elf squatting next to her. If he were human, he would be about twelve years old. His hair was cut short in the back, but there was a mop of dirty-blonde curls on the top of his head. His golden eyes betrayed curiosity. The smattering of freckles across the tanned skin of his nose made the child just cute enough to be trouble. Kindra imagined there were few people who could deny that face much of anything. That was until he spoke.

"Whadya need halfbreed?"

Kindra started at the use of the slur. It took her a moment to reconcile the innocent face before her with the hatred displayed by his words. Kindra reminded herself that she was in Alfheim and was a captive. Though the elf was young, he would be aware that anyone kept behind bars would logically be a criminal. At the very least, he would be smart not to trust a prisoner. Calling Kindra a half-breed could also be an attempt to appear tougher than he actually was. *After all, the kid isn't even five feet tall. He needs to make some attempt at intimidation, right?*

"Hello, my name is Kindra. Do you think it would be possible to get something to eat and a little water?"

The boy looked confused by her polite introduction and did not reply. Kindra wished Jess were here to help her with the calculation of the age of this elf. First she tried to remember if she was supposed to multiply his observed human age by ten-thirds or three-tenths. She then decided it didn't matter because she was pretty sure she wouldn't be able to multiply twelve by either fraction without pen and paper. She gave up and decided to use a rough estimation that this elf had been alive slightly longer than she had, even though he looked like one of the middle-school students she regularly worked with in the school counseling office. Without a word, the boy stood and opened the cell door. He exited the cell and locked the door behind his little body before walking away.

Kindra was reminded how silent elves were when the boy reappeared without a sound. He unlocked the door, entered, and locked the door behind him with one hand, while carrying a silver bowl in the other. When he placed the bowl on the ground next to Kindra, she stared at him incredulously. Narrowing her eyes, she decided to give the kid a piece of her mind. First, he called her names, and now he was serving her water from a dog bowl.

The kid spoke before Kindra could unleash her anger. "Listen, I am really sorry."

The kid's tough guy attitude was entirely gone. Instead, his face reddened with embarrassment. He went around to Kindra's back and worked to free her hands. Kindra wasn't sure if the little elf was showing kindness, or if he had determined Kindra would need her hands if he didn't want to find himself holding the dog bowl to her mouth so Kindra could drink.

"My name is Alek, and it seems I am not particularly good at being a prison guard. I usually help the houndsman, but now that you're here, I was promoted to the position of your guard. I've never even met a prison guard. All I know is I'm supposed to keep you alive and keep you locked up. It really didn't sound much different from taking care of the other pets, but then you started talking. The other pets can't talk. I wonder sometimes what they are thinking, but I just make it up in my head and pretend they are happy to see me and that they think of me as their friend."

There was a part of Kindra that wished the elf had never started speaking. The words poured from his mouth in a rush, as if he hadn't had the opportunity to speak much in the last few decades. Given her circumstances, Kindra was not sure it was fair that she should also have been charged with entertaining a lonely teenage elf. On the other hand, she might be able to use this to her advantage. If Alek liked to pretend that the other pets thought of him as a friend, it should be easy for Kindra to convince the boy she could be his friend too.

Kindra plastered a smile on her face and said, "It's nice to meet you, Alek. I guess there are no glasses available for the water?"

"Nope," Alek replied. "I looked for some food too, but I didn't think you'd want what we feed the pets. I don't live down here or anything. I stay in the barracks with the other slave kids. I usually bring a snack and I would've shared it, but I ate it while you were sleeping."

Kindra's breath caught in her throat. This young kid was a slave. She had figured he was the son of the kennel master. *Maybe he is the son of the kennel master and the kennel master is also a slave?* Kindra dismissed the thought when she considered that the kid had said he lived in the barracks with other slave kids. He was likely an orphan. *Then again, maybe all slave children are removed from their parents?*

"Where do your parents live?" Kindra asked.

"Ain't got none of those. Don't need 'em anyway. We all watch out for each other."

That question answered, Kindra asked another. "Where are we?"

"We're in Dredfall. The kennels at Fallholm to be exact. Like I said, I take care of Skalanis's pets."

Kindra froze. No, the kid had definitely not said those words. Kindra had assumed the pets this kid cared for were dogs and that they belonged to Ulford. She was horrified to hear the pets in this kennel belonged to Skalanis. There was no way the pets were ordinary dogs.

"I see," said Kindra. "How long was I asleep?"

"A couple of hours," replied Alek. "Listen, sit tight for a bit and I'll go get you something to eat."

The boy did not wait for a reply. He stood and exited the cell in the same silent manner as before. Kindra immediately concentrated on the lock for her cell. She thought about it opening, and it clicked.

She willed the door to swing open and it did. Kindra was on her feet and rushing for the door to the cell when a giant, shaggy, dog-like creature walked by the doorway. It sniffed the air and turned to look at Kindra. She quickly willed the door to shut again and it crashed closed with a loud clang. Mentally, Kindra locked the door. *Good to know. They really were not expecting that lock to keep me in here.* The hundespor were here to do that job.

Alek came back down the hallway. The young elf reached up and gave the hundespor a scratch on the neck as he walked by. Knowing hundespor were not actually dogs, and could take a humanoid form, Kindra wondered if what the kid had just done was actually an insult. The frightening creature did not seem to take offense, and it simply walked on, past Kindra's cell. The young male entered and closed the cell door behind him.

When he approached, Alek pulled a sack from under his shirt. He dumped out a few cakes, some sliced cheeses, and a quarter loaf of bread. Kindra smiled to herself. It seemed likely the male had pilfered the food from someone's table. She hoped he wouldn't get into too much trouble for it. She tore the bread and offered some of it to Alek. He accepted, and they chewed in silence for a time.

"So, Alek," Kindra began. "How long do you figure you'll be my guard?"

"I'm not really sure. No one told me an exact amount of time. They said they would check in every few weeks to be sure I was doing my job, though."

Kindra mulled that over. Checking in every few weeks made her think she might be held here for quite some time. She had so many questions, but she didn't want to spook Alek, or get him thinking he was not doing his duties appropriately, so she did not want to rattle them all off at once. For Kindra, this would take incredible strength. She anticipated she would have quite some time to ask her questions, though. Throughout the many hours she would undoubtedly spend in this cell, she would befriend Alek, ask him questions, and formulate a plan to get the hell out of this place.

ACKNOWLEDGMENTS

Writing a book is a journey, and I did not make this trip alone. Inspiration, support and time from others carried me through to the end. My gratitude goes to the people who joined me on the journey through the pages of this novel.

My parents, Lenore and Bob, as well as my in-laws, Millie and Willie, drove me to turn out this second adventure, demanding to know what happened next in the characters' stories.

My husband Phil deserves thanks for being supportive when I became frustrated. Also, I'd like him to know that I appreciate the time he gave up so I could write.

I need to thank my nephew Landon for the inspiration for the end of this book. Also, for creating Alek's character, who Landon has made me promise, will have a starring role in book 3.

Thank you to my cousin Darren for reprising his role in creating cover art for my book. This time, he was able to bring Jess, Butch and Cassidy to life for me.

Thank you to my Alpha/Beta and early readers for catching all of my mistakes throughout the writing process and pointing me in a better direction with the story. This list includes Dr. Suzanne Solomon-Hollander, Murial Roth, Davida De La Harpe, and Riley Rae Vanhoy. Special thanks to Ed Cooke for practically having me re-write the entire book for the better. At least he earned himself an American coffee franchise in exchange for all of his hard work and time.

Thank you to Elena A. Steele. Her narration and production of the Finding the Past audiobook was one of the best lessons I could get on writing. I had her character voices in my head while writing the speaking lines for book 2.

Lastly, thank you to Kim at High Point K9 Center for teaching me how to tame my crazy dog, Bernie. This was the inspiration for Jess's relationship with Butch and Cassidy. Special thanks to Luna, Scout, Phoebe, Patton, and Nero for lending many doggie personality traits to the canine duo. We would all be a little less human, without dogs.

www.ingramcontent.com/pod-product-compliance
Lightning Source LLC
Chambersburg PA
CBHW011517240626
47154CB00010B/3064